Beginnings

A Brady Trilogy

DEDICATION

Dedicated to those who seek for a new beginning and to those who've already found it. Keep love radiating brightly within your hearts.

*And a very special dedication to a man who's saved me in every possible way. Argo, you are my knight in shining armor and my prince charming come true.

TABLE OF CONTENTS

The blissful scents of the salty sea filled the air. Fresh patches of seaweed were pushed to the shore by powerful indigo waves. The fierce sun made it impossible to walk barefoot on the burning clear sands. Many came to tan under the merciless sun on a hot sizzling July afternoon. The rapid thumping of the volleyball being spiked over the net were equally pleasant to the chatter among the California tanners spread across the beach. Far in the distance, surfers challenged their boards up to the crest as the waves carried them gently back to the shore. A blond-haired little girl in her precious yellow swimsuit was joyfully collecting seashells in her red sand bucket. High school students were enjoying their last summer days before the fall arrived with its new agenda of scholarly plans. It was a wonderful scene. If travel agents had been present, these would be the very moments they would capture and advertise to their clients looking for a great California beach vacation.

Isabel Nicolette Stamos felt relaxed. Quitting her job at the agonizing law firm in Los Angeles and moving to San Diego was the best decision she had made this year. Thankfully, her free spirited mother was more than willing to give her the keys to the beach house. "Go enjoy life, Izzie baby. You work too hard," her mother had said. If anyone knew how hard Isabel had worked at that prestigious law firm, it was her mother. It was only her second day in town, and she wasn't going to waste it worrying about the life she left behind. Arms reaching over her head, she stretched like a lazy cat waking from slumber. Soon she'd have to polish her resume, drive into the city, and hunt for a new job, but right now she would just enjoy every divine moment of doing absolutely nothing. Especially since she hadn't been under the sun since her last vacation to Cancun, Mexico two summers ago, and her tan was long overdue. You simply couldn't live in California, particularly the beachfront, and have creamy white skin. Not that she was transparent, she still had some color remaining, but nothing compared to the tanned blonde a few feet away in her tiny string bikini. The blonde was lying on her stomach and had untangled the straps of her sparkly pink bikini top. Another thing Californians tried to avoid was tan lines, as much as possible.

Sitting up, Isabel grabbed her water bottle and began flipping through her magazines. Good thing she had stopped at a nearby mini market to purchase some water, snacks, and the month's latest issues before heading over to the beach. *"Hollywood Celebrity Marriage Ending in Outrage due to a Scandalous Affair"* was revealed in bold print on the cover of one of her celeb magazines. *What else is new,* Isabel mused to herself. She tossed the magazines aside and concentrated on the peaceful sight of the dancing waves, rising high above, yet landing lightly on the shore as if the echoes of the splashes were whispering secrets only the waters understood. *Ah, the beautiful secrecy of the bottomless sea,* she smiled to herself. This was the exact paradise she had hoped for on her two hour drive to San Diego. It had been a long and difficult year, and although it was barely July, the sequence of events that had taken place since early January was enough burden to last Isabel a lifetime. Endless hours put into work at the law firm had deprived her from enjoying the life she longed for. She hadn't planned to live a boring workaholic life with no room for socializing, but somehow had ended in the dead center of it. She all too quickly remembered her true reasons for leaving L.A., and she felt that dreadful pain in her chest threatening to return.

No, Isabel thought to herself, *it is all in the past, and it will remain there.* She was determined to start a new life, create a new beginning, and she refused to remain the helpless, pathetic girl she had left behind. She was stronger now and more capable. *Well at least that's what her therapist tells her.* She knew she was making quick recovery and from what Isabel had endured in the last couple months, it had taken great willpower to overcome the dreadful anxiety she had tried to fight alone. She was a loner with no friends, no lover, and no support group. Her mother was her only friend and family, and the only person there during the darkest period of her life. She had tried to keep the truth from her mother as long as possible, until she had reached her breaking point.

Isabel pushed all bleak thoughts out of her mind and concentrated on the pleasant beach around her. She had come to San Diego to change her life, not dwell on the past. She looked around and smiled to herself once again. Everyone was in bikinis and swim shorts. No desks, no law books, and no client files. She wiggled her toes deep into the burning hot sand and hugged her knees, breathing in the salty air. Her gaze fell upon a tall man in the distance, and she noticed that he had not come to the beach prepared. Standing close to the shore with his back toward the sands, he was dressed in well-tailored gray trousers and a white dress shirt. She noticed he had unbuttoned and rolled up his sleeves. *The complete executive type,* she concluded. He stood, with his hands in his pockets, staring far beyond into the sea. She couldn't see his face, but he certainly was tall, with wide shoulders and dark brown hair that blew unruly in the light breeze. Her eyes fell lower, seeing how well those gray trousers accommodated his nicely shaped behind. Isabel shook her head and brought her attention back to the ocean feeling like a complete creeper for gawking at a man who was fully clothed. She sure was tempted to go for a swim but felt a little rusty and defenseless against the powerful waves. *Going for a quick dip couldn't hurt,* she told herself as she adjusted her bikini and headed toward the ocean.

Luke Brady had a million things running through his head. He had left his office for a brief walk on the beach to clear his mind. It was the only way he could find some serenity and think. He loved the loud environment of his office but sometimes not even his closed doors gave him the opportunity to just think. Managing the nation's largest print and advertising company was no simple task. His father had left him in charge of their San Diego headquarters and now, as the Vice President, Luke was nothing but fully devoted to the company his grandfather had established decades ago. Luke, at the prime age of twenty-nine, was a determined man, and once he set his mind to something, he made sure it was done. He wasn't used to things not going his way, and he worked hard; countless hours spent in his office until things were as he pleased. Whatever Luke wanted, Luke got. His father, noticing the restless ambition in his eldest son from a young age, had no concerns leaving the headquarters to be managed by his firstborn. A few years ago his father had decided that it was Luke's turn to take over and continue the legacy his grandfather Sean Thomson Brady had started.

Luke first began working with his father at the young age of eighteen. At that time, most of his friends were moving to various college campuses, chasing after women, joining fraternities, and beginning their four-year long dorm party adventures. *But not Luke.* He stayed behind, spending half his days studying at San Diego University, and any remaining time he could find in his father's office. He avoided meaningless parties and meaningless relationships but would indulge himself casually in meaningless sex. From a young age, Luke had learned that there was no need to chase. With money, power, and status, women came to you. Now his father lightly managed their New York branch, even though his younger brother Andrew was fully in charge of that location, while Luke paid annual visits and kept a very close eye on all of B. Pentagon Print and Advertising locations. There was much to prepare for with new projects emerging and then his personal assistant of five years dropped a bomb by announcing that she was resigning from her position. It was going to be difficult to replace her. Rachel was very good at making sure his life ran smoothly by handling all the pesky errands he didn't have the time or patience for. Now, gleefully engaged, Rachel was in the process of planning for her wedding and starting a new life. This reminded him to pick out a nice wedding present for his well-deserved and reliable assistant. He had already sat through countless interviews and had not yet found her replacement. He continued to ponder on this thought and his next board meeting when his gaze fell upon a brunette who was wading near the water. He was amused by the way she was hesitant, as if debating if she should slowly walk in or jump in headfirst.

Isabel didn't expect the water to be freezing. Just leave it to the Pacific Ocean to be ice cold when the strong July sun was burning up the rest of the beach. She finally went in deep enough for the water to cover her knees. As cold as it was, she realized it must have been a lifetime ago since she felt this good. The chill of the water was surprisingly therapeutic. Reminding herself to glance toward her items, she squeaked at the sight of seagulls tearing through her bags and ran like a lunatic toward her possessions.

Luke watched in amazement as the brunette began to run like a mad woman while shouting. *What the hell is she doing*? He looked up ahead and noticed the woman was headed toward a large mob of seagulls and prepared himself for the disaster he was most likely about to witness.

"Oh come on, this isn't happening. SHOO… SHOO… stupid birds… get away! Go on now get out of here!" she yelled. But Isabel's attempt to get rid of the birds backfired when they attacked in retaliation. Losing her balance, she was about to hit the sand when strong arms caught her around the waist. The man in the gray trousers held one arm firmly around her waist and flapped the big birds away with the other. The noisy birds surrendered to Luke and gathered their herd and flew away. Isabel was trying hard to catch her breath before she could thank the man when he suddenly erupted in loud laughter.

"Are you all right?" he managed to ask.

"Yeah, yeah I'm fine," she whispered, still trying to catch her breath. "Thanks for helping," she said as she turned around to face her rescuer. She was stunned by his dark green eyes and incredible smile. He was even taller up close and had thick brown hair, a strong jawline, wide shoulders, and a hard chest she could feel since he was still holding her.

Holy hell. It was like cupid had backhanded her hard across the face. She couldn't remember ever facing a man this gorgeous or oozing with sex appeal. She quickly became embarrassed by her own racing thoughts and uncontrolled breathing.

Luke felt a quick pang in his stomach as the odd yet very attractive woman breathlessly staring into his eyes. From a distance he hadn't noticed how beautiful the brunette with the strange behavior was. She had the largest brown eyes he had ever gazed upon and long brown hair. She stared up at him with her hair half blown in her face and her lips slightly parted.

For a brief moment, they just gazed at each other with their breaths caught at their throats. Isabel's heart started beating faster when she realized the man with the God-like face still held his arm tightly wrapped around her waist. As if reading her mind, Luke released her quickly. She was stunned by her instant attraction toward a complete stranger.

"You should be careful what you leave out in the open around here." He gave her an easy smile, quickly wanting to ditch the awkward moment of just standing there and holding her. "These seagulls are more like vultures with the first sight of anything edible."

Isabel looked at her destroyed bag of snacks the so-called vultures had demolished. Still feeling a bit dazed, she didn't reply right away. *Just great, her first encounter with a stranger in a new city just has to be with a strikingly good-looking man. She doesn't have a social life, how was she to speak to Mister Sex Appeal? And why the hell is he in a suit?*

"You okay? You still seem pretty shaken up by it," Luke asked in concern.

"I'm okay, I'd just forgotten about the cardinal rule when it came to seagulls. It's been a while since I've been at the beach." She finally managed to give a friendly smile back.

He suddenly realized she had a warm, pleasant smile that contrasted with her intense eyes. "Not from around here?"

"I guess you can say that." Isabel laughed trying to cover her embarrassment as the stranger gave her a quick glance from head to toe. "I moved to San Diego two days ago."

"Oh? Where from?" Luke had to get back to his office as soon as possible and couldn't understand why he was so interested in making small talk with the brunette. He was known for romanticizing beautiful women without much effort, but he never let anyone, especially a woman, take away valuable time from his responsibilities. Other than his family, there was nothing more important than B. Pentagon. But for some reason he wasn't rushing back to his duties.

"I moved from L.A. Long story short I quit my job, put my condo up for sale, packed my bags, and now here I am," she said, smiling nervously. Panic hit her hard as she realized that once her condo was sold, there would be no going back. She also didn't know why she was standing there, telling a perfect stranger her personal business. But perfect he was. The more she looked at him the more she realized how utterly attractive he was. His green gaze could burn holes anywhere he looked, and they were currently leaving burn marks all over her face. *Wow,* she thought, *this man is intense.* She had to stop herself from fanning her face with her hands. But he suddenly looked familiar. She thought she had seen his face before, and she concentrated to place a name with the face.

"Oh wait, wait, I know who you are." She spoke a bit too loudly. So she *had* seen his face before. A girl didn't see a face like that and forget. She dived, hands first, into the salvaged pile of magazines, grabbed Times Corporate Man and began flipping through the pages frantically. "Here it is. That's you isn't it?" Isabel held the article up for him to see.

Luke grimaced as he stared at the article his PR manager had convinced him to do about America's top young corporate leaders. And way at the top he was. Luke was still annoyed with Rick for convincing him it would be good PR for the company. Maybe it was after all. "Uh yeah, that would be me." Luke gave Isabel a wide grin.

"Wow, that's amazing," Isabel replied. "You must be proud of your success."

"Well yeah, it has its advantages." Luke laughed. "I'm sorry, I didn't even introduce myself even though it seems there's no need now. But nonetheless, I'm Luke." He offered his hand, and Isabel shook it enthusiastically.

"I'm Isabel. Sorry about the whole seagull thing. I overreacted running here. It's great to meet you." She laughed even though she was mortified knowing she must have looked like a mad fool.

"No problem, it's no big deal. So you said you quit your job?" *What the hell is he doing? Why does he even care?* Rick was going to be in his office with their new client for a meeting in about an hour, and he was standing here, in his suit, making small talk with a half-naked woman.

"Yes, I did. Now I'm unemployed and don't know what the heck my next move is."

He could tell she was tense when she said it. She seemed like the type who organized her life down to the very last detail. Now she had made an impulsive judgment to leave everything behind and start somewhere new.

"Well I guess it's a good thing I ran into you then. I'm currently left trying to find an immediate replacement for my assistant. You can come to my office with your resume for a quick interview." Luke was surprised at his own impulsive judgment. *Did he just offer a job opportunity to a woman in her bikini? And not just any job but the position of being his personal assistant? A position that requires spending every waking moment of his office time with her?* The sun must have fried his brains, because he much rather have asked her out to dinner.

Isabel's stare showed she was just as stunned. "That would be wonderful actually. Wow, yes, yes that would be great, thank you." She silently cursed herself for sounding like a blabbering idiot instead of the professional woman she actually was.

"It's settled then. Come by my office tomorrow, two in the afternoon, and we can start from there," he said as he pulled out his business card and handed it to her. "My building is walking distance from here."

"Ha. That explains the suit." Isabel snorted and turned blood red. Luke bit the inside of his cheek to try not to laugh. She seemed a bit quirky, but he liked her honest reactions.

"Oh and even though our office is a few steps from the beach, it's still business attire so leave the bikini at home." He knew his comment might embarrass her, but it was entertaining to watch her cheeks burn red again. He stuck his hands back into his pockets and strolled off the beach. *Highly inappropriate comment,* he thought. Luke shook his head as he headed back toward his building. What was it about the beautiful brunette that made him act absurd?

~*~

The following afternoon Isabel debated about taking Luke up on his offer. Was it smart to work for a man she was outrageously attracted to? It was ridiculously bizarre considering she'd barely had a few minutes with him. *What exactly is he implying with that bikini comment?* she wondered as she stood in front of her closet fussing through her clothes. She couldn't tell if he was hitting on her or being serious. *This is ridiculous,* she told herself. *It's probably just the easygoing lingo in San Diego.* She was too accustomed to the stuffy old farts she worked with at the law firm that she forgot what a sense of humor sounded like. Obviously she knew how to dress for an interview. The man showed up to the beach in a suit pants for crying out loud. She sensed two very different personalities from that man. He was easygoing yet strong-minded. Whichever side of him it was that decided to offer her the job interview, she was grateful. It was not as though she needed the money right away, she had saved a bundle and would be getting a nice chunk once her condo was sold. Not to mention her mother was excessively wealthy, and Isabel had a massive trust fund from a young age. But nonetheless, she had to work, not only to make a living on her own but also to occupy her mind from the loneliness she felt deep inside. She remembered telling Joanne, her mother's real estate agent, that she didn't care to wait to find the highest bidder and to sell her condo to the first person who offered a reasonable price. She wanted the condo sold as fast as she wanted to forget L.A. and put it behind her. The best thing would be to keep busy with a new profession and leave the last one buried deep where it belonged. She was twenty-six years old and had never been more eager for a new beginning.

"Time to get your life back on track Isabel." She looked in the mirror and smoothed out her navy blue pencil skirt that lay a few inches above the knee. The cream colored silk blouse she chose made a marvelous contrast against the dark blue skirt and fit snugly against her skin. Appearance mattered a great deal to Isabel. She always made sure she was in her best business attire before heading to work. One of the perks for working at a high-status law firm was that the salary allowed her to splurge on shopping frequently. With her daily exercises and balanced diet she maintained a very good physique. She'd recently shed a bit of weight due to her lost appetite, but she was determined to become healthy again. However, she could thank her mother's great genes for her sheer smooth skin. Combing her long layered brown hair with her fingers, it laid passed her shoulders. Making last minute touches to her makeup, she grabbed her keys and resume and headed out. Fifteen minutes later Isabel found herself standing in front of the B. Pentagon skyscraper. She walked into the enormous lobby with polished gray marble floors and was greeted by the receptionist who informed her that Mr. Luke Brady was located on the top floor. The massive B. Pentagon logo dominated the wall behind the reception desk.

Walking out of the elevator on the top floor, Isabel noticed the modern design of the entire office. For one thing, the room was brightened with exquisite colors, and the walls were draped with enlarged front cover magazine ads and framed pictures. The office was pleasantly loud with some workers on the phones arranging deals while others hovered around desks laughing and discussing plans as papers were passed from hand to hand. She felt as if no one had noticed her walk into the room. Then all of a sudden, she noticed a young woman with a curvaceous body, long black hair, and a wide smile hurrying toward her.

"You must be Isabel," the woman said and swiftly took Isabel's hand in both of hers. "Hi, I'm Rachel Greyer, Mr. Brady's assistant. It's a pleasure to meet you."

"Isabel Stamos, pleasure's all mine." Isabel smiled back at the enthusiastic woman. So this was the person she was hoping to replace.

"Mr. Brady is finishing up a conference call. Why don't we walk to my desk and I can get you some coffee in the meantime?" Rachel led Isabel down toward the back of the building. There were two long rows of desks, but no cubicles, leading to one main office in the back. That office had large double doors that were currently closed. Isabel assumed it must be Luke's private office. She realized that Rachel's desk was the closest to Luke's office.

"No thank-you Rachel, I'll pass on the coffee." Isabel smiled and looked around the rest of the top floor. It was nothing like the quiet, conservative firm she was used to.

"Mr. Brady, your two o'clock appointment is here. Great, thank you." She heard Rachel hang up the phone. "He's ready to see you Isabel. You can just walk through those double doors."

Isabel took a deep breath while her hand hovered near Luke's door. She quickly knocked and entered once she was welcomed in. Stepping inside, she saw Luke sitting behind a large, dark wooden desk. He gestured her to come in as he hung up the phone, rose from his desk, and walked toward her.

"Hello Isabel. I apologize for the wait." He shook her hand and pulled the chair in front of his desk. "I hope you found our location easily?" he asked as he returned back to his chair. The playful man on the beach from the day before was gone and replaced by a stern, serious one.

"Yes, it's actually quite close to where I live." Isabel took a seat and placed her resume on his desk for Luke to view. She took a quick glance around his office and noticed the only thing that wasn't of modern design was the large oak desk he sat behind. The entire back wall was a window view of the grand Pacific Ocean. Isabel was entranced by the view of the beach behind Luke. She wondered if he stared out at the sea from his office the way he did yesterday afternoon. The rest of his office was quite spacious. In the left corner was a massive conference table, and in the right corner were black leather couches and lounge chairs surrounding a glass coffee table. Near the couches was a fine built-in bar with contemporary bar stools. *Does anyone need this much space in their office?* She looked at Luke who easily belonged where he sat. He was wearing trim black slacks, a black dress shirt, and a nicely fit charcoal vest, looking ever divine. He looked even more domineering in his office surrounded by the extravagant furniture. The place just screamed dominance and control. She wondered how many clients or women he entertained here and how often.

Luke had yet to make eye contact with her. "Isabel Nicolette Stamos." He read the top line, and his green gaze finally flicked toward her. "Greek?"

"Half, from my father's side," Isabel said and got a faint look in her eyes. She usually did when her father was mentioned. Luke caught the look but thought it best not to inquire.

"I see you worked as a paralegal for Preston D. Scotts Law Firm and Legal Associates for the last couple of years. Impressive. Mind if I ask how you came upon that position?" He watched her tense at the mention of her last employer.

Isabel reminded herself to stay calm when asked about her previous job. She had no choice but to include it on her resume since it was the highlight of her career backdrop.

"Certainly. My university placed me as an intern at the firm while I was studying for my Bachelors in Political Science, and once I was certified, I was hired permanently as a paralegal and assistant to Mr. Scotts, the founder of that practice."

Luke knew who Preston Scotts was. He had consulted with that particular firm in L.A. when B. Pentagon was dealing with a few legal issues. He knew Scotts was an extremely successful attorney, but for some reason Luke had decided against hiring his firm to represent his company. Therefore he had created and hired his own legal department here on his second floor.

"Did you want to become a lawyer yourself?"

"Yes and no. At first that was my primary goal, but I changed my mind and decided to proceed in another direction." *Far away from L.A. and that firm.* She also didn't want to mention that she quit halfway through her law degree.

"What changed your mind to remain employed with the prominent firm? It is a much respected law firm, and many would go through great lengths to obtain the position you held there." The way she was fidgeting with her hands gave Luke a feeling something wasn't right. He found her large, brown, haunted eyes mesmerizing as they grew wider. She was a petite woman with delicate features, but a bit too thin and fragile looking, Luke realized. *Why does she look so uneasy?* It was a job interview, and he was asking questions about her previous employer, yet the way she was reacting was as if he was prying into her personal life "You did mention yesterday you quit your job in Los Angeles, correct?"

Isabel stared at him without blinking. Just remembering the exact reason why she left that firm was causing an ache in her chest once again. She would stay calm, breathe evenly, and remember the breathing techniques her therapist had taught her. Struggling for the right words to say, she settled with, "It seemed the appropriate decision at the time."

Something is definitely not right, Luke thought. But seeing her shift uncomfortably in her chair caused him not to press the issue. Someday, somehow, he would get to the bottom of this. Why it quickly became so important to him, he didn't understand.

"Well then, let's discuss a few of your responsibilities as a paralegal." He noticed she exhaled the breath she was holding.

The next half hour she informed him of her duties and the firm's expectations of her in and out of the office. As Luke listened, he learned more about her work habits and realized she had an extremely demanding occupation. He knew all he had to do was place one call to Scotts to learn more about the woman sitting across from him, but he couldn't help but be impressed by her experience. She told him about the cases she had assisted with.

Her position as the thorough researcher involved preparing the attorney representing the firm with any pertinent information about the case, some of them being the infamous cases Scotts Law Firm had become known for in the first place. Luke only worked with well-developed individuals, and Isabel was clearly one well-accomplished worker. Finally, after the countless interviews Rachel and he had gone through, at last he had found someone who lived up to his standards, professionally and personally. But Luke wouldn't act upon the personal. The two did not mesh well. Yes, his first reaction to her was definitely a personal interest, but he made the decision to offer her an interview instead. Her proficiency was excellent, and she was just the type he would hire to work side by side with him on a daily basis. But did he risk hiring a woman he was tremendously attracted to? Well, Luke always loved a challenge.

"I must say I'm quite impressed with your background and work experience. I'd like to offer you the job as my personal assistant. I believe you'd be a great asset to our team," Luke announced as he grinned at Isabel.

She was instantly reminded how dangerous his smile could be, causing her heart to skip a beat. "I'd be more than happy to take that offer. Thank you Mr. Brady."

"Please. Call me Luke," he said with another one of his amazing grins. After all he had seen the woman half naked already, and they could at least be on a first name basis, he mused to himself. "Any questions?"

"Yes, when do I start?" Isabel was as ecstatic as a child heading toward Disneyland.

"Right away. Let me walk you back to Rachael's desk so she can begin training." As Isabel walked toward the door, Luke caught a glimpse of her legs and the rest of her snug, fit attire.

He'd seen her in a bikini but sure hadn't noticed her curves. Yes, she definitely did meet his personal standards. Silently cursing himself, he cleared his throat and walked her outside his office. He didn't understand why he was gawking over her like a teenager with uncontrollable hormones. But Isabel was part of his executive staff now, and she would be treated with professional respect like the rest of his team. He never mixed business with pleasure with staff or clients, and he didn't plan on starting now.

~*~

Rachel, being the cheerful high-spirited woman she was, enthusiastically began her training process, starting with Isabel's daily duties as the personal assistant. She learned Rachel worked very closely with Luke, tending to all his professional and personal needs. Rachel was usually the last one out of the office, staying back just in case Mr. Brady needed anything else before he left. She informed Isabel that Luke worked fast, and she had to play catch-up with him. He had a rapid paced working habit, and it was a challenge catching every word.

"Kind of keeps you on your toes." Rachel giggled. "But the day goes by very fast; there's always a lot to do around here. Here, why don't we go around and meet the rest of the staff?"

Isabel was introduced to all thirty-six executives that worked closely with Luke. She was later informed that he had personally hired every single one of them and designated the responsibilities of each. These positions weren't part of the executive team at the San Diego headquarters until Luke came along. He liked to take a different approach by stepping away from traditional. She met Jerry, a middle-aged man who was short, a bit chubby, and was one of the few on the advertisement committee. He had a jolly laugh and a twinkle in his eye. He was known for booking the most clients when it came to advertisement prints.

Then there was Linda, their chief editor, who was tall, blond, and had a sassy attitude. Brian, who looked like the youngest of the bunch, was their shy Tech Support Manager, who installed and managed all the latest software. There wasn't a single tech problem he couldn't solve. Brian had also designed a very elite security protection program making it impossible for hackers to access any of B. Pentagon files. Matt was a tall, gangly, former tattoo artist who was now in charge of graphic design. He looked like he belonged in a Motorcycle Club instead of sitting in an executive office. Then there was Ginger, who looked like she was in her forties, and had bright colored hair that matched her name. She was hired specifically as the events coordinator since she has an eye for detail. Isabel also got the chance to meet Rick, Luke's PR manager, who worked outside the office but stopped by occasionally for lunch or meetings.

Isabel liked the liveliness of the staff. Everyone was working hard, but they seemed to be enjoying what they were doing. She had enjoyed her job at the law firm as well until she became frantic to leave, but she hadn't felt this much energy before. Rachel was leaving in a week, and Isabel quickly realized how much she would be missed by the rest of the staff. Part of Rachel's duties was also assisting others if Luke needed her to work with them. Isabel recognized that Rachel had become the office favorite and many didn't want to see her leave but were happy for her. She had big shoes to fill, *but no pressure.*

"I'm sure going to miss this place," Rachel sighed as her and Isabel settled at her desk, "but I just can't wait to get married to my Mark. We're moving to Connecticut since Mark got the promotion he's been working toward for two years now. Plus we'll be closer to his family. Mr. Brady made sure I was placed in B. Pentagon's Connecticut location. Mark's mother is great. She said she can't wait to take care of her grandchildren. This way I can still work regular hours and start a family." She beamed with delight. Isabel found it fascinating how easily Rachel spoke about her personal life. She now knew more about her than she did about anyone she had worked with for four years at the firm. Must be the San Diego atmosphere.

"Because with this job, the traveling and all, it wasn't going to be easy to start a family you see," Rachel pointed out.

"Uh, traveling?" Isabel looked at her.

"Yes, didn't Mr. Brady tell you? As his personal assistant I traveled with him frequently wherever he went. It's part of the job actually. And it was already difficult maintaining my relationship with Mark. Imagine being married and flying out to different states each month. Especially with a man as attractive as Mr. Brady." She giggled softly. "Trust me, Mark wasn't so thrilled about that. There are many B. Pentagon locations spread out across the country and as Vice President, Luke is expected to show his face from time to time." Rachel noticed the frozen look on Isabel's face. "Oh Isabel is that going to be a problem for you? I hope I didn't worry you, I really thought you knew before accepting the job."

"Oh no, no it's okay. I should have expected traveling would be involved considering this is a nationwide corporation," Isabel reassured Rachel but more to herself. *Traveling with Luke? Is this a good thing or bad?* Looks like this job had more perks than she expected.

The next week Isabel worked close with Rachel, learning as much as she could about their clients and company procedures. She also learned how Luke liked his coffee, and that Luke ran every morning on the beach before coming in to work. Sometimes he showed up in his gym clothes, sweaty from his workout looking even more delicious as his sweat-drenched t-shirts clung to his muscular chest. He'd shower and change in the private bathroom of his office before the rest of the staff arrived. And since Isabel was an early bird, she was there to witness this glory.

Luke liked to take his favorite clients to Ricardo's, the laid-back Mexican restaurant in downtown San Diego, for lunch, margaritas, and business proposals. As his personal assistant, every so often she was expected to join their lunch meetings. He worked late almost every day, even on weekends, had constant meetings, and high expectations of his employees. She also learned Rachel would make frequent, exclusive dinner reservations at extravagant restaurants when Luke had a woman to entertain. Isabel realized that was going to be the most difficult part.

She also learned that Luke's family lived in New York where the second largest B. Pentagon was located. His mother Kathryn was a retired pediatrician who now managed their grand estate; his father Thomas was the CEO, his younger brother Andrew was third in charge after Luke, and his sister Emilia was a yoga instructor and personal trainer for the rich and the famous in New York. All in all, Rachel knew the tiniest details of Luke's life, and now it was Isabel's turn. In a matter of a week, she knew more about him than she had ever learned about any man in her life.

CHAPTER TWO

"Isabel, can I see you in my office please?" Luke hung up his phone. It was Isabel's first day without Rachel, and he noticed she made it to the office before anyone else.

"Yes Mr. Brady?" She appeared at his door.

"Have we heard back from Garrett for the new fonts we requested?" Luke asked without looking at her.

"Yes, he sent us samples just this morning."

"Good. I want you to work with Matt and see which one looks best for the job fair ad that the daily newspaper wants in their Sunday morning prints. It's their biggest event yet. Also, Rick is meeting with Joe for the press release so make sure you fax him the files we were working on last Friday. I want specific details to be mentioned in that press release, and I'm not taking my chances with unwanted publicity." He still continued to search through the papers on his desk.

"Yes sir, right away," Isabel added quickly.

"Where the hell are the damn magazine drafts? My meeting's in twenty minutes." This was one of those days where Luke had too much on his plate, but he wouldn't want it any other way.

"They're on the left side of your desk under the blue folder," Isabel informed him, which earned her the first look from Luke since she had walked into his office.

"Thank you." He smiled and her knees went a bit feeble. She really had to get over this crush she had developed on her boss.

"I better get going. I'm presenting these drafts to Timely Magazine so if you're looking for me I'll be in downtown," he informed her as he pushed away from his desk and reached for his suit jacket.

Today he was dressed in a trim navy suit. Isabel wondered if the man owned anything that didn't look irresistible on him. Grabbing the file, he headed for the door and spoke over his shoulder. Isabel rushed out after him jotting on her notepad as he spoke.

"Let me know how those fonts come out with Matt. I need those to be completed by the end of the day. I'll be in meetings all day but don't hesitate to interrupt me if a pressing issue is presented. Tell Brian to transfer and update my files on my laptop. I'll still want to take care of a few things from home. Call the hotel where Rachel will be honeymooning and make sure her and Mark receive a wine basket the day they arrive. Tell Rick I want to hear from him as soon as he sends out the press release. Make sure all my calls go to my office voicemail while I'm in this meeting with Timely. None of the staff should be calling me. The V.P. is a real pain in the ass to deal with as it is, and I don't want to hear from anyone other than you. Make sure you help Ginger with the upcoming charity dinner we have this Saturday. Also tell her to set a date for our annual beach event that should be held in mid-September. My clients look forward to that as much as our Holiday celebrations." He spoke quickly as he entered the elevator.

Turning around, Luke looked at Isabel and flashed his breathtaking grin. "Oh and welcome to the team, you're doing great here." He winked at her as the elevator doors closed, leaving her breathless, dizzy, and dumbfounded.

~*~

26

The rest of Isabel's week went by fast. By the time she blinked, the clock ticked to go home. Every day for the remainder of the week, time passed the same exact way it had since her first day without Rachel, with Luke rushing to the elevator doors while throwing requests over his shoulder as she eagerly followed him. He was constantly in and out of the office, sending orders to his employees as he left the building. No one seemed to mind the demanding environment. In fact, they all seemed to love it. They consumed it, ate it up, and savored every bite. Isabel saw that Luke's requests were met and spent a great amount of time working with Ginger on finishing last minute arrangements for the charity dinner. Luke and his family were avid donors to multiple charities but they held their own charity functions for a particular organization that helped domestically abused children. She found it strange, and was unable to make a connection as to why this specific group related to him or his family, but she did not question it. Ginger gave her a run-down of how the dinner would proceed. Apparently Luke always welcomed his top local clients to his events and none ever declined his invitations.

"I'll see you tomorrow at the charity," Ginger told Isabel on her way out. "I left the address on your desk."

"Thank you Ginger, I'll see you tomorrow," Isabel called out after her on late Friday evening. She poked her head inside Luke's open doors. "Need anything before I head out?" she asked him.

He stood in front of his grand windows peering toward the dark ocean. The sun had abandoned them leaving a dim shadow behind. Isabel loved the view of his striking back profile as much as she loved his gorgeous face and beautiful green eyes. He was dressed in black suit pants, a charcoal dress shirt, and a fitted black vest as his suit jacket hung on the holder near the door. Once again, hands in his pocket, he stared out into the far distance. He turned around and gave her a crooked smile. Isabel had been working with Luke for about two weeks now, and she still hadn't gotten over his appearance. His smile still made her heart struggle to beat like she was on a lifeline support. She didn't deny she was attracted to him and found no harm in admiring him from a distance. Besides, a face like that was made to be admired.

"Are we all prepared for tomorrow's event?" he asked.

"Yes, Ginger made sure it's perfection down to the last detail."

"I think you can give yourself some credit as well, don't you think?" He gave her *that smile* again, the one that made her stomach turn inside out.

"I guess I can." She blushed.

Luke was amused at how easily she became embarrassed and found her innocent glances very endearing. Sometimes he'd catch her staring at him and pretend that he didn't notice when she flushed red. Besides, he liked knowing he had such an effect on her. It definitely stroked his already confident ego.

"Nonetheless, I'm pleased you are part of my team. You picked up where Rachel left off with ease and that means a great deal for me considering we are at the peak of our busiest season. We're lucky to have you, and my staff speaks highly of you. I'm pleased you're here," he said and smiled.

His appraisal baffled her. Isabel wanted to tell him how much these two weeks had meant to her. All those years working in the firm had drained her energy and lowered her self-esteem, yet Luke and his staff were treating her as a prized possession and cherishing her in a matter of only two weeks. She wanted to blurt out that if it weren't for him, his company, the new job, and his wonderful staff, she would be at home curled up in the fetal position, desperately hating her life. She wanted to tell him how safe and comfortable she felt, what this place was doing for her, and how the change of lifestyle had made the greatest impact. She wanted to tell him that she was sleeping better, eating more, and for the first time in a long time, she'd found meaning in her life. She was beginning to find hope in her future. She wanted to say these things, wanted someone other than her therapist and mother to know what she had lived through, but the pain was too strong to speak of.

"Isabel?" Luke's brows drew together in confusion. He saw a distant look in her eyes and shuffled through his mind to recall any offensive statement he must have made but drew a blank. "Where did you go?"

She stared blankly at his face. "I'm very lucky to be here," she whispered a hoarse reply. Yes, she was very fortunate indeed. *Fortunate to be alive*, she thought. She could feel the tears burning in her eyes and cursed herself for it. Since the beginning of the year, she had been on a train wreck of emotions, crashing through every town of bad anxiety a person could feel, and none of the stops had ever reached Happville. But now she was overwhelmed with both joy and relief, stunned by how swiftly her life was changing, and she feared that this too would soon come to an end.

Luke was lost for words. He slowly walked toward her, held a hand gently to her elbow, and walked her toward his couch. She looked as though any minute now she'd break apart and begin crying. He lightly nudged her to sit, and she complied. He walked over to his bar and poured her a tall glass of water and when he reached her again, he noticed her face was pale and her hands were slightly shaking. He sat on his glass table directly across from her and held the glass to her lips urging her to drink. Once he set the glass down, he took her hands inside his.

"Your hands are freezing," he whispered. He rubbed his hands over hers to warm up her blood. When that didn't help, he brought them to his lips and blew warm breath to it. He lightly kissed her knuckles and went back to rubbing her hands.

The sweet gesture was what brought Isabel back to reality. Her therapist had told her that at times, during strong moments of emotion, she tended to block herself from reality to avoid experiencing mental pain. Her mental pain caused her physical torture, and her brain involuntarily ordered her body to shut down. It kept her mind from thinking and her lungs from breathing. But Luke's hands brought her back to consciousness. She quickly gasped, forcing herself to breathe, afraid that if air didn't hit her lungs soon, she'd faint on him. She was alone with a man she barely knew, on his territory, and not an ounce of fear warned her to get the hell out. She didn't fear him. In fact, what scared her more was that she was more drawn to him than ever before. She took desperate quick breaths urging her lungs to cooperate.

"It's okay," Luke murmured and soothed. "Breathe slowly. You're alright."

"I'm sorry," she choked out. She shut her eyes, furiously praying it would help hold back the tears.

"Don't be," he whispered back. He was too puzzled for coherent words. *What the hell did he just witness? A panic attack? Why?* "What happened to you?" he finally asked.

"Bad things," she cried out.

Her words shocked him. He wasn't expecting that answer, nor was he prepared on how to handle it. A thick wave of anger tightened his chest. He wanted to know who had hurt her, and how they had done it; he wanted to hunt down the bastard who had inflicted pain upon her and make them suffer. He had never been this livid with frustration and rage, but he fought back his own aggression. What she needed right now was help, not a violent reaction to scare her more. And that's exactly how Luke felt right now. Vicious toward anything that could have placed her in this position. His swift anger was so intensely deep it surprised and confused him.

"Do you want to talk about it?" he asked as calmly as he could force himself to. She only shook her head. He wouldn't pressure her, that's not what she needed. They sat there quietly for some time while Luke tried to rub some warmth back into her lifeless hands, and Isabel managed to collect herself. He told her that he would take her home, but she insisted on driving. She wouldn't embarrass herself any further. The least he could do was follow her home, and he wouldn't hear any argument about it. They pulled to the backstreet behind the house of her beachfront home. She parked and got out quickly, reaching Luke's door before he could exit his car.

"Are you going to be all right?" He wanted to walk her to her door but could sense her hesitation. She even avoided looking into his eyes. She shakily tugged her hair behind her ear numerous times.

"I'll be fine. Thank you and I'm really sorry," she managed to say.

Luke let out a harsh breath. He was the type of man who did not like complications and dark holes. He liked to know the truth right away, but he knew this wasn't his place to pry. It was killing him to know the truth, so he could help, her but he wouldn't push.

"Anything you need at any time, you let me know okay?" His voice was stern. It quickly became important for Luke to make her understand she could trust him. "Don't ever hesitate to come to me."

"I will," she agreed. "Good night." She walked inside her house, locked all the doors, turned on all her lights, and was thankful Luke waited until she was safely inside. She saw his headlights pull away and released a shaky breath. She checked the locks again and went to soak her misery in a long, hot bath.

~*~

Luke stood inside the central ballroom of the Grand Hotel. He had greeted his guests and spoke to the chairman of the organization. His entire executive staff was present, all but Isabel. *Where the hell is she?* She was supposed to have been there half an hour ago. He didn't care that his assistant was late. He feared more that she might not be feeling well again. He shouldn't have left her alone like that. She seemed unstable. But what other choice did he have? He couldn't invite himself into her house and pry into the life of a woman he barely knew. He was supposed to keep a platonic business relationship with her. He debated about calling her when Linda passed by, and he caught her arm.

"Linda, have you seen Isabel?" he asked his chief editor.

"My, my, is our prompt new assistant running late to her first B. Pentagon event?" Linda teased and earned a scolding look from Luke. "Relax, I'm sure she's on her way. Give the girl a break, she's probably lost, she's new to town."

Luke ran a hand through his hair. He was probably worried for no reason. She would call if she couldn't make it. It wouldn't be like Isabel to not show up. *Get a grip Brady.*

"Besides," Linda continued. "You have bigger issues to worry about." She pointed her chin to the dark-haired vixen that was cat-walking her way toward Luke.

"Shit, I forgot about Magda." He let out a harsh breath.

"She's a real pain in the ass, Luke. I really don't know how you deal with her," Linda said shaking her head.

"I invited her to this over a month ago. Damn it, I completely forgot."

"Well *she* apparently didn't," Linda mused. She couldn't help but enjoy the annoyed look on Luke's face. "Good thing you didn't invite another date."

He wanted to scold her again but couldn't help but laugh. At last year's event, Rachel had an accidental mix-up and sent the same invitation to two different women he was seeing. He barely escaped the scandal by canceling on one of them last minute.

"This one really thinks she's got you by the throat. Gloats about her dates with you everywhere she goes. She's so sprung, it's pathetic."

"Luke baby, there you are," Magda said, walking past Linda with no acknowledgement. She was in a fiery-red silk dress that was pressed so tightly against her body it left little to the imagination. She presented her cheek up to Luke, and he lightly kissed it.

"You bailed on me last night," she purred as she pressed her body against his.

"I had something very important come up that required my full attention." At least he wasn't lying. He felt no remorse for canceling on Magda to take care of Isabel.

"I was very lonely without you," she continued in a sexy, playful voice.

"Might I suggest next time you purchase a vibrator," Linda called out. Luke stared at her, stunned, and Magda's cheek's burned a red almost the same color as her dress. But years of practicing to be the perfect socialite had taught her to keep herself composed in public.

"Why Linda, I didn't even see you standing there. Then again, that dress is so bland you just blend in with the rest of the surroundings." Magda gave her a lethal smile just provoking her to continue.

Linda's blue eyes turned to ice. "Well only a slut like you thinks of displaying her tits at a charity function," she said, smiling ruthlessly.

"Enough!" Luke snapped before Magda could retaliate. This was going to be one annoying evening, and he couldn't let this continue. He knew Linda could spit fire better than any drill sergeant and as entertaining as it would be, he had a charity event to run and not a damn cat fight. *And damn it, where the hell is Isabel?*

"Linda, do me a huge favor and call to check on Isabel." The glare in Luke's eyes warned Linda not to continue. She rolled her eyes and walked away. Linda went over by Matt, and by the way Matt howled with laughter and high-fived her, Luke knew she must have told him about the conversation between her and Magda. He couldn't blame his staff for not liking her. At times Magda could be one uptight, prissy bitch. He dated her occasionally and from time to time invited her to accompany him to such events, but he had made it clear to her they had no chance of a relationship or future together. Associates with benefits is what he liked to call it.

"Who's Isabel?" Magda asked. Her smile didn't do well to cover her jealous curiosity.

"My new assistant," Luke replied.

"Shouldn't she have already been here? It's an hour past the invitation time," Magda instigated.

"Let me worry about my own staff Magda," he warned her.

Magda got a displeased look on her face. Luke was usually a better companion at such events, but today he was too tense. It annoyed her greatly.

Isabel pulled her car into the parking lot of Grand Hotel. A quick glance to the diamond Cartier watch on her slim wrist informed her she was ridiculously late. She had gotten lost twice getting there. Her mind was still working on the events of last night, and how she made a complete fool of herself in front of Luke. "I'm happy here so why did I have another episode?" she muttered to herself. *He must think I'm crazy.* Who wants or needs a personal assistant who has a nervous breakdown on the second week of work. But she couldn't help but smile at the way he took care of her. How sweet he was. The powerful, wealthy executive had a soft, caring side. It made her feel safe with him.

"Miss?" a young man tapped on her window. "Valet service?" he asked.

"Yes, please." She stepped out of the car and earned a look of approval from the young valet worker. *He must be at least in his late teens,* she thought to herself and smiled back when he began to blush.

The receptionist in the lobby informed her that the central ballroom was around the left corner. Isabel arrived and was greeted by a few of her co-workers. It warmed her heart how easily they all accepted her as one of their own. She felt part of the team with them, unlike back in the law firm where it was every man for himself. She spotted Luke standing intimately close to a tall, dark-haired woman in a sexy, revealing red dress. When he made eye contact with her, she almost turned away from the intensity of his green gaze but instead forced herself to walk toward him. The least she could do was thank him for last night.

Luke felt as though the air was knocked right out of his lungs. He felt as though he was looking at another woman. It was only hours ago that Isabel was fragile and vulnerable in his office and now she stood tall, confidant and radiating in a navy blue gown. The silk and lace hugged her body perfectly and floated down to her feet. She looked magnificent. As she walked toward him, he noticed that she turned more than a few heads, catching the attention of other men. This bothered him more than he would like to admit.

"Excuse me." He released Magda and went to her.

"Luke, I'm so sorry I'm late." Isabel placed her hand on his arm. "Like an idiot, I took a wrong turn—*twice*. I guess I'm still not too familiar driving in this area. I'm very sorry, I know it's my duty to be here before others and—"

His laugh interrupted her. "Isabel, it's okay. You look amazing. I feel as though there's no need to ask you how you are doing, because you look great."

She wasn't expecting that reply. Her cheeks turned slightly pink, and she couldn't help but let out a nervous giggle of relief. It made Luke grin widely. He liked the sound of her laugh, even more when *he* made her laugh.

"Well I feel much better," she continued smiling. "Listen, about last night. First, I'm sorry. I know it's not easy dealing with an emotional woman and second..." she paused, her deep brown eyes searching his piercing green, "thank you."

Luke watched the genuine emotion that filled her eyes. Before he'd met her he might have said brown was such a dull, boring color but the depth of Isabel's brown irises brought a whole new meaning to him.

"Let's not speak of what happened. I'm glad I was there. And the offer still stands Isabel, whenever you need anything, you come to me," he reassured her.

"I will," she promised again. "Great gathering." She smiled and looked around. "I never had a chance to ask you though. Why this organization that helps domestically abused children in particular? It's a great cause, of course, but I'm failing to make a connection."

Luke looked away. "Let's just say it hits close to home."

She was startled. Luke, abused as a child? She couldn't begin to imagine it. From what Rachel had told her, he had a loving family, and they were all extremely close.

Luke noticed her confusion. "No Isabel, it's not about me. I was fortunate to have a devoted father and a very caring mother who loved me unconditionally and gave me more than I needed. Someone very close to me had a bad upbringing in life. I saw firsthand how much he suffered, and I would like to personally help any organization that saves children from domestic abuse. The idea of an adult taking advantage of their strength toward a child's weakness leaves me bitterly disturbed and angry."

"Wow," was all Isabel managed to say. She admired his brilliance in his business, and now she admired his compassion. At that moment she fell for him a little more.

"Luke darling, aren't you going to introduce me?" The dark-haired woman appeared by his side and placed a possessive hand on his arm. From a distance, Isabel hadn't seen how beautiful she was. She had dramatic dark eyes and a long black mane. She looked of Latina heritage and was utterly gorgeous. "I'm Magda," she extended her hand to Isabel, "Luke's date for the evening." She smiled smugly.

"Isabel. It's great to meet you. Won't you excuse me for a moment? There are a few things I need to check on," she replied politely. "Let me know if anything is needed." She smiled warmly at Luke. No one could deny the affection in her eyes. A quick glance at Luke and Magda saw he shared the same impression. Luke did not look at women with this much heat. This made her burn with envy.

"You're a little too late sweetheart. By the time you arrived, everything was already taken care of. " Magda gave her a snotty smile.

Isabel was amazed by the woman's audacity. An angry shiver made the tiny hairs all over her body tingle from the reaction. "Miss Magda, I'd appreciate it if you didn't meddle in my conversation with my boss. Don't you worry your pretty little head about how we handle our business affairs, *sweetheart*." Isabel's unexpected reply was so sharp and crisp she had Magda gasping. She turned around and left, heading for her table and leaving Luke watching after her with a pleased, twisted smile on his face. *That was unexpected*, he thought. *Well, well, well, looks like Linda's not the only one with a bite.*

"Luke's going to be pissed for the way I talked to his date," Isabel told Linda as she took a seat next to her. She was still sweltering with irritation. How dare that woman. She had barely met her for two minutes, and she was trying to degrade her in front of Luke.

Linda turned around and was surprised to see the outraged face of Magda. *Damn it. Must have missed something good*, she thought regretfully. "Don't worry honey, she's a world-class bitch. If that were the case I would have been fired a long time ago," Linda said making Isabel giggle.

The rest of the evening went according to schedule. Luke gave an impressive opening speech welcoming his guests. The chairman shared a few words of his own, giving the background of how the organization started and gave his great gratitude to the Brady family for all their grand donations. Dinner would soon begin, followed by an auction. Luke and Magda were seated directly across from Isabel. Magda was becoming impatient with Luke's lack of acknowledgement toward her while his eyes kept shifting toward his assistant.

"Is this seat taken?" Someone placed a hand on Isabel's shoulder. She turned around to see an attractive man gesturing to the empty seat next to her. He was tall with olive skin, warm brown eyes and was very well dressed.

"Nope, it's all yours Nate," Linda called out before Isabel could speak.

"Thank you Linda." Nate smiled and took the seat next to Isabel. "Good evening. How do you do? I believe I recognize everyone at this table except for you." He flashed a smile.

"I'm Mr. Brady's new assistant."

"Ahh, Brady, you didn't tell me you had such a lovely assistant," Nate called out to Luke from across the table but kept his eyes pierced on Isabel.

Luke was reaching his boiling point. He didn't like the gleam in Nate's eyes as they roamed Isabel's face. "It's on a need to know basis Nate," Luke gave a crisp reply.

"Nathan Portacalas," he extended his hand.

"Isabel Stamos."

"Stamos? You're Greek!" he looked delighted and astounded at the same time.

"Yes, from my father's side." She laughed as she recognized his last name to be of the same heritage.

"If only my grandmother were here. Always badgering me to find a nice Greek girl and settle down. Wait 'til I tell her I was fortunate enough to sit next to Aphrodite herself," Nate hummed in a seductive voice.

Isabel flushed at the compliment. Her grandfather had called her Helen of Troy many times but being compared to the Greek Goddess of Love and Beauty had a whole other meaning.

"Still fast with your words there huh Nate?" Linda wiggled her brows at him. "Too bad your grandmother isn't here," she teased. God she loved how these events always ended in scandal or drama. The blazing look in Luke's eyes was telling her he was not as entertained as she was.

"I can't help but acknowledge true beauty when I see it," he said and continued to beam at Isabel.

"But it's such a small world, and Greece is such a small country. She might end up being a distant cousin," Magda suggested and earned a cautious look from Linda. "I mean how embarrassing would that be for you Isabel?" She laughed cynically.

"Jealous, Magda?" Linda gave her a mocking smile.

"Jealous? Oh please." She laughed. Yes, Isabel was beautiful, she thought, but she looked uncomfortable in her own skin. And no man was interested in a woman short of confidence.

"I'm willing to take that risk," Nate told Magda, but his eyes still lingered on Isabel.

They continued talking in this manner as Nate tried to work his flattery on Isabel; Magda made rude comments, and Linda jumped to her defense. Isabel scratched a non-existing itch on the back of her neck and shifted her eyes nervously away from the table. She didn't feel comfortable being the topic of discussion and didn't like where the conversation was going. She felt uneasy and wished the topic would shift toward someone else.

"Maybe I can persuade you for a dance?" Nate leaned into her still coaxing his bold approach when the music switched to a soft melody.

Luke noticed Isabel's hesitation. It didn't take a rocket scientist to see the clear discomfort written all over her face. But since Nate was so conceited, his head was too far up his own ass to notice Isabel's reluctance. "Careful. You don't want to cross me Nate. Keep gawking at *my* assistant and your company risks losing me as its representative." Luke's eyes burned into Nate's. He had put an emphasis on 'my.' He had just about enough of watching him make Isabel uncomfortable. Not only did he want to protect her, but an enormous sense of possession came over him. He was surprised by his intense feeling to claim her.

The table suddenly became quiet. It was one thing to be on Luke's bad side but to receive a threat or warning from him was an entirely different matter. Isabel was flabbergasted at how everyone held their breaths after Luke's words. He did not raise his voice nor get up from his seat yet they reacted as though he had flipped the table upside down. Even Linda, who was always prepared for a smart comeback, shut her mouth and looked down at her plate.

Isabel lightly cleared her throat after a full minute of excruciating silence. "Well I uh, I better go help Ginger prepare for the auction." All the men rose as she did. She left the table without another word heading toward the back door when Luke caught up with her. "Did I upset you?" she asked.

Her question caught him off guard. "Upset me? Why would you assume that?"

"Because I was rude to your date and caused a scene at your table," she said through lowered lashes. Her breathing was uneven. Though she hadn't done anything intentionally, she felt an extreme load of guilt.

He gently laughed, feeling relieved that he was able to put aside his anger. "It's not your fault. Magda's deserved worse from Linda. And as far as Nate goes, I'm sorry he made you feel uncomfortable. I'm more disappointed your first event with us is not going how I expected it to."

"No, I'm having a great time Luke. And that's sweet of you to care." She smiled. What was it about this man that melted her heart so much? He was utterly wonderful.

"And try to keep away from Nate. He tends to get too comfortable when given a little room. We do business with his grandfather, but since he's too old to appear at these functions he sends his juvenile grandson instead."

He kept searching her brown eyes. She wondered if there was more he wanted to say, but he didn't continue. He left her and walked back to their table. Isabel helped Ginger complete the auction and announced that she would soon be heading home. She avoided returning to the table as much as possible, staying more behind-the-scenes with Ginger. She wanted to leave before she witnessed Luke and Magda leaving together. Luke walked her to valet and waited until her car arrived. She wondered if he thought Nate might follow her out and was silently grateful he was there to ensure this didn't happen. She said good night and couldn't wait until Monday morning to see him again.

CHAPTER THREE

Every September B. Pentagon held an annual beach bonfire and invited all their local clients. It was Luke's way of bidding farewell to summer and hyping up his staff for the upcoming holiday projects. With the joyous season around the corner, it was going to be a demanding term for everyone. It had been one hell of a profitable year for B. Pentagon, and Luke would see to it that the year ended with a big bang.

Isabel arrived early to the beach to help Ginger set up before the guests arrived. Living beachfront had its bonuses; she was walking distance away. She took in a deep breath, filling her lungs with the salty sea air. She was in paradise. She recalled her second day in town, meeting Luke on this same beach, and smiled to herself at how a brief encounter with a gorgeous stranger had transformed her life immensely. A few hours later she was surrounded by their San Diego executive staff along with multiple clients. Some enjoyed surfing while others lay around on the sand. Luke was engaged in what seemed like a very intense volleyball match. The sun had started setting as Isabel joined the others around the fire, enjoying a nice glass of Merlot. She wasn't surprised that Luke had provided only the best of wines for his clients. God bless San Diego's private beaches that legally allowed visitors to indulge in beer and wine.

Isabel listened quietly as a few carried on a casual conversation, but occasionally she caught herself more interested in the volleyball game. Especially since Luke had stripped down to just swim shorts that sat dangerously low on his hips, revealing that well defined v-line that no sane woman would deny was mouthwatering. His chest was left gloriously bare. He had broad shoulders, a lean torso, and rock hard abs. The muscles on his forearms and back that flexed each time he sent the ball striking over the net were more than pleasant to look at. He high-fived his teammates every time they scored. Isabel was fascinated by the Celtic design shamrock tattoo engraved on the back of his left shoulder. Sweat gleamed all the way down his naked back from the high adrenaline he must be feeling. Her mouth went dry, and she licked her lips to hydrate them. She hadn't realized her hungry eyes were taking their fill of Luke's appearance. Had she ever met a man more irresistible? Isabel, so caught in her own daydream of Luke, hadn't noticed when Linda followed her gaze and came to sit next to her.

"Fantasizing about our boss?" Linda teased as she lightly elbowed Isabel back to reality.

Isabel instantly turned cherry tomato red. "What? No I was just, uh, so caught up in their game." She tried smiling, but could tell Linda wasn't fooled.

"Don't worry. He's great to look at isn't he?" Linda sighed then sipped her wine as her eyes narrowed on Luke. "I imagine he's a good lay. Strong muscular arms like that just make me wonder what else he can do. I know I wouldn't mind finding out," Linda added as she winked at Isabel and caused her to blush even more. "Too bad I have a strict rule called 'no sleeping with the boss'. Plus, I don't sleep with younger men. He's twenty-nine, and I'm at the fabulous age of thirty-two," Linda said and laughed, playfully fluffing her hair. "Unfortunately, it complicates things. And unfortunately, I love my job more than I love sex. Sounds pathetic huh?" She laughed as she indulged in more wine.

"See if it was his younger brother Andrew, I'd have no choice. That boy is sexy as sin. You'll meet him soon, I'm sure. He's another replica of Luke. But unlike Luke, Drew doesn't mind seducing staff or clients," Linda continued. "Nope not Luke. He's got his head too deep into this business."

"People really enjoy working for him, don't they?" Isabel realized. She was completely taken by how cheerfully they all waltzed into the office each morning.

"Well I'll tell you one thing, the man knows how to give a great Christmas bonus that's for damn sure. He's very generous with his pay as well. Not like he doesn't expect us to earn it, but I can't complain when it comes to that aspect," Linda said and nodded her head. "He's a clever man."

"How so?"

"Because he makes life in the office so gratifying, we prefer working behind our desks than resting at home," Linda snorted. "He also knew prior to hiring that most of us were single and bloodthirsty for a career versus starting a family. This way he gets more dedication from his staff."

Isabel hadn't realized this. No wonder Luke was successful at such a young age. "His grandfather started the business, but Luke made it what it is today," Linda continued. "Business grew rapidly once he was in charge, so he kept adding multiple new locations. Soon, B. Pentagon spread all across the nation."

Guess he's got brains and beauty, Isabel thought, but she had figured that out after the first week working for him.

"There goes Rick, always late to these events." Linda shook her head like a mother would toward a misbehaved child. "I'm going to go grill him about those PR reports he was supposed to have emailed me yesterday to edit." And just as quickly as she had appeared, Linda was gone.

Isabel smiled as Linda left. She certainly was a handful. The woman had an excessive amount of energy and was unable to stay in one spot for too long. *And what's the deal with these people and their blunt conversations?* Didn't any of them think of censoring their thoughts before speaking? Talking about their love lives like it was as casual as exchanging recipes. She wondered if the San Diego air would soon make her as bold as Linda. *Highly doubtful.* She was still thinking about the sassy blonde when Luke, beer in hand, sat down next to her.

"Having fun?" he asked, smiling.

Much to her immediate relief, Luke had put his shirt back on. If he sat next to her this close and was half naked, she was sure to hyperventilate and humiliate herself.

"I'm having a great time." She smiled back. "It's such a good way for your staff and clients to associate. Was there anything you needed? I can go set up for the barbeque."

He caught her arm to stop her from rising. "No, stay. Everything is where it's supposed to be. Besides, Ginger is beyond compulsive. She's planned everything to the last detail." Luke laughed.

Isabel had been working for him nearly two months now. It was challenging for Luke to keep his distance when he was constantly drawn to her, yet he fought every defying thought and kept his relationship with her professional. He refused to make her uncomfortable. Not only did he enjoy working with her but for some odd reason he couldn't explain, he liked knowing she was safe. Not a day passed by without a radiant smile glowing on her face. Though her eyes still kept their secrets, she looked to be better. He had become not only accustomed but addicted to her shy schoolgirl giggle. He liked walking into his office and seeing her there happily working with the rest of his staff. If he couldn't have a personal relationship with her, he'd at least appreciate her from a distance and keep an eye on her. He never wanted to see her vulnerable again.

"Thanks for helping Ginger out, by the way."

"It's what you pay me for. So what's the story behind your tattoo?" She regretted it as soon as she asked. "Sorry, it's none of my business," she said instantly. *How more obvious could she make that she'd been sitting here staring at him?* Luke's lips twisted into an amused smile.

"Don't be, I don't mind. I got it after I found out Matt was an ex-tattoo artist, and I asked him to design one for me a couple of years ago. You see, my grandfather had one right here," he said, pointing to the inside of his wrist, "So I told Matt to design a similar one for me. I don't know why I did. I had never planned on getting one. It was more of a spontaneous spur-of-the-moment thing in honor of my grandfather. Hurt like hell, I'll tell you that." He grinned.

"Well at least it looks really good."

His green eyes lingered over hers. "You think so? I'm glad you like it." He smirked.

Isabel let out a nervous laugh. She quietly cursed herself. *Way to go making it obvious you were checking him out Isabel.* "So why the Celtic design?"

"I guess because it's a symbol to my heritage." His arm brushed against hers, and her whole body heated from the slight touch.

"Irish?" she managed to continue.

"Half, from my father's side." He grinned and watched her eyes light up in amusement. God, her eyes were so hypnotically beautiful with those long, thick lashes. A man could just get lost staring into them. Not a speck of any other color than a solid warm brown. He'd never been one to pay much attention to any woman's eyes before, but Isabel's were mesmerizing. Reminding himself that his thoughts were getting ahead of him, he got up and casually excused himself to go help with the barbeque.

After the barbeque was served and the s'mores devoured, Isabel helped Ginger clean up. The event was over and most had already said their goodbyes and headed home. She finished placing the last of the remaining items in Ginger's trunk, bid her farewell, and headed back toward the beach to walk home. Luke noticed and followed her trail.

"Need a lift?" he asked as he caught up with her. *Damn it Brady, you can't even keep your distance for a full hour.*

"No, it's alright. I actually live really close remember? I walked here." The ocean winds sent a chill down her back making her shiver.

Luke frowned and threw his jacket over her shoulders. "Well then the least I can do is walk you home. It's late, and the street lamps don't give much light." There was no way in hell he'd watch her walk home alone no matter how close she lived.

Isabel bit back her hesitation once she realized the beach was darker than expected. The incident in L.A. had left her petrified of the dark. She mentally cursed herself for being a coward and began to walk with Luke. A few moments later, they were standing outside her mother's beach house. Both feeling a bit awkward as if it were the end of a first date, they silently hovered outside the door.

"Thanks for the jacket." Isabel finally broke the silence as she handed it back to Luke.

"You're welcome." He smiled. "Have a good night Isabel."

"Good night Luke," she smiled back and headed up the front steps as Luke left.

The nighttime breeze had enhanced the blissful ocean scents. Luke strolled back toward his car with his hands in his pockets, enjoying the feel of the cool breeze as it touched his skin. The loud splashes of the deep waves brought a sense of familiar serenity for him. He was halfway back when he heard a loud crashing sound and a woman screaming. He stopped dead in his tracks with impulse blaring at him that the voice belonged to only one person.

"Isabel," he choked.

In an instant he was flying up the steps toward her door. He pushed open her front entrance and ran inside as Isabel came crashing into him. He grabbed her by the shoulders to balance her, and an instant chill went down his back when he saw her pale face.

"What's wrong? Are you hurt? What is it?" He feared she might be injured and shuddered from the thought.

"It's the... it's the... I just couldn't..." She struggled to speak. Alarm took over her as she tried to catch her breath and speak to him. Finally, after gaining enough self-control she managed to speak in a loud trembling voice. "RAT... the, the rat, it's a huge rat." Embarrassment colored her face when all Luke did was stare at her. How could she explain it wasn't the rat she feared? How did she tell him when she walked inside and heard the slightest of noises she dreaded the thought of someone being inside her house? She'd seen the mouse, but it was too late to stop her uncontrollable panic that tended to blur any rational thoughts.

Luke was still holding on to her shoulders tightly. He didn't know if he should curse her for scaring him half to death or erupt in laughter, but when he saw the startled look on her face, he decided either reaction might frighten her more. Not sure what to say or do next he absent-mindedly began stroking his hands up and down her arms.

"Okay…umm…well, uh, where is it? Do you want to show me?"

"Over there," Isabel managed to choke out. Luke looked around but didn't know exactly where "over there" meant. "I'll show you," she quickly added. "The kitchen."

Luke turned around as Isabel nudged him out of the living room. It amused him how she followed closely clenching both fists into the back of his t- shirt.

"THERE IT IS!" she screamed and started pulling Luke's shirt while strengthening her grip. She wrapped her arms around his waist pressing the front of her body tightly to his back leaving zero distance between them. He turned hard when he felt her breasts press firmly against his back and took a deep breath for control.

"Sweetheart, I can't catch the bastard if you're pulling me back," Luke gently explained.

"Oh, right. Sorry. Wait, DON'T kill it." She panicked at the thought of a dead rat in her kitchen and quickly handed Luke an empty jar and towel sitting on the counter. She squealed when Luke managed to grab the rodent from the tail and placed it in the jar. He left and reappeared a few moments later with an empty jar.

"I'm guessing you only do well with humans," he teased when he found her still frightened in the kitchen. "You might want to look around and find the hole that little guy crawled in from."

"I guess I overreacted again," Isabel sighed, with her hand pressed to her forehead. *First seagulls and now rats.*

Luke lightly laughed. "Well I better get going."

"Thanks again," she said and gave a shaky laugh back as she walked him toward the door.

As they stopped at the front entrance, he turned around facing her. He subconsciously brushed her hair away from her face, lightly touching her cheek. She had such delicate bone structure. For a moment, he studied her face and watched her nervously shift her weight from one foot to the other. She must have been spending more time on the beach; her face was slightly tanned. He let his fingers caress her cheek, no longer denying himself the temptation. Slowly lifting her chin, he lightly kissed the corner of her mouth, dangerously close to her lips. It took every willpower he could possess to not brush his lips against hers. What he would give to just taste that beautiful mouth. He pulled away and stared into her eyes and sensed no hesitation.

Heat rushed to Luke's brain when he realized her eyes were inviting him to take more. If this were a date, Luke would have greedily taken her lips and pushed his hands up her shirt with no reluctance. It alarmed him how physically attracted he was to his own assistant, and her body language showed she was no stranger to the enticing lure between them. He scrubbed his hand over his chin. He couldn't take another step. He either had to have all of her or none at all. As he began to talk, she interrupted him.

"Don't apologize. It will just make things awkward." She paused for a moment then released a muffled laugh trying to grab a hold of her jumping nerves and racing hormones. Without saying a word, he gave her a crooked grin, shuffled his hands through his already unruly hair and watched her eyes light up in amusement. He walked away and heard her close the door. Luke counted the sound of numerous clicks. She must have at least five locks on that door. As he walked back to his car, he promised himself that someday soon he would find out why Isabel Stamos felt the need for that much protection.

~*~

The days flew by rapidly inside the exciting walls of B. Pentagon Corporation. Isabel realized she was more productive in an energetic, high paced environment than in a quiet office. She had become better acquainted with the staff and enjoyed working with them. As for Luke, she tried not to dwell too much on what happened the night of the bonfire, especially since he hadn't made anything of it. Isabel wondered if Luke was deliberately avoiding her. He hadn't been calling her into his office as often as he used to, and when he did, he barely made eye contact. Three times this week she had made a "dinner for two" reservation at a local swanky restaurant and knew there was nothing business related about it. But she convinced herself she was once again overreacting because Luke was a busy man and had his reasons to be locked up inside his office.

Isabel had a good view of Luke from her desk when his double doors were open. Occasionally, she'd find him standing with his hands in his pockets, gazing out his window toward the sea just as he had the day they met. A serious frown molded his face when working countless hours in front of his computer. When on the phone with an old client, his tone would become light and friendly as he'd lean back in his chair and discuss business casually, but when negotiating, he became calculating and persuasive. Isabel couldn't imagine anyone turning down a business proposal from Luke. In fact, she couldn't imagine anyone turning down any type of proposal from Luke. He certainly had his way with people; his voice was just as hypnotizing as his good looks. Isabel scolded herself each time she caught herself daydreaming about her boss.

Always on queue to interrupt her racing thoughts, Linda appeared at her desk. "Not planning on leaving yet? It's Friday." Linda gave her a wide excited grin. "So what are your plans this weekend? Any hot dates?" She wiggled her brows.

"Nope. Not this weekend." Isabel laughed lightly. She didn't remember the last time she'd even had a date, yet alone a hot one. Before joining the law firm, she dated occasionally and had a moderate social life. Then her world had darkened once she became an associate of Preston Scotts.

"Then, in that case, a few of us are going over to Clay's tonight for some drinks. It's our usual hangout spot in downtown and has the best bar in town. You have to join us, I promise it's worth it," Linda continued in her energetic tone.

Isabel had heard numerous co-workers talk about Clay's. They said it had a nice bar, an old karaoke machine, and a small dance floor. *Not her usual scene*, Isabel thought. But when she moved away from L.A., she promised herself and her mother that she would have a life outside the office. "I don't drink, but I'd love to check out the place. What time?"

"Nine pm, drinks and dancing. And I don't want to hear any of that 'I don't drink or dance' crap when you get there tonight," Linda said as she placed her hands on her hips and wondered what the hell this chick did for fun. "Here's the address. Wear something sexy and don't be late."

~*~

Isabel's cab pulled into the busy parking lot of the well-known bar. After a few outfit changes, she settled on a deep plum cocktail dress that exposed her slim, tanned legs and nude-colored pumps. Walking through the crowded doorway, Isabel spotted Linda and a few others laughing at the bar. Linda's gaze immediately caught Isabel's, and she came dashing toward her.

"You made it." Linda grabbed her hand leading her toward their group. "Wow, you look great. I love the dress."

"The same goes to you. You cut your hair." Isabel spoke loud to be heard over the music and loud chatter amongst the large crowd. Linda had chopped off her medium length blond hair to a short sleek bob revealing her long neck. She wore a short black dress with strappy black heels. Isabel looked around and noticed the rather racy attire the rest of the women were wearing and for once was glad she took the risk and put on the shortest dress in her closet. Isabel giggled shyly as she watched Linda wave and wink at a few men before they reached their group.

Everyone was excited to see Isabel, and it warmed her heart how easily she'd made friends. She waved to Matt who was sitting on a stool and openly flirting with the cute bartender he'd just met. Since he was currently sporting a t-shirt and not his usual dress shirts, Isabel noticed both of Matt's arms were covered in sleeved tattoos. He sent her an instant smile and raised his beer to salute.

"So what are you having? I already started a tab," Linda told Isabel. "Your first night here at Clay's needs be unforgettable, and I'm buying."

Before Isabel could object Linda gave her an exasperated *don't start with me* look. "I'll have whatever you're having."

"Good girl. Hey sweetie, give me two double shots of your best tequila," Linda called out in an alluring voice to the male bartender. His name was Josh, and he had tattoos covering most of his arms and parts of his neck. It didn't take much observation to figure out he was one of Matt's friends. Josh gave Isabel a quick teasing wink at the sight of her alarmed face.

"Tequila?" Isabel stressed. "I've never had a tequila shot yet alone a double." She laughed nervously.

"Isabel, we're here to get a little tipsy, meet a few fine men, dance our sexy heels off, and have a good time. Look around you honey. The place is swarming with hot guys. If you're going to hang out with me tonight, you have to pick up the pace so let's go," Linda said as she handed Isabel her glass. "Now follow my lead."

She watched Linda lick her wrist, sprinkle some salt on it, throw her head back taking the shot, lick the salt off her wrist, and bite into a lime. "Well, here goes nothing." Isabel shrugged and mimicked Linda's lead. She squinted her eyes and sucked in her cheeks from the sour taste of the lime causing Linda to burst into laughter.

"That's more like it rookie. A few more of these and you'll be pulling *me* to the dance floor." She laughed and ordered another round. "Speaking of hot guys, there goes our boss," Linda said as she bumped her shoulder to Isabel. She noticed Isabel tensed and instantly turn toward the door. Linda was right. *Their little Isabel had developed a crush on Luke.*

Luke hadn't spotted them yet. Isabel tried not to stare, but she couldn't help herself, especially since she was excited he was there. She hadn't expected Luke to show up to the same bar his staff was always occupying during the weekend. She took quick glimpses from the corner of her eye and noticed the way his arm was wrapped around the tall, leggy blonde he'd walked in with. She wore a skintight, black mini skirt with a white tank top revealing her voluptuous breasts. A few, including Matt, approached Luke to greet him. The blonde had a smug look on her face, knowing many recognized the man she had walked in with. Isabel's heart fluttered as she caught Luke's surprised look when he saw her. She flashed him a quick smile and turned her attention back to Linda. She couldn't help but feel a tang of disappointment. She didn't want to feel jealous but couldn't help it. It was for these exact inappropriate reasons she had to overcome her attraction toward him because he would never be hers.

"Why am I not surprised?" Linda shook her head. "That whore finally got her paws on Luke," she looked at the blonde with disgust.

"You know her?"

"That's Stacey," Linda said in a sickened voice. "She used to work at B. Pentagon in the mailing room, making occasional bullshit excuses to come to the top floor just to flirt with Luke. Rumor has it, she quit the second she figured out Luke wasn't going to sleep with one of his own employees. Can you believe her?" Linda said with a disgusted laugh. "People kill to get into that company, and she quit to bone the V.P."

"You really don't like her huh?" Isabel noticed Linda's instant change of mood.

"No, I don't. She got me in trouble with Luke's father, our CEO. He had specifically ordered some editorial prints from me, saying it was urgent. I worked on them all night and the next morning. Handed it to her when she came collecting the mail and made it crystal clear it was vital and needed to be sent out certified. Leave it to that brainless bimbo to misplace the file. I had another rough draft copy but by the time I realized Mr. Brady Senior hadn't received it, it was too late. We lost the potential client, and I was called into Luke's office to explain myself. I always wondered if it was intentional on her part or if she really is that careless." Linda sighed. "Anyway, we're here to have some fun, not talk about that little twit." Linda immediately changed her mood and placed her bright smile back on. She liked Isabel and didn't want to bore her with a sob story when she had promised her an entertaining night. And when Linda promised, she delivered. "Let's get drunk and dance." She wiggled her hips.

Luke hadn't expected to see her there. He became completely oblivious to the woman next to him as he watched Linda hand Isabel a shot and nudge her to drink. She looked good. Really good. The way that dress hugged her body was causing a reaction below the belt that he didn't want to acknowledge. And he was right, she definitely had been spending some time on the beach. Her long, beautifully tanned legs were proof enough. Luke noticed he wasn't the only guy staring as Linda caught the attention of a few guys and gestured them toward Isabel and herself. After a few more drinks, he noticed the newly formed group turn toward the dance floor. Isabel hesitated, but Linda lightly pushed her toward one of the men they had attracted. One who didn't pass the opportunity to grab Isabel's hand and walk her toward center stage. Luke's Irish blood boiled as the man ran his hand up and down Isabel's back after pulling her close.

Linda, with her eagle eyes, caught Luke's furious look as he watched Isabel. *Well, well,* she thought to herself, *seems like the feeling between these two is mutual. Things are going to get quite interesting in the office soon,* she mused.

He cursed himself for being irritated. After almost kissing her at her front door, Luke had become more determined to stay away from her. He forcefully turned his attention to his date. Unfortunately, the woman couldn't carry on a decent conversation, and her only talents were in bed. Luke told himself he would only stay there for a while longer and then continue his date as planned. But his raging curiosity had him staying behind and secretly watching Isabel most of the night like some kind of obsessed creep. He didn't like the way her head fell on the shoulder of the guy she was dancing with when he made her laugh. He didn't like how she giggled when he attempted to dip her while dancing. And he sure didn't like the way the douchebag didn't take his hands off of her by caressing her back and touching her hair. But most of all, he didn't like the way all of this made him feel. Why did he care who she danced with, and how they touched her? It was none of his concern. She was his employee, not his possession. He knew he could never be that free with Isabel; it just wasn't set out that way for them. Yet he almost broke into a wild frenzy when he watched Isabel leave the scene with that same man's arm draped over her shoulder.

~*~

Monday morning Isabel sat at her desk nursing a massive headache. Massaging her throbbing temples, she was glad that the office was empty, allowing her to enjoy the complete silence. For some reason, her hangover had lasted a few days. Just goes to show how weak she was against alcohol, and she could just kill Linda for it. But she smiled to herself. For once in a long time she had a great social night and had to be *grateful* to Linda.

"Rough night?" Luke startled her as he dropped a handful of heavy files on top of her desk.

"Geez, you scared me. I didn't know anyone was in the office." Isabel quickly began organizing the files he had dropped.

Ignoring her accusation, Luke continued to look at her. He had never been more frustrated with a woman than he was with her, and it irritated him that he allowed it. He was tempted to ask if she went home with that guy from Clay's, but he knew it would be out of line. So he took out his anger another way.

"I had asked that these files be completed and on my desk last week," he scolded.

"I thought I had completed them and returned them back to you," Isabel said confused.

"They aren't complete. I don't like the format of the prints. I want it redone," he continued in the same annoyed tone.

"I'm sorry Luke, I will definitely look through it again." Isabel's hands hurried through the files.

"I don't pay you to be sorry. I pay you to get the job done right the first time. If men at Clay's bar are going to be a distraction and impair your judgment at work then I suggest you figure a way around it." Luke was more irritated with himself than he realized. *What the hell was he doing speaking to her like that and bringing up Clay's?* Two whole days had passed by, and he still couldn't get the image of another man's hands on her out of his head. He'd barely known the woman a few months so why had he developed this possessive attitude? Maybe because he sure as hell didn't want another man having what he couldn't. What he was frantically and painfully aching for yet denying himself of since it was forbidden.

"I'm sorry Luke, but is there a problem from Friday night?" Isabel asked as she followed him into his office.

Luke noticed the rest of his employees began to arrive as he sat behind his desk. "No, there's no problem. I just need those files completed please," he said more calmly and watched her nod and leave without saying another word.

The rest of the day Luke worked silently behind closed doors and told Isabel to hold all his calls. He didn't call her into his office again, didn't allow anyone to disturb him, and didn't even leave for lunch. He must have been overworking himself, because he was beginning to not recognize his own rash behavior. It was that damn woman who was making him lose his mind. He couldn't get her out of his head and as much as he had tried to distract himself with Stacey on Friday night, he had failed miserably. He wanted Isabel so badly it burned. Why? Why did he want her? What was it about Isabel Stamos that constantly managed to get under his skin? Maybe that was the problem. Maybe that was why he was losing his mind. Luke never came across anything he wanted and couldn't have, and that's why he was on edge when it came to his attraction toward Isabel. He would just have to find a way to get over it. When the holidays were over he would take a quick weekend vacation to his cabin in Big Lake and clear his head. Feeling like a complete jackass for the way he treated her earlier that morning, he picked up his phone.

"Isabel can I see you in my office?" He hung up, and she was instantly at the door. "Close the door please," he said, watching her nervous moves. "Have a seat." She hesitantly pulled the chair and sat.

"I want to apologize for my behavior this morning. I've got a lot going on and didn't mean to take it out on you. I'm actually very impressed by the additional changes you have made around here. Hiring you was beneficial to my company and it wasn't fair to you the way I reacted. I didn't mean to take on the role of the scary boss," he finished and sent her a warm smile.

Her heart melted. She knew he was bombarded with work and knew how much pressure the holiday projects were bringing upon everyone. But she knew that wasn't the only problem. Strong instinct told her Luke was fighting his attraction toward her. He was constantly hot and cold toward her. She didn't know which direction he would turn next.

"I'm sorry too, Luke. I didn't know the prints weren't to your standards, and I should have received a final confirmation first before leaving on Friday."

After they finished talking, she got up to leave. Pausing at the front doors she looked at him. "I know this is irrelevant and has nothing to do with work but for what it's worth nothing happened between me and that guy from Friday night. He just escorted me home and left. Nothing happened," she repeated. "I was just uh…" She swallowed the lump in her throat. "I was just too scared to go home alone since it was pretty late."

Silence hung heavily between them. Luke opened his mouth to speak but didn't trust himself to comment.

"I just wanted to clear the air and needed you to know how the night ended," Isabel rushed out her words. "It's been a long time since I've been out with friends and besides, it will definitely take some time until I can work up the nerve in that department again," she snorted and immediately turned red, realizing she had spoken without thinking. Was she seriously standing her and speaking to her boss about her non-existing sex life? Ever since the incident in L.A. she had become self-conscience and a bit insecure. She herself was surprised at her bold behavior Friday night and immediately blamed the tequila. She quickly excused herself leaving Luke to stare at the closed doors.

"What are you hiding Isabel?" he whispered.

CHAPTER FOUR

December arrived with promises of it being a very cold winter. B. Pentagon Prints was at the peak of its season as Luke's staff merrily worked overtime and most weekends. Ginger, with Isabel's help, had decked the halls to bring in holiday cheer. The Annual Christmas Gala and New Year's Bash held in New York was rapidly approaching. Ginger and Isabel had been in constant contact with the Manhattan location's events coordinator working on the details. The CEO, Luke's father, wanted specific arrangements and sent them a long guest list. Most of their clients were back east and had gladly RSVP'd to the celebrations. B. Pentagon was known for throwing the largest and most exquisite holiday celebrations for its clients. Since Luke's father had started the tradition, the event was to be held in his New York estate. As Luke's personal assistant, Isabel was expected to join the event just as Rachel had every year.

Luke worked in silence the next few months behind closed doors. When his doors were open, he usually wasn't in his office. Isabel also noticed his dinner for two reservations had decreased. He was acting strange, and she knew she was the reason. One minute he was pleased to see her, and the next he struggled to keep away. It looked as though he was fighting himself around her, and she wanted to convince him to stop wrestling with his thoughts. She was sure of how he felt from the way his eyes lingered over hers; how occasionally he'd brush his fingers over her cheek when they were alone. Whenever he was close enough to touch he didn't fight the urge to gently stroke her face with the tips of his fingers and softly brush her arms with his hands. Yet she would see him hesitate and pull back. It distressed her to know she was falling for a man who refused to want her back. She told herself it was because he was trying to maintain a professional relationship but a large part of her insecurities told her maybe he just wasn't that into her. *Maybe* she wasn't worth the risk for him to take.

Luke realized the best way to stop thinking about Isabel was to be buried deep in his work. He desperately tried to distract himself with exclusive dates hoping meaningless sex would relax his unsettled nerves. He thought in order to get his mind off the woman he denied himself, he could distract himself with casual dating. Unfortunately, he failed miserably. He would sit across the dinner table from a beautiful, intelligent woman and think about Isabel instead. He hadn't touch, kissed, or slept with a woman since he'd met her. She had spoiled him for anyone else. His travel arrangements with Isabel were approaching, and he had to prepare himself to see her as his assistant and nothing more. He was going to spend a lot of close time with her and needed to bury his need for her. The busy holiday schedule was a definite bonus with helping him keep his distance.

He sat at his desk and was planning his next meeting when his phone rang. He looked at the receiver and realized the call was coming directly to his line instead of a transfer from Isabel. Only a handful of people had Luke's direct line. Debating if he should pick up or leave it to voicemail, like he had most of the day, he finally picked up the phone.

"Brady," he called out.

"Luke? It's Preston Scotts. Hope it's not a bad time." Luke recognized the old voice in an instant.

"Can you please hold a moment?" Luke placed the call on hold and quickly went to shut his double doors. "How can I help you Scotts?"

"Well I haven't called to discuss business Luke. I've actually called to ask you about your assistant. A few of my contacts have discovered her to be working closely with you. I'm sure by now you're aware she used to work for me."

Luke paused. He predicted this call was one he wasn't going to like. "Yes, Ms. Stamos has been my personal assistant the last couple of months. Is there a message you'd like me to pass along to her?"

"No, it's alright. I rather have her not know about this call," Scotts hesitated. "How is she doing? Is she alright? Does she seem fine?"

Luke recognized worry in the old man's voice and for once had received a call he wasn't prepared to handle. "She seems fine, I haven't noticed anything wrong." A lie of course. Isabel cringed each time in mention of the firm.

There was an awkward silence for a moment. One of those long pregnant pauses where both parties are too stubborn to speak first. Finally, Scotts cleared his throat and continued. "She quit my firm and left town so fast I didn't have a chance to talk to her and figure out what the hell was going on. I was away on a long trip to Nevada representing a client of mine and when I got back there was no sign of her. My partner told me he was unable to get a hold of her. I loved having Isabel working here. She was young, energetic, and the best researcher I have ever come across my thirty plus years in this profession. And from my understanding, she loved working here too. She was more than halfway through her law degree and knew she had a permanent job here so it came as a surprise as to why she left in January. I contacted her law school and found out she dropped out short after that. I tried to reach her at home but found her condo empty. I'm not trying to scare the poor girl; I'm just trying to figure out what the hell happened."

Luke sighed heavily but continued to remain quiet. The fact that he didn't even know that Isabel had once tried to obtain a law degree bothered him. *Why hadn't she told him about this?*

"I understand your concern Scotts, but I assure you she seems perfectly fine. If I find out anything, you'll be the first to know." Another lie. He had worked with the man before and respected who he was, but he wasn't ready to discuss the personal life of his assistant with her former employer, especially since she seemed troubled by something neither of them knew about. Yet Luke had a feeling it must have something to do with that damn firm. *But what?* If the firm was the problem surely Scotts would know.

Luke hung up the phone and walked out of his office to find her, but Isabel wasn't at her desk. "Hey Brian, where's Isabel?" Luke asked his savvy tech who was troubleshooting Isabel's computer.

"She took the mail downstairs. The mail clerk called out sick today." Brian shrugged as he continued to hit the keys on the board.

"It seems like I need to start hiring who should be working in that damn mail room," Luke muttered irritably.

His attention was brought to the large huddle his staff had formed around a tall woman with wild curly brown hair. Her back was toward Luke, and he couldn't see her face, but he watched his staff beam in excitement as the woman was clearly signing and passing out autographs. When she turned around he recognized her instantly and was amazed. *Vivian Taylor.* What in the world was Vivian Taylor, the famous artist, doing here?

"Ms. Vivian Taylor. This is a pleasant surprise. To what do we owe the pleasure of your company?" The woman was exquisitely beautiful with a slightly tanned face and large brown eyes. Luke had never met her but felt as though he had seen her eyes in person before. "Luke Brady", he said as he gently shook her hand.

"It's a pleasure, Luke. Sorry I arrived here unannounced. I was in town and wanted to see my daughter." Vivian saw the puzzled look on his face.

"Your daughter?" Before Luke could put two and two together, Isabel walked through the elevator doors.

"Mom? What are you doing here?" she said. Her face lit up with excitement as she rushed toward her mother and enveloped her in a warm embrace.

"Izzie, my baby." Vivian smiled as she watched her daughter teasingly roll her eyes at her childhood nickname. "I missed you so much. I'm sorry, I should have let you know I was coming here, but I like surprising you. How are you doing sweetheart? Are you eating well?" Vivian cupped Isabel's face with both hands and studied her with concern. The rest had returned back to their desks except for Luke. "I wanted to finish the gallery in Malibu sooner so I could come here to be with you, but I was right in the middle of it. I'm sorry I didn't get here faster honey. You should have stayed with me in Malibu, I really didn't want you to be alone out here after what happened Izzie. I thought you were just taking a trip, but you've been here for months. I want you to come back with me."

Isabel realized Luke caught the worried tone in her mother's voice as he held his hand to his chin and studied her through narrowed eyes. Her mother kept rambling about how she was concerned about her, and Luke's green gaze became more intense with every word as he watched her. She became desperate to stop her mother from talking before she revealed too much.

"Mom, I'm fine, I already told you that," Isabel widened her eyes, warning her mother.

Vivian recognized her daughter's silent plea to change the subject. She also caught the unsettled glances she kept sending the man next to them, the man that continued to watch her daughter with heavy, penetrating inquisition. She released her face and folded her hands. In an instant she was bright and cheerful again trying to shadow her wariness.

"Well I just wanted to stop by for a quick hello." She sent her best smile, but Isabel wasn't fooled. "I'm having a late lunch with a few friends in town and I'll see you at home for dinner okay?" Vivian hugged her daughter. "It was so wonderful meeting you Luke." She smiled and waved a quick goodbye to her admirers and left.

"So you're the daughter of a world famous artist. You continue to shock me Isabel. I didn't even know Vivian Taylor had a daughter."

"She didn't want the press suffocating me. She left her personal life out of her work," Isabel said. *And thank God for that.* She wasn't the type that would have done well with the constant paparazzi her mother was so enthralled by.

"She did a pretty good job with that. You don't seem the sort of person who'd thrive off of being in front of persistent cameras."

Isabel's eyes widened. *How did he know? Was she that transparent?* Or did Luke seem to always have this special vision that saw right through her.

"She seemed quite concerned about your well-being. Why is that?" he probed.

Isabel looked away.

"Offer still stands," Luke continued. "I'm here to help. You only need to ask."

Luke walked back to his office. He tried his best not to pry but the call from Preston Scotts, and Vivian Taylor's concern if her daughter was eating well, pestered him. He had a horrifying thought that whatever it was Isabel had ran from wasn't so far away, and he'd be damned if it tried to even come close to her. He silently vowed they'd have to go through him first.

~*~

Ecstatic joy swelled Isabel's heart to have her mother home. This year would have been the first time in all of her life she would spend the holidays without her. She missed the warm feeling of sitting around a cozy dinner table with just the two of them. During winter, they usually ended the night drinking wine by the fireplace and indulging in their favorite chocolate mousse dessert. Her mother would tell her all about her thrilling travel adventures, and the new collections she had added to each of her exhibits. Two years ago, Vivian had purchased and moved to an oceanfront loft in Malibu with large rooms and high ceilings. Her latest project was the art gallery she recently opened a few miles away from her new home. Isabel knew her mother didn't like cramped areas. Wide spaces made her feel more comfortable so the only property she would purchase would be beachfront.

"You can't get more space than the ocean," her mother had once pointed out.

They had identical features. Having her first and only child at a young age Vivian looked better than ever. With gold rings scattered on her fingers, dangling earrings, and forever dressed in bright-colored clothes that hugged her body, showing her great physique, Vivian brought life into any room she stepped into. Now they were together again, chatting away and laughing while they relaxed by the fire. It was times like these Isabel missed her father greatly. She wished she had the chance to feel his big strong arms hold her again and make her feel safe. During her darkest times was when she yearned for that sense of security the most. But as fate would have it, her father died from a fatal heart attack, leaving her feeling incomplete and her mother heartbroken.

"You look to be doing well baby." Vivian sadly smiled while watching her daughter pour them another glass of their favorite *Fat Bastard Merlot*.

"It's this beautiful San Diego atmosphere." Isabel settled next to her mother on the wide cream colored couch. "I still can't get over this beautiful ocean. No wonder you love the beach so much Mom. I feel so alive being here. You know I've always loved the beach as much as you and Dad. As weird as this may sound, I used to keep a bottle of sunscreen in my bottom drawer at the firm and smell it when I missed our summers on the Mediterranean." She laughed at her confession. "I never want to go back to L.A.," she murmured.

"I never want to see you back in that town." Vivian remembered well that all too disturbing call she received from her daughter. First thing she did was rush to L.A., got Isabel out of that town, and hired the best therapist money could buy. She had never seen her lively Izzie so terrified and broken. It broke her heart to see her struggle so much. Working at the firm wasn't the life Vivian wanted for her. All her life she imagined her little girl growing up and living a euphoric life. She desperately wanted to see her happy. When Isabel made the decision to temporarily vacation in San Diego, she knew it was a fantastic idea. She looked much healthier. No, she definitely did not want her daughter going back.

"You sold your condo pretty fast." Vivian smiled.

"Yes, in less than a month after I put it up for sale. Your real estate agent Joanne said she wasn't surprised how fast it sold considering the great location." Isabel sighed with relief. Now that her condo was sold she felt more at ease. Another dark memory of her past put to rest.

"Good. I'm glad that's over and done with. Joanne's good at what she does and is worth hiring." Vivian indulged in more wine. "So tell me about your new job, and that gorgeous new boss of yours," she asked with excitement. "Oh, that office was lovely! So much life and color and just a few minutes away from the beach."

Isabel laughed. "You'd definitely love working there. Words can't describe how much I love it there Mom. Not only is the job fast paced and exciting but the people are just fabulous. I've made good friends there."

"And your boss? Luke, was it? Is he treating you well?" Vivian was surprised to see her daughter blush. "Well?" she continued when her daughter didn't speak.

"Luke's great. He's part of the reason why I'm doing so great here," she paused, "and it doesn't hurt that he's just so damn sexy." Isabel giggled and flushed a little more.

"Why Isabel Stamos, I have never heard you speak about a man like that." Vivian was shocked yet entertained. She watched her coy Izzie turn red as a tomato.

"Well I've never met a man like Luke before. He's just so incredible."

"So I take it something is going on between you two?" Her daughter, age twenty-six, had never spoke about a man as profoundly. She knew her daughter had been involved with men before, even dating casually at one point, but never got this doe-eyed look. It somewhat worried her. After all, Luke was her boss.

"Oh no, no. Nothing at all. Just a little cliché crush on the hot boss I need to get over." Isabel laughed. "I'm probably just drawn to him so much because of how well he took care of me when I had another episode." *Shit.* She bit her lower lip and regretted it as soon as the words escaped her mouth.

"Another episode?" Vivian's eyes widened in alarm. "What happened? Damn it, why didn't you call me Isabel?"

"Mom I'm fine, I promise it wasn't a big deal. It wasn't a bad episode. Luke was just having a brief meeting with me telling me how well I'm doing, and I guess I just became overwhelmed with emotion and reacted by freezing up again." Isabel hoped the situation sounded as casual as she tried to make it seem.

"I worry so much about you Izzie. Especially you living here all alone. I wish you would at least bring Johnny here to watch out for you."

"What? Johnny? No Mom, I'm fine, I promise you. Please don't make anything of this," Isabel tried to reassure her mother. The last thing she wanted was to have Johnny, aka Big John, her mother's head of security for her exhibits, watching her every move like the hawk that he was. If someone needed to watch her then it meant she wasn't safe. Isabel felt secure here and didn't need that image tampered. "Mom, I'm fine," she said again.

"So you're saying he took care of you huh?" her mother finally spoke.

"Yes he did." Isabel smiled remembering how Luke rubbed warmth back into her shaking hands.

"I'm not sure it's such a smart idea being involved with your boss Isabel." Vivian worried. She knew her daughter hadn't been involved with a man in ages. When it came to relationships Isabel had always been naïve and didn't take many risks. No doubt life had made her this way. But the look in her eyes was telling Vivian this was more than just a minor crush. Her daughter was deeply affected by this man and did not care to hide it. Not Isabel's usual behavior. "I don't want to see you get hurt," Vivian said.

Isabel sighed heavily. "I'm not going to get hurt, because I'm not involved with him. And as much as I'd like to be, it's unrealistic. He's my boss. You know the whole look but can't touch sort of deal."

"Well if you do get involved with him, just please be careful. I want you to be wary of every move you make. Being involved with the boss isn't going to be a normal and casual relationship. It's going to be complicated, and Luke looks like a complicated man."

Isabel snorted, "Oh he's the complicated one huh? *Hello,* you're sitting next to a head case here." She laughed and earned a displeased side glance from her mother.

"Ha, ha, very funny. I'm just saying guard your emotions, that's all."

"Mom."

"And use protection. Are you on the pill? I know you haven't slept with anyone for a while but protection is important," Vivian continued.

"Oh my God. Mom. Really? Eww. Can you please just stop talking? Please."

"I'm serious Izzie."

"Oh God. Mom if I get involved with any man, I promise to be as careful as possible. I'm not a child so let's please just drop this and go to sleep, it's past midnight."

Arm in arm, mother and daughter walked upstairs to their bedrooms. Vivian spent a few short days with her daughter. She had to be certain Isabel was truly doing as well as she looked. She made her daughter promise to have a safe trip to New York, call her often, and visit her in Malibu when she returned. Isabel watched as her mother sat in her car, waved good-bye, and headed for the road.

~*~

On Friday evening, Isabel began clearing her desk. She had missed her mother the moment her car had pulled away. She couldn't wait to visit her in Malibu and see her new exhibit. Luke walked through his double doors and approached her. "Busy day."

"I'll say. And loved every minute of it."

"What are you doing tonight?" Luke asked.

Her heart skipped then began thudding an abnormal beat. *Relax,* she told herself, *you have no idea why he is asking and are getting ahead of yourself.*

"Nothing planned." She tried to sound casual. "Dinner at home, a good book, and a glass of wine. Maybe two." She laughed. "I earned it this week."

Luke smiled down at her. "That you did. I'll tell you what. I'll buy you that glass of wine if you will join me for dinner tonight. I'm meeting with a new client. Wait, let me rephrase that. I'm meeting with a new, potentially very *big* client. We need to discuss contract details and—"

"And you need me to write down these details and terms," she finished his sentence.

He couldn't help but grin at her. "Oh you know me well. I'm sorry, I know it's the weekend, but I promise it will be one hell of a dinner and wine. Heck, you can have the whole bottle if you want." He laughed.

She wondered how could anyone resist that face. Isabel drew her brows together as if considering his offer. "Hmmm. Very tempting. I'll take it." *Not like she had better plans.*

"Good, I knew you wouldn't let me down. We're meeting at Marcio's at eight o'clock sharp. Here's the address," he said as he jotted down on her note pad.

"Marcio's? Never been there but heard a lot about it. Very upscale."

"Like I said, a potentially very big client, so dress to impress. And don't be late." He winked and left back to his office.

Isabel went quickly home to get ready for her dinner plans with Luke. She knew it wasn't a date, yet she couldn't control her giddy excitement. She showered, dressed, styled her hair, and made sure her eye shadow was the right shade of smoky. She grabbed her purse and rushed to the kitchen to call for a cab. The last event she drove to she got lost and would not risk running late on Luke again. As she ended her call she noticed the window above the sink was lifted open.

That's strange, she thought as she fiddled with her diamond stud earrings. She didn't remember opening that window. It was cold, and she hadn't cooked for days so why would she open the window? Frantic waves of panic shook her body. *No, it couldn't be.* She alarmingly looked around the house. Everything was in place. If someone broke in, didn't they usually do it to steal? Unless it meant someone hadn't come for her possessions. They were here looking for her. Wild hysteria shook her to the bone as she frantically ran out her door. *You're overreacting and hallucinating again, Isabel. You promised to no longer live in fear.*

She forced herself to regain composure and quietly waited for her cab on the street while ordering her breathing to become normal again. An hour later, Isabel walked into the grand entrance of Marcio's. The place was as classy as these restaurants could be with rich Italian décor, sleek glossy floors, high ceilings, and dimmed chandeliers. The restaurant was lit by candles and decorated with white orchids in every corner. She heard her own Prada heels clicking on the white glossy marble as she approached the large reception desk.

"Hello. Here to meet Mr. Luke Brady."

"Right this way, miss," the tall red-haired hostess gestured toward the grand double doors.

Luke immediately turned his attention to the entrance as if he sensed her presence. She was dressed in a black cocktail dress hugging her petite curves that revealed those same tanned legs that had yet to leave Luke's mind since seeing her at Clay's. She looked sexy, yet breathtakingly classy. She was the most beautiful woman he had ever seen. He had seen many beautiful women, but he did not understand what it was he felt inside every time he set eyes on her. He liked having a hold on his emotions but when it came to Isabel Stamos, he lacked control.

"Your guest has arrived Mr. Brady," the hostess quietly announced as she led Isabel to him. "Would you like to be seated now or wait for the rest of your party?"

"We'll be seated now, thank you," Luke answered without taking his eyes off Isabel.

"Right this way please." The hostess noticed Luke's hot gaze and felt an immediate twitch of envy toward Isabel as she led the way.

"You look stunning," Luke whispered in her ear as he helped her to her seat.

"Thank you," Isabel spoke softly. He was dressed in one of his black power suits again, and she told herself not to gawk at him. He sat next to her as they were approached quickly by one staff member after the next. It didn't take long to realize he was a highly admired customer.

Their client arrived shortly after their drink order was taken. Mr. Benjamin Steins was the owner of a major technology company. Naturally, he wanted to discuss business first and dinner later. Steins had started in a small local office but in a matter of two years had grown his empire into a very large corporation. He had new products to advertise and wanted to take his clients by storm.

"Smart and brilliant advertisement is what I want," he said. This was where Luke came in. Isabel took quick notes as Luke and Mr. Steins discussed business. He wanted billboards everywhere, his company name printed and advertised in every major magazine, and even a magazine of his own. Based on his research, he admitted to Luke that he was told B. Pentagon had the best graphic designers. He wanted Luke to have his company name printed all across the nation.

Isabel quietly listened as Luke executed the deal smoothly. Mr. Steins hadn't cracked a smile all night and by the end of the deal he had transformed his cold exterior into a more friendly expression. Isabel was amazed at Luke's sharp tongue. He knew exactly what to say to make the deal work. Finally, business was discussed and dinner was served. All three became more relaxed once the agreement was settled, and Isabel began to enjoy their luscious steaks and the fabulous Chianti as promised by Luke.

An hour later, Luke escorted his now happy and satisfied client to his waiting limo and returned back to Isabel.

"That went well." She smiled to him.

He sent her a glorious grin that once again made her heart beat faster. "I think I'm going to consider you my good luck charm, Isabel. Mr. Steins is one hard ass to impress, but the deal went smoother than I expected." His eyes gleamed with satisfaction. "Thank you for joining me tonight."

"Oh it was my pleasure." She smiled back as she gestured to her empty wine glass. Luke laughed.

"Would you like another glass?"

"I'm okay."

"Did I tell you how beautiful you look tonight?" Luke whispered as he leaned in dangerously close.

"I don't mind hearing it again," she murmured and watched his eyes light up with appreciation. She didn't mind showing the lack of hesitation in her eyes. She wanted this man. Wanted him more than she was verbally willing to admit. If words couldn't speak for her then she hoped her eyes would send a clear message.

He caught the tips of her hair between his fingers and was slowly twirling it, close enough to smell the sweet scent of her perfume. That wild jasmine scent filled his lungs; the same scent that left him light-headed and yearning every morning when he walked past her desk. All he had to do was lean in a bit closer and his lips would be on hers. The look in her eyes was inviting him to do just that. It surprised him how welcoming her glance was as if she could read his mind and silently willed him to kiss her. The moment was overwhelming, and he almost caved in but he'd come this far without ruining things with her, so he lifted her hand and kissed her fingers instead.

"Come, let's get you home." And just like that the moment was broken.

He closed the bill and they walked outside toward valet. "Where's the ticket for your car?" Luke asked as he handed his to a young gentleman wearing a red vest.

"I came with a cab. I didn't want to risk running late again."

Luke chuckled. "Well the least I can do is drive you home. My car is already here." He casually took her hand and walked her to his car. He couldn't resist the urge so he kissed the back of her hand once more before opening the passenger door. He bit back a groan as he watched her dress rise seductively up her slender tanned thighs as she slipped into the seat.

"Why do you torture yourself Brady," he muttered to himself. He tipped the red vested gentleman generously and got behind the wheel.

Isabel examined the expensive interior of his black BMW M6 convertible. "New car?" she asked when he sat inside.

"Yes, it was an early Christmas bonus I gave myself." He grinned and took the road.

Isabel was silent most of the ride back home. Luke watched as she clung to her small purse. She didn't make any small talk and just kept her eyes straight on the road. He felt the immediate switch in her mood and wondered what was making her unsteady. In his opinion, the evening had gone well. But as he pulled near her house, he noticed her breathing became unstable and heavy and her hand trembled when she reached for the door.

Isabel silently cursed herself supremely for being a coward. She'd become weak and frightened once again. She thought she was stronger now but couldn't push away the unwanted fearful thought of someone slipping inside her kitchen window, waiting for her to return. She shut her eyes tight and told herself to control her breathing. She felt Luke's hard hand on her shoulder.

"Isabel, what is it?" His voice was in deep concern. She opened her mouth to speak but no words came out and panic struck her even more. *Oh God,* she hoped she wouldn't hyperventilate again. Luke looked at the empty dark house and immediately realized her problem. "Are you scared to go in?" He began to gently rub her shoulder. "Come on," he said as he got out the car. He opened her door and put a protective arm around her waist pulling her out. She leaned against him limply still failing to gain her strength and feeling mortified.

Luke walked her to her door. "Keys in there?" He gestured to her purse. She nodded, and he took it from her stiff hand and dug out her keys. Once they were inside, Luke turned on every light and lamp he could find while still holding a tight arm around her waist. "It's alright," he quietly said and moved her to face him. "You're safe I promise. I'm right here," he whispered.

"I'm sorry," she said, finally catching her breath. "I'm stupid. Don't mind me, I'm just being ridiculous." She managed to release a weak laugh. She looked up for an answer only to find his eyes searching hers.

"What the hell happened to you? Tell me," Luke quietly demanded. "What has hurt you Isabel?" He took a strand of her brown hair and gently tucked it behind her ear. It pained him to see her so pale and scared.

"I think someone tried to break in today while I was at work," she managed to say with a shaky voice.

"WHAT?" his voice rose in alarm. "You're fucking kidding me. Did you call the cops?"

"No," she whispered.

"Why not? Why didn't you at least tell me earlier or called me to come get you Isabel?" His grip on her tightened. He could sense his own fear choking him. He didn't want to allow his mind to even think about what could have happened if Isabel walked inside alone and was faced with an intruder.

"I didn't want to overreact. I saw the kitchen window open and couldn't remember opening it myself and panicked. I'm sure I'm the one who opened it, and I just forgot. It's happened before." She shut her eyes.

Luke became silent. He pulled her into his arms and held her firmly against his chest for quite some time. He finally pulled her away, gripped her face in both of his hands and looked into her deep brown eyes. "Well I'm not leaving you alone tonight. And don't bother arguing with me, because I can assure you I will win. Go get ready for bed, and I'll bunk here on the couch."

"Luke, really. You don't have to—"

"I mean it Isabel, don't argue with me. Go to bed. You need to get some sleep."

This should be the most awkward situation Isabel could possibly find herself in. *A sleepover with the boss,* how out of place does *that* sound? She waited for the discomfort to kick in, but she was oddly at ease. She threw her arms around his neck and tightly embraced him in relief. "Thank you," she whispered.

He stroked a hand down her hair. "You can thank me by going and getting some rest." She kissed him lightly on the cheek and headed upstairs. Once Luke was alone he looked around the house making sure all the windows and doors were locked. He didn't notice any tampering or evidence of a possible break-in. He looked for an alarm system but failed to find one.

"Unbelievable," he muttered to himself. "The woman has her mother's art pieces worth twenty grand each lying around with no damn alarm."

Luke stripped down to just his boxer briefs and sprawled on the wide couch. His mind pondered upon all the unanswered questions regarding Isabel's behavior and wanted to know what triggered her panic so easily. *Is she getting any help? Is this why her mother is so concerned?* He finally drifted to a light sleep. Two hours later he was awakened to the sounds of sobbing. He sprung to his feet and realized the sound came from upstairs. He followed the noise to Isabel's bedroom and realized she was crying in her sleep. It broke his heart to see her distressed. She struggled and continued to cry in a helpless voice, too drowned in her dream to separate it from reality. With hands fisting the sheets, she shook her head trying to wake herself up. The sight was too agonizing to watch. Luke kneeled at her bedside and began to wake her. He just couldn't stand there and watch her being tortured.

"Baby wake up. It's just a bad dream," he murmured to her while stroking her hair. He watched her struggle to break from her spellbound nightmare. He continued to stroke her hair and speak softly into her ear hoping to comfort her.

"I can't breathe." She gasped. "I can't breathe."

"Yes you can. Just concentrate."

It took a great deal of effort, but she finally stirred away from her demons. "Luke?" She cried out and fluttered her wet eyes. It was as if his voice had finally broken the curse.

"I'm here baby." He kissed her forehead. "You're safe, I promise." He brushed his lips over her tear stained cheek.

"Oh God Luke, hold me please. I'm so scared." She continued to weep.

Luke hesitated but finally got into her cold bed. He pulled her close in a warm embrace and held her. Soon, his heated body warmed her sheets, and Isabel settled into his comforting arms. She rested her cheek on his bare chest and wrapped her arms tight around his waist. She held on to him firmly, afraid that if she relaxed her hold she might lose him. Luke continued stroking her hair and whispering to her until he felt her body become limp as she slipped away into deep slumber. Her thin silky night gown barely left any barriers between them as she pressed her body snugly to his. It was the first time in Luke's life that he spent the night in a woman's bed without being sexually involved with her first. But for some reason, he felt this to be the most intimate situation he had ever been in.

CHAPTER FIVE

Isabel awoke with her face buried into her pillow to an empty bed with Luke's scent still lingering on her sheets. She went downstairs, but he was already gone. As she checked the time, she noticed how late it was. Jeez had she really slept until noon? *How is that possible?* She never slept passed eight. It could be because she felt all too comfortable and safe in Luke's arms last night. Her cheeks heated when she remembered Luke holding her as his hands had ran up and down her arms and spine until she was in peaceful serenity.

"I need some coffee," she mumbled and headed for the kitchen. A note placed on her counter read:

Morning,

Had an early brunch meeting. Jake will be there at noon sharp. Don't argue. Just let him work. You'll be safe.

Luke

Jake? Isabel wondered who Jake was as the doorbell rang, 12pm sharp. This Jake must be prompt. She opened the door to a tall, buzz cut, dark-haired, incredibly handsome man. He had to be at least six foot two, the same height as Luke.

"Guessing you're Isabel? Jake Callaghan," he said. He didn't offer a hand. He wore denim jeans ripped at his right knee, a black shirt, leather jacket, and combat boots with dog tags hanging around his neck. He had a serious rugged face and dangerously intense icy green eyes that showed no sign of emotion. A little scar cut across his left brow made him look outrageously threatening. Nothing about this man said 'friendly and approachable,' yet Luke's note had ensured her safety.

"Well are you going to let me in or leave me to freeze to death?" he asked irritably as she hesitated at the door.

"Oh right, sorry. Please come in."

"I'm guessing Brady didn't give you much detail. I'm here to install a security system."

"Oh." Isabel was confused. She began to protest but stopped herself. "Alright." She smiled. "Can I get you some coffee?"

"Sure." Jake was already walking around the living room, scanning ceiling corners and windows. She immediately realized that she was still in her nightgown, though he had hardly even looked at her. "I'll be right back," she said and dashed upstairs to change. She came back to the living room and placed a tray of sugar, cream, and a large cup of coffee on the coffee table.

"Thanks," Jake said. "Ever had a system before?"

"No. Just moved in a few months ago." It never crossed her mind to get one. Her condo in L.A. didn't have one either, and since she was barely ever home, she never thought she'd needed one.

"And what do you suppose was going to guard these Vivian Taylor paintings you have scattered around your living room?" He raised his brows and spoke sarcastically.

Isabel smiled widely. "I don't know. She hadn't warned me her art was all over the place before giving me the keys to her house."

"You know her?" Jake asked.

"I'm her daughter," she said and was satisfied by the shocked look on his face.

"No shit?" He stared at her in amazement. "Alright, well this shouldn't take more than an hour. I'll explain the system and coding once you're fully equipped. You shouldn't need much done. Three control panels will be enough. I'll put one near the front door, one on the back, and another in the upstairs hallway. You'll have a few motion detectors, alarms on all the doors and windows, of course, and from what I saw outside, four surveillances should do it. But just in case, I'll walk around the outside once more and maybe place a fifth cam as well."

"Surveillance? As in cameras?" Isabel nervously laughed and shook her hands in front of her. "All that really isn't necessary."

Jake crossed his arms across his chest. "Either I can do my full job now or half-ass it and be back tomorrow morning. If you know Brady as well as I *think* you know him, he's not going to settle for less than full security."

Isabel wanted to tell the man that Luke didn't live here, and it wasn't his decision. She didn't need his system or security cameras surrounding her premises. But she knew he was right because she did know Luke and if he had sent Jake here, then he doubted she *"accidentally forgot"* to close her window. This meant he must have already made up his mind that Jake should install a system. There was no changing Luke's mind once it was set. She sighed and nodded her head in agreement. After all, she still couldn't remember ever opening that window.

Jake began working without another word. He worked fast and didn't bother asking for permission when entering any room, even her bedroom. He didn't acknowledge her or ask her further questions. He looked like the type of man who didn't bother with many words. He had stripped off his leather jacket and his black t-shirt stretched across his muscular upper body. He had a tattoo on the back of his right triceps all the way down to his elbow that spelled something out, but Isabel wasn't close enough to read the words. He looked like he had just escaped an Army prison with his worn-out combat boots and dog tags dangling from his neck. His exterior appearance screamed *caution, danger, keep away.* This was the type of man every mother warned her innocent daughters about. But Isabel was at ease with him because she knew Luke wouldn't leave her alone with a man unless he fully trusted him.

After Jake set up the complicated system, he handed her a guide book and told her to pay close attention. Isabel stared at the complex screen and frowned. "This doesn't look like a typical home security system."

"It's not," Jake said as he began gathering his equipment and tools. "I don't make house calls." He looked at the petite brunette in front of him, arms crossed over her chest, waiting for him to elaborate. "It's a corporate system. Similar to the ones I install for Brady's company."

"Oh." *So he works for B. Pentagon as well?* "How weird that I've never met you before."

Jake was about to be a dickhead and blurt out that Luke didn't get into the habit of introducing his short-lived flings to his best friend and family. He had gotten a call from his best friend at eight am asking if he was available to do a new location installment. Much to his surprise, the address he was given was to a local house and not a B. Pentagon building. Nothing about this woman said she was one of Brady's one-night stands. He watched the pretty woman hover across her new control panel, testing it out.

"So how long have you two been dating?" Jake asked. He figured it must not have been for long since he was just finding out about her.

It took Isabel a moment to realize he was asking her about Luke. "Oh, no I'm not with Luke. I work for him. Personal assistant." She smiled.

Jake stared at her stunned as if she had slapped him hard across the face. *Well I'll be damned,* he mused to himself. Brady must be infatuated with his own assistant. This was a definite first. Sure, he always cared for his employees, but Jake would bet his Harley that his old pal Brady paid special attention to this one. Isabel flushed when Jake stood there bluntly sizing her up from head to toe.

"Well then," he finally said, "card is on the table. Tell Brady I'll see him later." Duffle bag in hand he headed for the door.

"Wait, what do I owe you? You haven't given me an invoice," Isabel called after him.

He turned around, smug smile spread across his face. "Brady's already picked up the tab." He closed the door quietly behind him and walked toward his car. As he dumped his bag behind his work truck, he saw Luke approaching him.

"Well if it isn't the generous boss himself. Hello Romeo," Jake said with a wide grin on his face as he lit up his cigarette.

"Shut it Callaghan. Everything set?" Luke uneasily nodded his head toward Isabel's door. Jake took a long look at the house and then his childhood friend. Something was definitely going on. He took a long deep inhale of his smoke.

"Just as you asked. So what's the deal with you and the babe? Didn't know you started sleeping with your employees." Luke sent him a warning look that made Jake's grin grow even wider.

"I'm not sleeping with her," he said, "And I thought you were quitting," he indicated to the cigarette.

"Starting tomorrow. You said you spent the night here," Jake continued with his probing.

"Doesn't mean I slept with her," Luke snapped. "It's not like that with Isabel. I care about her." It surprised him how easily the words came out. And since last night he'd been worrying about her even more.

Jake studied Luke's face and sensed his restlessness. His eyes kept anxiously shifting toward Isabel's house, watching it as if any minute now he'd finally see what he was looking for. He easily read the signs that this wouldn't be a good time to ask Luke any further questions. That was the beauty behind their friendship. They only needed to exchange a few words to know exactly how the other felt.

"Huh, I think you might be doing more than just caring about her pal. The Brady I know doesn't send me to just any random woman's house to ensure her safety. If you're going to act on this Luke, be careful, and don't fuck it up. Shit like this usually gets messy and you know that." But Jake received no answer which told him his assumptions were right. Luke was enthralled by this woman more than he thought and wasn't sure how to handle it.

"I've got to run. I'll see you in New York." He tossed out his cigarette and climbed into his truck.

Luke stayed outside Isabel's door debating if he should go in. Finally, he made the decision that it would be best to stay away. The lines were beginning to blur, and he was confused what side he was on. He was losing his mind and never thought he'd use so much energy to force himself to stay away from a single person. That's how strong Isabel's magnetic pull was toward him. Right when he thought he was in control of things and had placed a safe distance between them, she pulled him right back toward her. He needed to clear his mind since Jake's words still echoed in his head. He knew what was at stake if he and Isabel became involved, and it ended badly. He knew he sure didn't want to fuck it up.

He walked away from Isabel's house disputing between what his mind told him to do and what his heart yearned for, yet his heart refused to follow his mind. He got into his car and headed for his office, *his sanctuary,* where he could work and gain an ounce of peace to clear his head of all things Isabel.

He was working behind his desk when he heard the sound of the elevator announcing someone's arrival to the top floor. He wondered if maybe one of his employees came in to work on a Saturday. He continued working when Isabel walked into his office. He leaned back in his chair watching her walk toward him. She was dressed in a dark gray sweater dress and black boots. Just the sight of her made Luke's desire burn. *There's just no escaping her*, he groaned to himself. This woman was subconsciously out to torture him.

"Hi," she said, smiling nervously.

"Hey." He smiled back. "Forget something in the office?"

"I needed to pick up a few files to take with me to New York tomorrow. Plus, I was hoping to catch you here." She saw his brows rise in surprise. "I wanted to thank you for sending Jake to install the system."

"You're welcome," he said, smiling.

"And also to thank you for helping me again." She looked to the floor. "I managed to embarrass myself yet again didn't I?

It's just so damn pathetic already." She let out a weak pitiful laugh. Luke walked in front of her and lifted her chin.

"Hey. How many times do I have to repeat that I'm here for you?" he asked with a stern voice.

"I know you are. You've proved that tremendously." She searched his emerald green eyes. "But why?"

Her question caught him off guard. *Why Brady? She wants to know why?* He didn't dare admit it. He could just bluff his way out of this one as well and play the 'boss ensuring the safety of his employee' card. But he was tired of hiding his true interest in her. He took a deep breath and brushed his index finger lightly above her brow.

"Because I care about you," he admitted. "I care deeply for you Isabel." He lightly stroked her face with the back of his fingers then traced her lower lip with his thumb. It was all the assurance Isabel needed. She placed her delicate hands on his chest, slowly rose and closed the distance between their lips. She kissed him with confidence. Gently at first but then very profoundly as her lips became slightly demanding. Luke groaned and placed his hands firmly on her hips. He slowly pulled her closer until their bodies molded against each other. As much as his mind had warned him to prevent this very moment from happening, his heart had ignored it. He softly sucked on her lower lip causing her to slightly moan. It was the sweetest music to his ears. He wanted to take her on his wide wooden desk which had enough surface to support them both. He thrust his tongue into her parted mouth and turned the embrace into a moment of heat and passion.

Isabel's mind became clouded and her skin burned. Need, sensation, and thrill shook her entire body, a reaction she thought she would never feel again. She felt it deep in her core—the powerful urge that made her want more. The slow strokes of their tongues continued, and Luke's mouth became harder on hers. He ran his hands up and down her back slowly and seductively, pulling them both into a heated frenzy. At this moment, he realized he was pressing a very hard part of his anatomy against her lower stomach. It took all his willpower, any sense he still had left, to pull away and stop himself from ripping her clothes away and devouring her.

"Isabel." He forced away to break the kiss. He placed his forehead on hers and was struck for words. Both breathing heavily, they gazed into each other's eyes. He'd reached entirely too close to losing his edge. He wanted her more than anything he had ever wanted and the strong yearning desire thrilled yet frightened him deeply.

"Don't say anything," she breathlessly whispered against his lips. "It was the exact thing I needed." Her chest felt heavy, because she could not distinguish the look in his eyes. She was unable to read satisfaction or regret in them, though either way she did not want to know. She wasn't sure she was ready for either answer.

They stood in silence until the burning heat cooled down, and Luke desperately wanted to ask her if they could try to make this work. He feared he might scare her; that if he pushed, she'd run away. He still didn't know what she was running away from when she arrived here, but he didn't want to make any mistakes and lose her before he even had her. He'd let her figure things out at her own pace. He already knew what he felt and knew what he wanted. He wanted Isabel, but he knew he'd never risk hurting her.

"Promise you'll still come to New York with me?" he asked, searching her brown eyes. "I hope that this hasn't changed anything and won't hold you back from coming with me." She laughed nervously. *This kiss has changed everything*, she thought.

If only he knew how much it had changed her. She was no longer denying how quickly she was falling for him.

"I'll be there. Which reminds me, I better go finish packing." Luke hesitated to let her go, but he finally released her.

"See you tomorrow morning," he called out after her as she closed his double doors. Isabel didn't know how she made it to her desk on shaky legs. *Wow*, she thought, *that was intense*. She began arranging her files with shaking hands when moments later Linda appeared.

"Hot date with the boss last night?" Linda leaned on Isabel's desk as if the woman had radar every time she thought about Luke.

"Yes, discussing contact details with a big shot client. Pretty hot." Isabel was still flushed.

"Uh huh," Linda said and raised a brow and studied her. "Don't act like you don't possess a fatal attraction toward our sexy as sin boss over there. I see how you get those puppy dog eyes every time you look at him. It's written all over your face sweetie. I must say he shares the same attraction toward you. He looks a heartbeat away from breaking control and dry humping you."

"I do not!" Isabel shrieked, turning red as a tomato. "And no he does not." *Oh my God, did Linda just see them kissing in Luke's office*? Her mortification brightened her face with an even deeper red.

"Not buying it. Look how flushed you are just thinking about it. It's actually pretty cute. Don't get all shy with me Isabel, I have a sixth sense when it comes to these things. And don't be embarrassed about it either." She pointed a finger at her. "We're all adults, and we can speak about sex openly."

"Okay, fine. Maybe I've developed a little crush on Luke." Isabel lowered her voice. "But it's out of the question and I need to get over it."

"Why?"

"Why? Because he is our boss that's why. I'm just attracted to him because he's the first good-looking man I have been around in such a long time."

"How long?" Linda raised a brow.

"Too long." Isabel laughed.

Linda stared her down. "When was the last time you had sex?"

Isabel began rearranging random items on her desk to avoid Linda's inquisitive eyes. "Four years ago," she mumbled under her breath.

"I'm sorry, what? I didn't hear you." Linda leaned in closer cupping her ear dramatically.

"Four years ago," Isabel repeated louder.

"WHAT? Are you crazy? How is that possible? How did you even manage that? I mean look at you?" Linda's shocked voice made Isabel cringe.

"Hey, it's not that bad," she said defensively and earned an *'oh really?'* look from Linda. "Okay fine, it is that bad." Isabel burst out laughing, and Linda joined her. She had developed a great friendship with Linda. In the short period of time they had become good gal pals inside and outside the office and one night after another round of tequilas at Linda's house, Isabel had trusted her and blurted out everything that had happened to her in L.A.

Linda now knew the big dark secret that lurked in Isabel's mind. She had told Isabel to get the proper help, but she made her promise she would let her deal with it the way she thought best.

"Besides, that's not why I'm so flushed right now. I've completely embarrassed myself in front of Luke. I had an episode in his office a couple of months ago and last night another one of those dreadful nightmares." She sighed and ran a hand through her hair.

"Oh shit Isabel." Linda voiced with concern.

"It's not a big deal. Please don't worry. I guess it's because I talked to my mother and you about it recently which freshened the memory and opened old wounds."

"You can't open wounds that haven't yet been healed sweetie. You never got closure from what happened, that's why it will never leave you. You should do something to cope with it."

"I'm fine, Linda."

Linda sighed. She tried to talk to her numerous times, but Isabel just wouldn't budge. She actually thought if she ignored it then it would go away.

"Okay fine, have it your way. Just take better care of yourself for me please. You know what would get your mind off of all that? Hot and sweaty sex with our delicious boss over there. Trust me, it would be great therapy for you."

"Oh my God Linda," Isabel chuckled and covering her face with both hands, "you are just too much. Can we please stop talking about Luke? He's in his office and might hear you."

"Not until you admit it's more than just a crush." Isabel glanced quickly toward Luke's closed doors.

"I'm really attracted to him. Never been this drawn to any man before," she admitted.

"Oh my God. *I knew it!*" Linda yelled and excitedly jumped up and down.

"*Shhhh,* Linda."

"So do you think something will happen in New York? You do know that you and Luke will be alone on his private plane don't you?" Linda's eyes were gleaming with enough mischief that slightly alarmed Isabel.

"No, I did not know that. Thank you, that's just great. Another thing to be nervous about. And to answer your question, no I don't think anything will happen. I know he cares about me, but he's not going to get involved with me. We've been spending a lot of time together because my position requires it but I can tell Luke prefers to not complicate things and keeps his distance. Every time we get a little too close he pulls away, and I need to accept that." Isabel recalled Luke's face after she kissed him. He wasn't exactly rushing to declare any feelings toward her, and it hurt, but she knew he wasn't the type of man to rush into anything.

"Besides, who'd want to get involved with a woman as emotionally unstable as I am? I've had a few episodes in front of him Linda, I'm sure I totally freaked him out."

"Luke's not shallow Isabel," Linda scolded.

"I know, I'm just saying I understand his reasons for staying away."

"Well, I, on the other hand, think he won't be able to control himself sooner or later, so my money's on him. Four years Isabel. Four freakin' years." Linda shook her head still stunned how anyone went through life that long without releasing some sexual tension. "Anyway, have a safe trip sweetie," Linda said, tightly hugging Isabel. "And call me if you have another nightmare, and I'll stay on the phone with you okay? And as for Luke, I'm rooting for him so don't forget to shave your legs." Linda playfully swatted Isabel's butt before she left.

~*~

For most, annoyance toward airports came easily. Having to find the right terminal, dealing with security, flight delays, and the long dragging departure to their destination was a great nuisance. But to Isabel, it was a familiarity all too comforting. Her parents loved to travel and by the age of twelve she had already seen more than most would in a lifetime. Isabel hadn't had an ordinary childhood. She hadn't attended the same school for more than two years. Through constant traveling with her parents, she'd had the luxury of seeing many beautiful foreign countries. It wasn't until her father's death that her mother finally settled in California.

Now she sat in B. Pentagon Prints' plush and very spacious company plane and watched Luke speak to his pilot. The soft royal blue carpet felt like velvet underneath her feet, and the smooth plump white seating made her feel as though she was floating on a fluffy, weightless cloud. She ran her hand slowly on the exterior of her armrest and felt the softness of the fabric. She observed Luke in his trim fit, three-piece dark charcoal suit and fiddled nervously with her heart locket. She wondered how many times he had stood in that exact spot speaking to his staff. How many times had he used this lavish plane for business? And how many women sat in her exact seat waiting for him to join her?

She remembered vividly how Luke's hands had felt the day before when he was holding her firmly against him. She remembered how desperately her mouth had roamed against his, how his demanding lips and tongue had stroked hers. She would give anything to taste him again. Since the minute they'd met, her need for him had kept building and building. She feared she'd soon explode like an uncontrollable, erupting volcano. She did not recognize the woman within herself when she was with Luke. It was as though an unknown source was feeding her the confidence to take what she wanted, yet her lack of experience kept pulling her back.

As if reading her thoughts, Luke shifted his attention to Isabel and looked directly into her eyes. She could have sworn the world stopped orbiting as his intense green eyes bore into hers. That in some odd bizarre way, he could read her mind. She felt naked and slightly vulnerable. Here was the man she was most intimidated by—who she had allowed herself to become close to despite her better judgment—and he could see right through her. That's what she loved and feared most about Luke. That he saw her as clear as day. He witnessed her strengths and insecurities yet she did not bother to hide herself from him.

"Nervous about flying?" He smiled down at her as she shifted to become more comfortable in her seat. She was wearing black slacks and a white, chiffon shirt. Her dark brown hair rounded her beautifully tanned face and her big, bright brown eyes intensified as she gazed upon him. Anticipation began choking him. *This is going to be one long flight to New York.*

Isabel watched as Luke stripped off his suit jacket and handed it to the flight attendant.
"No actually," she said and smiled back. "I've done this quite a few times. Well nothing like *this*, though." She laughed as she looked around the plane.

"Oh? Had a few adventures of your own?" Luke asked as he took his seat. Though the seats were wide, Luke sat close with just the armrest separating them.

"Fortunately, my parents' professions allowed us to travel quite excessively," she said and smiled in fond memory.

"Your father was an artist as well?"

"No, he was a philosopher." She remembered the two very different people her parents had been. "There's my mother—the free spirited artist who talks until she is out of breath—and then there was my silent, serious father who didn't talk often and would have much rather observed. We traveled anywhere and everywhere. My mother has a passion for any type of art she can find. It doesn't matter if she's staring at a da Vince masterpiece at the Louvre or being mesmerized by the breathtaking sight of the Taj Mahal. To her, if you consider yourself an artist, you have to appreciate and understand all forms of talent and beauty."

"And your father?" Luke asked as the plane took off. He wanted her to continue talking. He liked watching her steady eyes as she spoke. She was too caught up in her own travel back in time to notice the shake and rattle of the plane. He recognized how poised she was and liked seeing her this way. Too often he had seen her nervous and unsettled, and it pleased him to see her at ease for a change. He guessed it was because she spoke so fondly of her parents and that caused her to relax. He had to admit he loved seeing her in his private plane. She looked as though she belonged right there next to him.

"He loved it. Every minute of it. He found every opportunity he could to observe the different cultures we came upon. He wrote about their social styles, living habits, their affection toward family, and devotion to their professions. For my father, he'd much rather have pondered upon what people were thinking than stare at colorful pictures, as he would refer to it. He was a good man, and he loved us so much." With a low sigh, Isabel looked at Luke as he looked back with wondering eyes. She knew he had caught the past-tense tone when she spoke of her father and since he didn't ask, she felt comfortable telling him. "He passed away from a heart attack when I was twelve years old."

Luke saw the grief behind her eyes. He knew pain when he saw it. He waited in long silence before asking, "Where's your favorite place to have traveled?" The relief in her eyes showed she was grateful he changed the subject.

"Well," a slow smile curved at the corner of her lips, "every year during summer we would visit one of the Greek Islands." She remembered all too clearly dipping her toes in the Mediterranean. "But my favorite place was this small village in Naxos where my father's parents lived. Legend has it, the land was the birthplace of many gifted, brilliant philosophers; that there was something in the water they drank and air they breathed that caused them to be so extraordinary. We'd always have a picnic at one of the local beaches and eat the goat cheese my grandmother had made while my father would tell us the stories of the mythical Greek Gods. Sometimes, my grandfather would sneak me a sip of his red wine. He said wine was the drink of the gods and it gave strength. He thought my arms were too skinny and weak, and I could use all the strength I could find." Luke grinned at the way Isabel laughed. God, he loved hearing her sweet laughter and seeing her this way. He deliberately kept silent so she would continue.

"I remember how my grandmother would yell out "Zabel" every time I'd eagerly take the wine from my grandpa. That's what she called me," Isabel explained, "as if that was my Greek name or something." She giggled at the memory of it. "It was a beautiful village. There was this overpowering feeling of peace and security, and the locals were all one big, happy family. The death of my father devastated both of my grandparents immensely, and they all too soon followed him. Now I imagine they must be with my father eating goat cheese and sipping wine with the gods my father so respectfully spoke of."

Luke listened silently as Isabel spoke of her childhood. The stories she knew of how her mother—during a summer trip to Greece—had met her father, fallen hopelessly in love, and married him all in same summer. Everyone in her father's village had attended to see the local resident marry the beautiful American. He didn't know anyone other than himself who felt so passionately toward family. He loved listening about the history of the villagers she spoke of and promised that one day he would visit that very same island in Greece.

He was so enthralled with her childhood tales that he almost forgot they were on a plane to New York until Isabel turned off the light above her head and closed her eyes to rest. He continued to study her face as she drifted to sleep. While he gazed at her, his own eyes became heavy from sleep and within seconds he was dreaming of the serene waves of the Mediterranean Sea.

Later, Luke awoke, shifted in his seat and felt his right arm captured. He looked over to find Isabel curled up tightly against his arm, her warm slender body pressed against his. She laid her head more on his headrest than hers, leaving her lips just an inch away from his. She looked so peaceful and smelled of sweet jasmine flowers. Luke couldn't help but to gently touch her cheek with the tips of his fingers and feel her soft skin. He pushed her hair lightly away from her face knowing the gesture might awaken her. She fluttered her eyes half open still heavy from sleep.

"What time is it? Are we almost there?" she whispered, half mumbling her words.

"We still have another hour. Go back to sleep," he whispered back while watching her eyes close again. Her lips looked so soft it made him wonder if her lips would once again taste as sweet as her scent. He leaned forward and gently brushed his lips against hers as she parted her lips inviting more. He softly touched his tongue to hers as she welcomed a long lingering kiss. The slow strokes began heightening his desire. She moved her lips in a lazy yet seductive movement against his while a magnetic force pulled him toward the exact measures he knew he shouldn't take. He caressed her face and kissed her sensually while his trusty pilot soared them toward the city that never sleeps.

CHAPTER SIX

By the time they arrived at his father's estate, Luke's burning need for Isabel was blazing at the core of his stomach. She looked even more appealing with her cheeks flushed and her lips slightly swollen from the hour-long kiss. It made him ache for her intensely. He almost lost control when his mind ran wild with images of taking her then and there on the soft airplane seats. She wasn't speaking which only made him more anxious. Maybe he shouldn't have kissed her, but he couldn't manage not wanting to touch or taste her when she sat so close. Now they sat silently in the black stretch limo that took them to his father's house.

Isabel was vaguely confused if the kiss really happened or if it was all just a sensual dream. He wasn't apologizing so either it didn't occur, or he didn't want to discuss it. She cringed from the thought that he might regret kissing her again. This was exactly what she couldn't understand. One minute Luke was hot and practically undressing her with his eyes and the next he acted hesitantly as though the smallest gesture might break her in half. She snapped back to reality when the limo came to a stop in front of tall iron gates. The gates opened, and the limo pulled into a long stoned path leading toward the house. They had arrived at Luke's father's estate and now her heart pounded for other reasons. She didn't understand why she'd become nervous about meeting Luke's family. She examined the large stone brick house with French vintage windows. The structure was so massive she wondered if the word "house" was even the right term to describe it. *Oh, but it is breathtaking.* Larger than life, it looked like a vintage castle mirage. No wonder Mr. Brady senior wanted to entertain his guests here for the holidays. It was captivatingly beautiful. Enchanted, she stepped out of the limo and beamed with appreciation. Her mother would definitely call this a work of art.

"Amazing isn't it?" Luke asked, standing next to her and watching her instead of the house. "And this would be my most beloved childhood memory. It used to belong to my grandparents. Once my grandfather passed away my family moved here while I stayed in San Diego. Come on, let's go inside and get settled," he said and took a hold of her hand.

"It's beautiful," was all Isabel could say as she let Luke lead her inside. The interior was as exquisite as the exterior. They walked into an immense foyer with white poinsettias in an antique, tall vase displayed on a round table located in the center of the room. After handing both of their coats to a door man who appeared out of nowhere, Luke took Isabel's hand again and guided her toward the living room. She was surprised how firmly he held her hand; not worrying what others might think if they saw them.

"Luke." A beautiful woman with light golden hair hurried toward them. Isabel noticed the lady shooting a quick look toward their joined hands and gracefully slid her hand out of Luke's.

"Hi Mom." Luke's grin was as wide as ever as he embraced his mother, burying his face in her light golden hair. Isabel easily caught the affection in Luke's gesture, and it made her smile.

"I missed you so much," she said and cupped his face and kissed both cheeks.

"And I missed you," he said, kissing both of her hands. "Mom I'd like you to meet my new assistant. This is Isabel Stamos." *The woman who has been driving me into a sexual frenzy,* he thought.

"Kathryn Brady," she said and took Isabel's hand in both of hers. She hadn't missed the way her son had been holding his assistant's hand when they entered her living room. She was half expecting him to have introduced her as his girlfriend instead. "It's such a pleasure to meet you."

"Pleasure's all mine Mrs. Brady." Isabel smiled warmly.

"Oh please, call me Kathryn my dear. How was your flight?" Kathryn noticed the quick glance Isabel and Luke exchanged with that question and bit the inside of her cheek to avoid grinning.

"Uh, it was good, thank you." Isabel prayed her face wasn't red while Kathryn's bright blue eyes studied her.

"I've heard great things about you and am so glad Luke was able to find another wonderful assistant. When I first heard Rachel was leaving I was devastated. She's such a sweet girl, and I guess in the last few years I had become used to her spending the holidays here with us. But let me be the first to welcome you to our family." Kathryn smiled brightly. Another quick glance was exchanged by her son and Isabel. She wondered when Luke had developed a personal interest in his new employee. No one knew her son better than her, and she recognized all the visible signs plastered on his face.

"Luke my boy," a loud deep voice echoed the room. Everyone's attention shifted to the man who walked toward them. He slapped a strong hand on Luke's back and pulled him into a solid stern hug.

"How are you Dad?" Luke said. He looked happy to see his father.

"Thomas, this is Isabel, Luke's new assistant." Kathryn smiled at her husband without blinking.

Thomas had been married to his wife enough years to catch the hidden message behind her tone. Her eyes were telling him to pay close attention. "Ah, Isabel," he shook her hand, "Great to have you working with us. I believe we spoke once over the phone correct? The plans for the holiday events are looking very promising. "

"Glad you're pleased with the arrangements, Mr. Brady. I'm here to make sure all last minute details go smoothly. Anything you need, please let me know." Luke had his father's green eyes, and now she knew where he got his height from as well. "You have such a lovely home," Isabel said to Kathryn. "I can just picture how beautiful the holiday events will be here."

"Thank you, my dear. Luke, why don't you boys catch up while I show Isabel where she will be staying." Kathryn casually hooked her arm with Isabel's and showed her the way.

An hour later, Isabel was unpacking her clothes and organizing the dresser in the guest bedroom. Kathryn was such a sweet woman as she had kindly showed her most of the house along with the stunning rose gardens she was sincerely proud of. She was also shown the ballroom hall where both events would be held along with the office she could work from. The spacious office had a large center desk which belonged to Luke's father and a few smaller ones surrounding it. Kathryn told her that Rachel worked out of this office and to make herself feel comfortable.

"Please be sure to let housekeeping know if you need anything," she had said. After settling into her room, Isabel headed toward the office. She selected a corner desk closest to the window and began organizing the files she had brought along. Completely oblivious that it was Sunday, Isabel went right to work. She still had to make a few arrangements for the Christmas Gala. Once she was done in the office, she would tend to the ballroom. She let out a relieved, gleeful sigh as she took a seat behind the desk. She felt relaxed, energized, and happy, almost disbelieving how quickly her life had changed.

~*~

Two days passed as Isabel, Luke, and his father worked silently in the estate office. Luke was keeping in constant contact with his staff back home while his father continued to secure deals with his lifelong clients. During the day, Isabel kept to herself behind a computer and the rest of the evening worked in the ballroom. She occupied herself with the décor, catering menu, and flower arrangements. She had a keen eye for detail and wanted both events to sparkle. There was still much to be done, and she was silently grateful for the busy schedules that placed some space between Luke and herself. Luke realized the distance only made the fire inside him flame even higher. He burned to touch, kiss, and taste her. They hadn't had a single minute alone in the last two days, but he clearly remembered how good her soft skin felt under his hands. He ached to have more of her, which caused him pained discomfort. He occasionally caught himself watching her as she worked. They spent hours in the same office barely speaking to each other. The quiet setting of his father's office was driving him *crazy*.

Thomas wondered if either of them noticed the sparks they set off each other. He was surprised the office hadn't caught on fire by the amount of sizzling chemistry that lingered heavily between them. He saw the restlessness in his son as Luke's eyes shifted to the door each time Isabel walked in or out of the room. If someone had told him that Luke had cut his attention from work due to his distraction for a woman, he never would have believed it. His second born, Andrew, however, was a different story. He was a playboy who didn't deny his lack of indifference toward women. But no, not Luke. Yet there it was, right in front of his eyes. His eldest son was completely crazed by his assistant, and the tension was making Thomas edgy. He either had to get out or push these two out. Otherwise, he would never get any work done.

"Luke, my boy, I have to head out for a quick meeting with legal and discuss contract renewal with Realtor Mag," Thomas said as he left his desk. "Have you talked to your brother?"

"I spoke to him this morning. He's still in Detroit closing up the Jefferson deal. He said he wasn't sure when he'll fly back, but it will be before the Christmas Gala," Luke informed his father. "And I haven't been able to reach Emilia. Where the hell is she?" he asked about his sister.

"She's in Paris."

"Still?" Luke was surprised. His younger sister went to Europe for vacation often, but it wasn't like her to stay in one location for more than two weeks.

"Amanda flew out a few days ago, and she ended up staying there longer. They both will be back in time for the Gala." Thomas picked up his briefcase and pulled out a file. "If you're planning on going into the city, do me a favor and drop these off at my office so Nancy can review them. Also, tell them to close early today. Tomorrow is Christmas Eve, and those people won't leave till I kick them out." Thomas released a deep hearty laugh. "Besides, it will give Isabel a chance to meet some of our staff here. You two have been locked up in here for two days straight and should get out for some fresh air," Thomas added as he grabbed his briefcase and left without leaving any room for discussion.

"Up for a visit to the Big Apple?" Luke gave Isabel a quick smile.

"I'd like that. I hear the city is beautiful this time of year."

"That and much, much more. Bundle up, it's been snowing. I'll meet you outside in ten minutes," he called out as he left the room. She couldn't tell if his tone was filled with relief or annoyance.

Isabel dashed upstairs and changed into dark blue, denim skinny jeans, a cream-colored sweater, and flat, brown leather boots. She reached the foyer, grabbed her white winter coat from the hallway closest, and walked out through the grand wooden doors. Instantly, the cold winter air slapped her in the face. "Wow, can New York get any colder?" she burred. She took a step to walk down the stairs and her boot slipped on the icy pavement. Just as her bottom was about to hit the ground, Luke's swift arms caught around her waist and hauled her up. She gasped in surprise when her back crushed against his hard chest.

"Looks like I'd better stay near you at all times to catch you when you fall," he murmured in her ear and sent a chill of excitement streaming down her neck. She shivered when he dug his fingers deep into her clothes, holding her tighter. "Not that I'm complaining." He released her waist and hooked her hand in the crook of his arm. "Hold on to my arm." He smiled at her with amusement in his eyes. Isabel realized his eyes turned into a more vibrant green during cold weather. She bit her lower lip but managed to smile as he led her to a sleek gray Mercedes SL.

After a quick visit to B. Pentagon's New York office, Luke drove around town showing Isabel the highlights of the city. She told him the last time she was in New York was at the tender age of five with her parents, and that she had very vague memories. Luke handed his car to a valet service of a luxurious hotel on a busy, main street. They walked around through the crowded streets of New York while Isabel kept herself warm and snug against Luke's arm. They watched a few street performers and laughed hysterically when a mime tripped and fell during his act and began cursing vigorously. She dragged him to a street vendor and convinced him to try a thick slice of pizza with her. Luke tried to persuade her they could have lunch at the hotel where he left his car, but Isabel told him she always wanted to try New York pizza. Luke watched her take a big bite of the greasy slice as she closed her eyes and licked her lips with satisfaction. He had to force himself to swallow the lump in his throat. He never imagined that watching a woman eat a slice of pizza could be this utterly seductive. Then again, he constantly felt seduced by Isabel, and the worst part of it was she wasn't even trying. He was naturally drawn to her. Unable to help himself, he leaned forward and brushed a soft kiss on her cold cheek. Isabel's eyes fluttered open and her chest tightened and quivered from the sweet gesture.

They walked toward an outdoors ice-skating arena crowded by jolly tourists. Luke pulled Isabel toward the ring and began purchasing ice skating shoes from a vendor. Isabel shrieked and ran the other direction, bursting into frantic, screaming laughs when he caught her around the waist and brought her back toward the ring. After a small amount of pleading, Luke was able to convince her to put on the skating shoes. He held on to her waist tightly while they slowly circled around the ring. Each time her feet threatened to slip, Isabel pulled Luke closer. He occasionally sent her wide grins as he encouraged her that she was doing great and to keep going.

Finally after what seemed like an hour of skating, they headed back to the hotel to pick up Luke's car. Isabel sat in the passenger seat and was unable to remove the wide grin on her face. She felt as though her heart would burst from overwhelming joy. This would go down in record as her favorite day with Luke Brady. Luke listened as Isabel happily chattered on about their day, how much she loved New York, and how different life here was compared to California. He himself hadn't imaged how much fun they could have together. For those few hours, he had been able to forget what their roles in reality were. Now that they were back in the car, it dawned on him that they had to go back to playing boss and assistant. He desperately wanted them to have what they just had on the streets of New York. Any onlooker would have assumed they were a couple out and about in the city, enjoying the winter air and each other's company. But they weren't a couple. He couldn't break that wall between them no matter how much he wanted to. He was falling for her, and it frustrated him that he couldn't have her. *What could he do to make things right? What could he do to make Isabel his?*

"Luke? Did you hear what I said?" Isabel broke through his thoughts.

Luke blinked a few times and then turned to glance at her. "What? No, sorry can you say that again please?"

"I was just saying that little girl with the pink scarf was so adorable. The one who was trying to help me skate." Isabel giggled.

"Yeah, yeah. Real adorable," Luke said absentmindedly.

Isabel noticed his inattentive answer, and her brows drew together in concern. He seemed really distracted by his own thoughts. Her brows rose in surprise when he abruptly pulled the car to a halt on the side of the road and jumped out of the door.

"Luke what is it? What's wrong?" she yelled, hurrying out of the car. Luke was already on her side of the car.

"I can't breathe, I just need some fresh air. I can't take it anymore. I'm a man with a lot of control, and I can't seem to control myself around you." He placed both hands on the car capturing Isabel between. He leaned forward and watched her body tense.

"Luke. What are you doing?" Isabel barely heard herself say.

"I don't think I can hide how much I want you anymore. I've wanted to kiss you since the day we met and since I already have, now I can't get the thought of taking you to bed out of my mind. I want you Isabel. I want all of you. I want to make love to you. I want to feel your naked body pressed underneath mine." Luke himself couldn't understand what had come over him. He had a basic animal need clouding his mind, and he wanted his hands on her.

Now it was Isabel's turn to worry about self-control, about how she might explode with desire that was rapidly growing inside her. His words burned into her ears and despite the cold, icy air she felt her body burning in fever from need. She had never been more aroused by any man other than Luke. Her heart was pounding. She couldn't breathe. Isabel thought she saw his eyes become darker. More wild. More intense. His eyes were burning into hers as he watched her while making no attempt to cover his desire for her. Bracing herself for the impact, Isabel felt a strong, violent shake rock her body as Luke crashed his lips to hers. This time she could feel heat, passion, and impatience. These would be nothing like his gentle kisses from before. These were *raw and intimate*. He wanted her, and every movement of his hard lips on hers sent a whole new shiver of excitement racing through her body.

He pushed her roughly, pressing her back on the car even more. His hands were roaming all over her body, slightly pulling her hair to tilt her head back and deepen the kiss. He caressed her

110

arms until they came down to her hips. He moved his hands over her butt, gripped her, and pulled her even closer to him. He didn't want any distance between them. He wanted to feel every part of her body touching his. He bit her lower lip and exploded with fire when a loud moan escaped her lips. He heard her breathing become uneven from pleasure, and it made him want to touch and feel her even more. He snaked his hand under her blouse and cupped her breast making the peaks turn hard. He stroked and teased her breast until her moans against his lips became higher.

Luke knew if he didn't stop himself soon, he would end up dragging her to the back seat of his sleek Mercedes, undressing her, spreading her legs and taking her. *But Isabel deserves more than this,* his mind screamed at him. He broke free of the kiss and rested his forehead on hers. Both gasping for air as they stared into each other's eyes, his wild green burning into her chocolate brown irises. Neither dared share a word. They stayed in this position for what seemed like an eternity until they managed to catch their breaths. Isabel's cheeks were burning. *Had she just been moaning on the side of the road?* This thought made her yearn for more. She hadn't realized how ready and willfully she would give her body to Luke if he demanded it.

"I'm, uh, sorry," Luke finally broke the silence. He pushed himself away from her, not daring to touch her again. "I don't know what came over me. Did I hurt you?" he tried to release a laugh but failed. His mind was too clouded for humor.

"Umm, no, I'm fine." Head still swimming with pleasure, Isabel grabbed Luke's arm. "Just give me a minute to regain my balance. For a moment I forgot we were outside." She laughed. Luke took a look at their surroundings and cursed. They were parked in the middle of the road just a few miles away from his father's home.

"Shit, me too. We should head back," he said but made no attempt to move or take his hands off her hips. Somehow his hands had found their way back to her body. He stared at her swollen lips and lowered his to hers again and kissed her softly. "Last one for the road." He grinned and helped her into the car.

The drive back home was in silence as neither of them wanted to discuss their situation. They both mutely feared that if they talked about it they might agree against their own wants and needs and keep the relationship platonic and professional. It would be the rational thing to do. But at this state of mind, with this much pent-up sexual turmoil clouding their judgment, neither one wanted to be rational.

~*~

The smell of fresh pine filled the room. The tall tree that towered toward the ceiling was dressed in oversized ornaments and glittered with white lights. This year's colors were royal blue, forest green, and bright turquoise, resembling the remarkable feathers of a peacock. The long anticipated day of the Christmas Gala had finally arrived. Isabel, in dark denim jeans and a thin black sweater, stood center stage in the ballroom, hacking out last minute details. She had pulled back her long, layered, brown hair into a loose braid. The guests would arrive in an hour, and she wouldn't leave to get ready until everything was as perfect as she had planned.

"Hey Jack, can we have more lighting on the ice sculpture?" Isabel spoke to one of the workers hired to help her with arrangements. "I want it to be bright in that corner. And let's push some of these tables further back so the center can be wide and open."

"I was hoping you'd wear something a bit more formal." Someone spoke directly from behind. A bit startled, Isabel turned around to face Luke.

"I, uh, I'm almost done here I promise."

Luke was already dressed in his black trim fit tuxedo. He looked deadly gorgeous, and her heart began to pound profoundly.

Every time she looked into his very green eyes she was quickly reminded of how it felt when he held her close and kissed her. She had loved his tender soft kisses but after yesterday, she had to admit she could easily become addicted to the taste of his impatient, eager, and demanding lips taking over hers.

Luke noticed her tense as he leaned closer. He knew he was attracting a few wandering eyes in their direction but at the moment he didn't care. As if challenging himself more than her, he lightly pushed a strand of hair away from her face and neatly tucked it behind her ear. It was becoming more and more difficult not to touch her.

"Not that those jeans don't look great on you." He watched her blush as he sent her a wide grin. "But I'd like it if you'd stop working and go get ready. Guests will be here soon. Besides, doesn't it take women hours to get ready for these types of formal events?"

"I'm not like most women," Isabel said and noticed his eyes become more serious as if he all too quickly agreed with her. "I mean I don't take as much time as most women do. But you're absolutely right, I should go get ready." She stepped away from him and couldn't get out of the room any faster.

~*~

Half an hour had passed as Luke and his father began greeting guests that were escorted into the grand ballroom and compliments were given for the extraordinary décor. Guests indulged in champagne and hors d'oeuvres while enjoying the pleasant symphonies played by the orchestra.

Kathryn, dressed in an exquisite royal blue gown, joined her husband and son in welcoming new clients and old friends. Her eyes met Thomas' and implied for him to look toward Luke. The uneasy look was back in his son's eyes, and he noticed Isabel hadn't yet joined them. Luke's eyes continuously shifted to the entrance door. *Where the hell is she?* Luke impatiently thought. He cursed himself for acting worse than a lovesick teenager.

"Where's your lovely assistant?" his mother asked reading his thoughts.

"Oh, Isabel? She should be here shortly, she was working late." Luke attempted to play off his anxiousness about seeing her. Was his impatience that noticeable? Why was he even waiting for her? She would be here soon enough. But his eyes froze at the door when he saw Isabel effortlessly glide into the room. Dressed in a cream chiffon gown with a ruffle-edged skirt that flowed to the floor, she was a vision worth worshipping. When she turned to greet a guest, he saw that her back was slightly exposed through heavy patterns of lace that ran from her shoulders all the way down dangerously low. Luke felt his own breath choking him. He watched her possessively as she greeted others while certain male guests were quite delighted to meet her. This didn't settle well with Luke, but he was a professional at keeping his composure. Isabel gracefully made her way toward Luke and his parents and couldn't avoid noticing Luke's heated gaze watching her.

"Oh Isabel, everything looks marvelous," Kathryn said and took both of Isabel's hands in hers.

"Yes, you've certainly outdone yourself. Such a fantastic job, we've never had exquisite décor such as this before." Thomas nodded in agreement.

"Trust me the pleasure was all mine. I enjoyed every minute of it." Isabel smiled but her eyes nervously flickered to Luke's who had yet to speak.

"Kathryn my dear, why don't we take a spin on the dance floor? I feel like dancing," Thomas said as he led his wife away.

"You look incredible," Luke rasped with such intensity it earned him a blush.

"Thank you." Isabel let out a nervous laugh. Just the day before the man had his hand up her shirt, and she still managed to flush from his compliments and yearning, green gaze.

Luke's lips twitched with amusement. God, how much he loved putting that shy look on her face. "Live orchestra, snowflake ice sculptures, walls decked with boughs of holly. I must say Isabel, I'm quite impressed," Luke said and nodded with approval while glancing around the room. He grabbed two flutes of champagne from a passing butler and handed one to her.

"Like I told your parents, it was entirely my pleasure," Isabel said as she accepted the glass. "I hadn't realized how much I had missed Christmas. I had so much fun planning these events. For certain reasons earlier this year, I thought I would never enjoy the holiday seasons again."

"And what reasons would that be?" he asked in a serious demanding tone.

She realized she had said too much. Once again, the uncomfortable look was back in her eyes as she glanced away. He saw her hand slightly shake and took the champagne from her hand before she could spill it. It greatly irritated Luke that he still hadn't figured out what motive had made her pack her bags and move to San Diego. A pang of jealousy told him he wouldn't like finding out if she had ran away from a lover to nurse a broken heart. What if she was still in love and had feelings for some jerk that had hurt her?

Isabel didn't want to face Luke so she tried to roam her eyes toward the guests. He gently grabbed her chin and turned her head forcing her gaze to meet his. She knew the questioning look would be back in his eyes.

"I know you've ran away from something Isabel," he lowered his voice. "It's just a matter of time until I find out exactly what," he promised.

"Uh, it's nothing Luke. Just some complications earlier this year that had somewhat left me thinking I would forget how to enjoy the greater things in life." She gave him a warm smile, but he wasn't fooled nor satisfied with her answer. He still stared at her through a narrowed glance as though she was a difficult puzzle he was trying to solve.

"I'm fine now, Luke. I admit I wasn't before but after meeting you and joining your company I got better. I'm happy here," she smiled again and thanked God when she noticed him relax. His eyes became more sincere at her small confession.

"Uhm uhm." Someone cleared their throat to catch their attention. Luke took a step back from Isabel not realizing he had closed the distance between them again. His gaze locked with Jake's very amused eyes. "I knew if I found Isabel I'd easily locate you Brady," he said with a smirk on his face.

"Jake, what's up man, how you doing? When did you get here?" Luke babbled, and Jake grinned at him.

"Just now. Guess you were too busy to notice." He turned his attention to Isabel. "You look absolutely beautiful Isabel." Jake leaned in and gently kissed her cheek. "Merry Christmas." Isabel flushed.

"Thank you Jake. Merry Christmas." She smiled. "Are you wearing an earpiece?" She noticed the security device in his ear.

"I'm on duty," Jake confessed.

"Jake handles security and surveillance at our larger functions," Luke informed her. "We tell him to lose the earpiece, enjoy the party, and let his team handle it, but he refuses." Isabel looked at Jake who just shrugged. He was dressed in a trim fitted, black tuxedo with a black shirt underneath. No tie. He looked like a dangerous James Bond with a daring edge. The black attire brightened his icy green eyes bringing out the little scar on his left brow.

"We need to head toward the security room Brady. Something I need to show you. I'll see you around Isabel." Jake gave a curt nod and headed for the exit. Luke narrowed his eyes watching his best friend leave. What was that about?

"I'll be back soon," he assured Isabel and gently touched her cheek. She smiled and nodded as Luke followed after Jake.

~*~

"What's so important Callaghan?" Luke asked as he entered their surveillance room that Jake had built himself. Jake let out a harsh breath and scratched his chin.

"I think your girl is in more shit than you know Brady."

"What?" Luke snapped. "What the hell are you talking about?"

"I went over to her house two days ago to check on her outside surveillance. Just to make sure everything's working properly," Jake paused.

"And?" Luke asked with raging impatience.

"I noticed large fingerprints on her kitchen window from the outside. Now I know Isabel isn't tall enough to touch that window from the outside, and her hands aren't big enough to leave such large prints, so my curiosity got the best of me. I tapped into her system and logged on from my laptop. I've already told her she can easily access the cameras from any location through a computer but realized she hasn't logged on even once to check. There wasn't even a pass-code setting on her account so it didn't take me too long to access her cameras," Jake confessed.

"Where are you going with this Jake?" Luke demanded.

Jake paused then shook his head. "How about I just show you." He moved to one of the computers and began typing. In a matter of seconds the outside of Isabel's house was displayed on the screen. Jake selected a date from a few days ago and clicked play. Luke watched with anticipation as a man, close to their age, with a jacket zipped up all the way to his chin, began roaming around Isabel's house. He was caught from various angles on all five cameras. He placed his hands on the kitchen window attempting to look inside. He began trying to nudge open the window with a tool when he turned around and came face to face with the surveillance camera. Instantly realizing he was staring into a security camera, the unknown man stumbled back and disappeared from view.

"Who the fuck was that?" Luke yelled.

"I'm not sure." Jake shook his head. The glare in Luke's eyes made his anger very evident. "I took a sample from the finger prints and a copy of this video to one of my guys. He's going to run this through his files and find a match. We'll know soon enough," Jake assured him.

"I've got to know who that fucking bastard is Jake. Can you imagine if Isabel was home alone or walking out of her house when he was there?" Luke began irritably pacing the room and running his hands through his thick brown hair.

"Well has she informed you of anything? Anyone who might be stalking her?" Jake asked. He paused for a moment before continuing. "An ex-boyfriend maybe?" He saw a cloud of rage blur Luke's vision.

"I don't know. She won't fucking tell me," he said through gritted teeth. Jake studied his friend. He had never seen Luke this twisted with emotion. Whatever hold it was that Isabel had on him must be fierce. He placed a supportive hand on Luke's shoulder.

"We'll figure it out. You'd better get out there, you've got more guests coming. I promise you Luke, I take it upon myself to ensure Isabel's safety. That douche won't get anywhere near her, even if I have to stand outside her door every damn day and guard it myself till I catch him."

Luke watched the ice in Jake's eyes frost. He wasn't surprised at Jake's reaction, protecting the innocent was his weakness. If he ever found a guiltless person victimized he couldn't help but to place himself in their shoes. Jake had an obsession with shielding those he cared for from harm. If he said he'd help with Isabel's safety then Luke trusted him. He nodded to his best friend and headed back to the ball room.

CHAPTER SEVEN

Most of the evening, Isabel engaged in delightful conversation with B. Pentagon's clients. Still on duty, she made occasional visits to the kitchen, making sure the catering service was on schedule. She noticed Luke standing with his hands in his pockets, his back toward her, examining the ice sculpture. She walked toward him and gently touched his arm.

"Luke? Everything alright with Jake?" she asked. He turned around and let a wide grin spread across his face.

"I'm not Luke sweetheart, but I can if you want me to be," he said. He winked then laughed when he noticed Isabel's surprised face. The resemblance was shocking, and Isabel took a step back. She was staring at a man who was not Luke but had striking similarities. Though his hair was a bit lighter shade of dark brown compared to Luke's, he still had those same gorgeous green eyes. But Luke's eyes were intense, whereas the eyes staring at her right now were playful and mischievous.

"Oh I'm so sorry," she quickly said.

"Don't be. A beautiful woman like you can call me whatever she wants darling." He grinned and caused her to blush. *Luke isn't the only one with a deadly smile*, she thought. It should be illegal for anyone to look as gorgeous as Luke and this man. She stared at him a little longer until reality hit her hard.

"Andrew?" she asked hesitantly. He threw his head back and laughed.

"I'm guessing you've heard about me then? Yes, Andrew Brady," he said and offered his hand, "but you can call me Drew if you like. Drew, Luke, Tom, Smith, whatever you please sweetheart." His eyes gleamed with humor. *Oh, he's good,* she thought. Isabel couldn't help but laugh at his bold approach. Luke and his brother were a spitting image. But when it came to personality, they had great lengths between them.

"It's nice to meet you." She shook his hand. "Isabel Stamos."

"Ahh, the Greek beauty all the men here are talking about," Andrew said and earned another bashful glance from Isabel. This one sure blushed a lot. And he thought his best friend Amanda was shy. "There goes Luke if you're still looking for him." He nodded his head toward the double door entrance.

Isabel turned to see Luke standing with two blond women in stunning gowns. One had shoulder length, very light golden hair and was dressed in a silk, ice blue evening dress. The other had dirty blond hair that was stylishly curled that fell all the way to her hips and was dressed in a vibrant, red gown. The upper part of her red dress was skintight and became loose after her hips flowing gently to the floor with a strikingly high slit on her right leg. Isabel noticed the way Luke's arm circled around the red dressed woman's waist as he pulled her close and kissed her cheek. The woman didn't flush or flutter as if a gesture like that from Luke was too commonly familiar. Luke noticed Isabel's gaze from across the room as she stood with Drew. He hooked the hands of both women through his arms and escorted them toward her. Before they reached them, the woman in the ice blue gown left Luke's arm and rushed into a tight embrace with Drew. Isabel watched with amazement as Andrew lifted the woman slightly off the floor holding her tightly around the waist.

"Welcome back angel face," Drew murmured into her ear. After he released her, he reached for the woman in red and kissed both her cheeks.

"Girls, I'd like you to meet Isabel Stamos," Luke smiled warmly at Isabel. He failed to mention she was his personal assistant, which felt oddly comforting, as though he was declaring there was more between them. Both women's attention turned to Isabel.

"It's so nice to meet you. I'm Amanda Bennett," the young woman in ice blue said. She shook her hand lightly and had a genuine, pretty smile on her face. Isabel noticed her petite features, small nose, pretty mouth and light blue eyes that sparkled. She had that all American 'girl next door' beauty.

"Likewise," Isabel smiled back and noticed how the woman easily leaned back against Andrew's shoulder. *Must be his girlfriend,* she mused.

"And this is Emilia, my sister," Luke announced.

Isabel noticed sea blue eyes studying her. She immediately saw the remarkable resemblance to their mother Kathryn with the blond hair, high cheekbones, and flawless skin. Luke and Andrew had their father's green eyes, but Emilia had deep blue irises like her mother's. Amanda had friendly, twinkling eyes, but Emilia's blue gaze was mesmerizing and alluring. Isabel felt as though she was under a microscope. After a moment Emilia's lips twitched into a welcoming smile as she took Isabel's hand.

"I'm glad Amanda and I made it back in time for the party. My mother told me you're behind all these beautiful decorations. I feel like I've walked into a winter wonderland. This place looks amazing. I almost didn't recognize my own home." She laughed, looking around.

"Thank you." Isabel laughed, feeling a bit relieved. For some odd reason she couldn't explain, she felt as though she had just gained Emilia's approval. "Oh and welcome back. How was Paris?"

"Ahh, it was amazing. Can't go wrong when you're shopping on Champs-Élysées. Have you been there before?" Emilia asked.

"Twice, but a long time ago when I was nine and ten; a trip with my parents for an art gallery opening."

"That's right, I heard your mother is Vivian Taylor." Emilia held back a smirk when Isabel took a quick glance toward Luke. She knew Isabel just acknowledged the fact that Luke had been speaking about her to his family. It didn't matter how many miles away they lived, Luke and Emilia were close. And the way he spoke about his new assistant, Emilia recognized all the signs that her brother was involved with her.

Emilia immediately wondered if the woman was worthy of her brother's attention. And so far, from what she could tell, she realized that she was. She always despised the gold digging floozies her brothers occasionally dated and slept with. Thank God her Brady men weren't dumb enough to let some unworthy woman get a grip on them. And Emilia was concerned about the woman who had currently been occupying her older brother's mind. He may be years older than her, but she felt just as protective over her older brothers as they did for her. But as she stood chatting with Isabel, she realized she liked her and wasn't surprised Luke was falling for her. He hadn't admitted this yet, but Luke's lovesick gaze wouldn't leave Isabel's face. *Yup, her brother is in too deep,* she smiled to herself.

"Amanda and I actually came across a few of your mother's pieces in Paris," Emilia continued, "when we met this fabulous French Duke who immediately fell in love with Amanda and invited us over to a cocktail party at his villa. Turns out he's a fanatical art collector and had a few of your mother's pieces. I fell in love with her *Lost Souls* piece and asked Amanda to seduce our wealthy Duke into gifting it to her but she refused," Emilia teased and loved seeing her brother Andrew become tense next to Amanda. They all grew up together, and she knew Amanda was in love with her brother though she would never admit it. And her playboy brother wouldn't get off his high horse and just be with her. Yet, anytime a man approached their shy, sweet Amanda, Andrew's evident jealousy was written all over his face.

"So a rich French Duke fell in love with you huh?" Drew asked Amanda and watched her cheeks burn red.

"Oh, it was nothing. You know how Emma likes to exaggerate," Amanda said and sent a scolding look toward Emilia, which only made her grin grow wider. Isabel continued to watch in amusement. She caught on to exactly what Emilia was attempting to do, and Andrew was taking the bait.

"It was nothing?" Emilia tried to sound shocked. "The man invited you to a weekend getaway on his yacht in Saint Tropez. He was gorgeous, and I mean *gorgeous*," Emilia cooed to Isabel, who couldn't help but giggle.

Amanda nervously shifted and tucked a golden curl behind her ear. "Anyway, where's Jake?" she asked desperately trying to change the subject since Andrew was watching her with his intense green eyes.

"Yeah, where is Jake?" Emilia asked all too eagerly.

"He's in the security room," Luke informed. "Working," he added when he saw his sister's eyes shift toward the main camera knowing Jake could see her.

"Of course he is. What else would he be doing?" Emilia snickered and rolled her eyes.

Andrew was barely listening to their conversation. His mind was too riled up to concentrate. He couldn't explain his irritation thinking about Amanda with some sleazy French guy who clearly had been trying to seduce her. So what if they were both single and unattached and she had every right to date whomever she chose? Andrew had always been protective over his sweet Mandy. Ever since he rescued her from three horrible, jackass bullies when she was still in pigtails, he had sworn to himself no one would ever cause her pain again. He wondered how far this slime ball French bastard had gone. *Only one way to find out*, he thought as he cleared his throat.

"Would you like to dance, angel face?" he asked Amanda and her heart melted from the endearment.

124

"I'd love to," she said, smiling, as she accepted his hand. The only man who could flutter her heart, and he was unavailable for relationships.

Isabel noticed Emilia's lips twitch with amusement. "I knew he couldn't wait to get her alone. He's going to grill her about the French Duke." Emilia laughed and clapped her hands with joy. She sighed with relief while Isabel continued to giggle. Luke shook his head but remained silent. "Well I should probably go see if Jake needs any help," she announced and was about to leave when Luke caught her arm.

"I think you've caused enough trouble for tonight Emma," Luke scolded her.

"Who me?" Emilia's shocked voice was back. "Relax Luke, I'm not going to bother him. I'm just going to stop by and say hello."

"I mean it Emilia," Luke warned. Emilia rolled her eyes but was finally released by Luke's strong grip and shimmied her way out of the ballroom.

"She seems like a handful." Isabel laughed. "I like her."

Luke narrowed his eyes as he watched his sister leave the room. "Yeah, she is. It's difficult maintaining a handle on her since she has a mind of her own," he said and finally turned his attention to Isabel. He watched her beautiful face and lightly brushed a finger across her cheek.

"Luke, if you don't stop doing that people will start talking," she whispered but her heart accelerated from his touch.

"I don't care. Come dance with me." He offered his hand. Isabel smiled and allowed him to direct her toward the dance floor. The orchestra was playing a beautifully sweet symphony, and she wouldn't mind enjoying it with Luke. They reached the dance floor and she couldn't help but notice how closely Drew held Amanda. She still couldn't figure those two out.

"Amanda's in love with your brother," she announced. Luke looked at her amused.

"You caught that, did you?" He laughed.

"Yes. I did. And I see that he's not so indifferent toward her. They aren't together though," she exclaimed. Luke released a small sigh.

"No, they're not. They should be but they aren't," he confessed.

"How come?"

"Because Andrew won't allow himself to become that way with her. He's too much of a player. He's probably afraid he might hurt her. I'm not sure," Luke said as his glance drifted toward them.

"But he cares about her deeply and it's obvious he wants her. I can tell by his body language."

Luke's eyes shifted back to Isabel's. "Oh really? You can read body language huh?" he teased amusingly.

"Yup," Isabel smiled. "See how he keeps caressing her back, kissing her shoulder, and touching her face?" She continued to observe as she slowly danced with Luke. "He wants her to be his without actually claiming her."

"And what does my body language tell you Isabel?" Luke asked as he slid his hand dangerously low on her back and pulled her close until there was no distance between them. He stared into her large brown eyes as they widened from astonishment.

After a long moment Isabel found some momentum to speak. "You want me," she whispered. "You keep trying to deny it and push yourself far away. You've been doing that since we met but you can't fight it or control it any longer. I know you want me Luke, and I'm sure by now you've figured out the feeling is mutual." Her heart was racing as she uttered the words. How bold and daring she had become with showing her sexuality with this man. He made her body yearn for things she didn't know were possible to want. Luke came to an abrupt halt in the middle of the dance floor. His intense green eyes were burning into her deep brown, and he released a struggled groan and rested his forehead on hers. She realized he did this each time he felt defeated by his own emotions.

"I don't want to ruin things between us. I don't want to hurt you or scare you away." He closed his eyes tightly.

"You're not going to," she assured him.

He pulled away but continued to stare at her. His gaze was too mesmerizing for her to look away. They began slowly dancing again but Isabel became aware of the many wandering eyes that had landed on them, including Drew's, Amanda's and Luke's parents.

"What happens now?" she asked hoping the onlookers assumed they were having a casual conversation. *Fat chance in that happening*, she thought.

"I'm not sure but I'd like to find out. Slowly though, if that works for you?" he murmured. "I'm scared if things progress as fast as that kiss from yesterday, you'll run away." Isabel searched his eyes. He really did believe he could push her that far. Did she look as fragile as he treated her? Didn't he see how badly she yearned for him?

"I'm not going anywhere," she whispered.

~*~

Andrew continued swaying with Amanda on the dance floor. Her thin, silky gown felt good on his hands. He rarely slow danced with women, but he loved dancing with her. It was too sensual and romantic, and he usually wanted to seduce women, not romanticize them. But his sweet Mandy wasn't just any woman. She was his closest and dearest friend, a friend he knew he felt a little more for than he should allow himself to. Nonetheless, she was his. She'd been in Paris with his sister for about a week, and he had missed her ridiculously. Now, there was talk of some Duke being interested in her, and he all but burned with jealousy.

"So tell me about this Duke," he purred into her ear.

Amanda looked into his wondering green eyes and rolled hers playfully and smirked. "I told you. Your sister was exaggerating."

"So he didn't invite you to spend a weekend with him?" Drew asked as he caressed her back with his hand, holding her closely as they swayed to the music. The slow caress of his hand was making her lose concentration.

"Uh…well yes, he did, but who's to say if he was serious or being hospitable. I barely understood the man. You know I'm not as fluent in French as Emilia is," Amanda said, attempting to sound casual.

Hospitable my ass, Drew thought. The scum was clearly trying to find a way into Amanda's panties, and he winced from the thought. "And are you going to find out if his offer was genuine?" Andrew continued to question her as he stared into her light blue eyes. The color of her icy blue dress was brightening her eyes, making them look even more irresistible.

"No I'm not, if that makes you feel better," she teased and couldn't help but laugh when Drew's face split into a wide grin. *God he could be so tempting*, she thought.

"Good." Drew smiled. "I'm glad you won't be going back to Paris then."

"And why is that?" Amanda arched her brows.

"Because I missed you like crazy," he confessed and leaned his head and gently kissed her bare shoulder.

Amanda held her breath. *This is Drew*, she told herself. He's a sweet talker and her closest friend. His gestures and words aren't supposed to mean anything other than affection toward her. All these years being so close, she had trained well to brace herself when he got too affectionate. Touching and being flirty was in Drew's nature, she knew this, but she couldn't help feeling a need for him. Years of training had taught her to keep a composed face and not allow his gentle hands to show the appeal she felt from them.

"Uh huh," she sighed as if she was exasperated. "Oh, I'm sure all the women you occupied yourself with really couldn't get your mind off of how much you missed me."

"No woman compares to you my angel face," he murmured to her. "My sweet, sweet Mandy."

Amanda's heart dissolved. He always managed to win her over with his sugar coated words. 'Angel face' and 'Sweet Mandy' had become her two favorite nicknames he had been using for her since they were children. "Oh Drew, you frustratingly charming man," she sighed and kissed him on his cheek. "Let's get something to drink, I'm thirsty," she said and pulled him toward the bar.

~*~

Meanwhile, the sassy and brazen Emilia was making her way toward the surveillance room. A quick glance in the hallway mirror ensured her makeup and hair were intact. She slowed her walk and swayed her hips as she entered the room she knew Jake was in. She sighed with pure female satisfaction when she found his lean muscular body hovered over a surveillance screen. The sight of him always made her mouth water.

Jake mumbled and cursed under his breath. He didn't have to glance toward the door to know Emilia had just walked in; he'd seen her heading toward the security room through his cameras. Maybe if he didn't make a sound she'd just leave and go away, he thought, but shook his head from the unlikeliness of that ever happening. Emma was a brat he was always trying to get rid of—a beautiful, sexy, uncontrollably alluring brat—but a pesky brat nonetheless. And what bothered him most wasn't that she bothered him but because he couldn't control his wild thoughts about her. He'd ached to touch or kiss her since she'd turned fifteen and was no longer his best friend's annoying sister who constantly tried to follow them around but his best friend's suddenly gorgeous sister. When she'd turned eighteen, he had made the mistake of kissing her. He'd come home one day, belligerently drunk, deep in his dark, twisted sorrows, and she taken care of him. Ever since that single kiss it was like she knew the power she had over him and wouldn't leave him alone. But he'd be damned if he ever took another bite of that forbidden fruit again.

"Hello Jake," she called out in her alluring voice.

Jake cursed in his head. He had no choice but to acknowledge her now. He turned around to see her casually leaning on the door frame with her arms folded across her chest. *Damn her, damn her, damn her,* he thought. Did she have to look this ravishing? He'd seen her through the cameras, and his eyes sure had appreciated the sexy, red number she had on. But the cameras did no justice compared to the vision in front of him right now. However, Jake was a man with immense control, and he could keep his composure and be a man of few words.

"Hello Emilia," he said and leaned back in his chair. His icy green gaze locked with her sea blue one. She let a slow seductive smile creep into her face as she slowly cat-walked toward him. Her dirty blond locks wrapped around her shoulders and tumbled their way to her hips. Emilia had perfect golden hair most women would gladly pay dearly for.

"Well aren't you going to kiss me Merry Christmas or at least hug me hello?" She gave her sweetest smile possible. She loved getting under Jake's skin and *damn him for looking so delicious in his dark tuxedo*, she thought. She'd love to remove that frost from his icy green eyes by tempting him, but Jake was very stern and never let her get too close. Except for that one kiss they shared a few years ago that had stolen her heart, he made sure to keep his distance.

Jake managed to give her a fake smile. He would play nice. Emilia always managed to trigger his anger and frustration which led him sexually craving her even more. But tonight, since she was in this risky dress, he'd keep his cool. "I'm working. Is there anything you needed from here?"

"No, I just came to admire the view," she purred.

Jake immediately knew he was in hot water as he recognized the change in her voice. Emilia was in one of her moods to make him suffer. He hadn't seen her for a few months which meant she'd been saving up for this moment dearly. Jake was always thankful he had business to attend to in San Diego that kept him months away from New York and Emilia, but avoiding her wasn't always possible. The Brady's were his only family, he loved all of them, and he desperately wanted to love Emilia like a little sister but other parts of his anatomy strongly disagreed with him.

"This isn't a playground babe." He said the word 'babe' knowing how much she disliked it and watched her eyes glitter with amusement. He always teased her about their age difference, trying to make it seem like she was too immature for his taste. "If you have nothing to do here you should head back to the party. I'm working," he said and turned his attention back to his computer.

"Oh Jake, play nice will you? I won't get in your way I promise." She almost laughed at her own lie as she made her way closer toward him. "Besides, I'm bored at that party. Luke is too busy gawking over his new assistant, and Andrew's going to be hogging Amanda all night since he hasn't seen her for over a week." She sat on his desk and let the slit of her dress fall open exposing her legs. She scooted closer until his hand that was resting on the desk touched her upper thigh. "And you're all alone in here so I figured I'd keep you company," she continued to hum in her tempting voice. She noticed Jake's gaze uncomfortably shift back and forth from her exposed legs to the camera screens. She wanted to hoot from triumph.

Jake swallowed his groan. He wouldn't give her the satisfaction of knowing he was tempted by her. "You're sitting on a file I need. You'll need to move," he said roughly.

Instead of moving out of the way, Emilia scooted over landing directly in front of Jake. She bumped her dangling feet against his knees and knew the shift in movement raised the slit of her dress higher. A wicked smile spread across her face as his eyes landed on her exposed skin. Any higher and Jake wouldn't have to guess what color panties she was wearing. She slipped her foot out of her sandal and slowly caressed it all the way up his leg, past his knee and toward his middle bulge.

"Emilia," Jake warned.

"What?" she asked all too innocently but let her foot caress down his leg again.

"We've been through this a million times." Jake's green gaze was blazing as he watched her flutter her lashes naively. But Jake was no fool. There was only mischief behind her sea blue irises. "I've advised you to stay away and stop playing these games."

"That's the problem Jake," she whispered, "I'm not playing games. I'm dead serious," she replied as her foot traveled back up and landed on his crotch.

Jake jerked out of his seat, grabbed her arms, and pushed her flat on her back until her sandy blond locks were spread on the surface of his desk. Emilia gasped as Jake's grip tightened on her arms. Boy, did she love watching his whole muscular body flex and hover over hers.

"You don't know what the hell you're asking for Emma. I'm not one of your soft college preppy boys. If I have you I won't be treating you like a lady," he hissed with his face just an inch away from hers. "Now I'm going to walk out of this room so do us both a favor and don't follow me because once certain steps are taken there will be no going back. You don't want to get involved with me beyond what we have. Trust me," he growled. He released her with a shocked look on her face and left.

Emilia stared out after him with her eyes wide and her chest pumping. She finally took in a deep breath, not realizing she was holding it. "Wow," she breathed. She couldn't know for sure if her skin was burning from fury or if Jake's aggressive behavior had turned her on even more. She realized it was both. She yearned for him and the swell in his pants she felt with her foot only told her how badly she affected him as well. She knew Jake wanted her, and every time he turned her down and rejected her, it tinted her rage even further and she promised herself to make him suffer more.

~*~

Isabel watched as Thomas Brady spoke into the microphone, welcoming his guests to their annual Christmas Gala. He reminded his guests that just like previous years, the sole purpose of these Holiday gatherings was to collect charitable donations for a particular association. Isabel realized it was the same organization that helped domestically abused children that Luke had sponsored in San Diego. She remembered Luke telling her the reason for their dedication to this particular establishment was because someone close to him had had a bad childhood. Isabel scanned the room spotting Jake as he walked in. A moment later Emilia walked into the ballroom a bit flushed and angry, just as her father announced how the organization had managed to save thousands of children this year by placing them into protective care. That once again this year, an anonymous donor had given the charity a hefty amount of money to ensure the safety of these children. Emilia stopped dead in her tracks as her eyes locked with Jake's. She held her breath along with Jake's icy green gaze throughout her father's speech. When Thomas stopped speaking and the room erupted in loud applause, Jake quietly slipped out of the ballroom.

~*~

As the clock chimed midnight, Isabel joined Luke and his family to bid farewell to their merrily content guests. She was profoundly pleased at how successful the Christmas Gala had turned out. Starting tomorrow, she'd have to dive in headfirst into completing all arrangements for their New Year's bash. She smiled at the exiting guests, knowing she'd soon see them at the next function. The cleanup crew she had hired arrived shortly after the last guests had left the premises. They were hovering outside the entrance door where the guests had been departing when Jake joined them.

"Everything set?" Luke asked Jake who was momentarily distracted looking at Emilia through narrowed eyes.

"Yeah, I sent my guys to do a last thorough look around the premises and gardens before they start locking up," Jake answered, his eyes still assessing Emilia. Isabel watched in wonder but was unable to read the expression in Jake's eyes. She glanced toward Luke's sister, and realized she wasn't looking back but softly speaking to Amanda and Drew. Emilia had come back into the ballroom but something was different about her. She kept to herself the remainder and looked a bit angry, distracted, and unsocial, which Isabel realized was very unlike her.

Kathryn caught Isabel off guard when she turned around from talking to her husband and embraced her in a tight warm hug. "Oh, darling girl, everything was so wonderful. I just love Christmas and it was absolutely beautiful this year," she beamed with appreciation.

"I can't wait to party again for New Year's," Thomas told his family, and they laughed. "Jake are you staying here tonight son?"

"No sir, I'll be heading back to my apartment," Jake replied.

"How about you three?" he asked Amanda, Andrew and Emilia. Drew had his own apartment in the city, and Emilia occasionally stayed at Amanda's apartment, but all four of them had their own bedrooms in the large estate. Even Jake and Amanda, whom he loved just as much as his own children, were welcome to come and go as they pleased. His home doors were always open for them.

"I'm staying here," Drew announced as he snaked a hand around Kathryn's shoulders. "I missed my mom." He smiled his oh so charming smile and earned a laugh with a playful swat on the arm from his mother.

"I'm going home too," Amanda laughed. "Emilia?" she asked and looked at her friend strongly hoping Emma would agree to go home with her so she could ask her what the hell happened that made her leave the surveillance room differently.

"I'm going to stay at Amanda's tonight Dad," Emilia said as she hooked her arm with Amanda's. "I left my luggage there when we came back."

"It's settled then. Jake, if you could please take the girls to Amanda's place?" Thomas asked.

"That's not necessary," Emilia interrupted her father and realized her voice rose higher than she wanted it to. Amanda's brows raised in surprise. Jake must have done something to really piss her off.

"No problem, I'll wait for you both here when you're ready," Jake ignored Emilia and directed his comment to Amanda.

"I have my car. I'm capable of driving us home," Emilia answered coldly without looking at him.

Jake's icy green eyes froze on Emilia's face. "You're not driving this late at night," he hissed. The woman made it nearly impossible to stay calm.

Emma made an unladylike snort and said, "Oh I'll be fine." She turned her arctic blue eyes on him. "I'm perfectly capable of taking care of myself. Amanda, I'm going to grab our purses and I'll be right back," she said as she turned inside.

It was then that Jake realized everyone had stopped talking and were waiting to see if this conversation would turn into a quarrel between him and Emilia. It usually did. "She's impossible," he muttered to Luke and walked toward his car. "Have a good night everyone."

"Good night," they called out after him, relieved.

After the cleaning crew and Jake's security team left, Isabel said good night to Luke's family and headed toward her room. Luke caught her arm gently at the bottom of the stairs. "Heading for bed?" he asked.

"Yes, I'm exhausted. By the way, you have meetings scheduled back to back tomorrow. Are you sure you don't want to cancel some of them?" she asked concerned. He worked too much.

"No, I'll be fine. I need to make my usual stops with clients when I come to New York." He paused and searched her eyes. "I'm more concerned about you," he confessed.

Isabel's eyes widened with surprise. "Why?"

"I haven't asked you how you've been sleeping," Luke murmured. "Are you alright? Is your room comfortable?"

"You mean have I been having any more dreadful and humiliating nightmares?" Isabel released a sneering laugh. She waited for him to speak but Luke continued to study her with his usual inquisitive gaze. She looked away. She had always been a bad liar.

"Damn it, Isabel," Luke seethed with impatience. "What's the problem, do you not trust me?" he asked angrily and noticed her mouth open from shock.

"What? No, of course I trust you Luke. I trust you more than anyone, it's just…" she paused. Why was he always doing this, making her discuss a subject she much rather forget? Why was he forcing her to remember? *Because he's a good guy and cares about you, idiot,* she silently scolded herself. "I'm just not ready to talk about it."

Luke opened his mouth to speak but the sound of his father clearing his throat from the end of the hall caught his attention. "Before you head over to bed I'd like a word with you in the library son." Thomas smiled casually.

"Sure dad, I'll be right there," he said as his father left them alone again. "Call my cell if you wake up in the middle of the night," he told Isabel, lifting his hand to caress her cheek. "I'll come hold you till you fall asleep," he whispered softly.

Isabel's heart melted. Luke was making it impossible to not fall for him. Who was she kidding? She was already in the deep end. "I promise I will," she whispered back. "Goodnight Luke."

Luke watched until the tip of Isabel's flowing gown disappeared from view before heading headed toward the library where he found his father pouring a healthy portion of whiskey at the wooden bar.

"Bourbon?" he asked when Luke entered.

Luke raised his brows but answered, "Sure." If his father was pouring drinks at this hour then it must be something serious. Luke took a seat on the dark brown leather couch until his father sat across from him. He assessed his son with thoughtful eyes before taking a sip of his drink.

"Luke, I'm going to ask you a serious question, and I want the truth because I'll know if you're lying."

Luke's eyebrows arched again. "Sure Dad, what is it?" *This has to be good*, he thought.

"What's going on with you and Isabel?" Thomas asked with worry lacing his voice. "It seems like your relationship with her is more than just business."

He watched Luke maintain control of his face. This was one of the reasons why Thomas felt confident having his son run B. Pentagon. Expressions weren't easily read off of Luke's face, and you could never be sure what he was thinking. But he'd raised the boy and knew he'd eventually start talking.

"Now I wouldn't normally ask you these questions," Thomas continued. "What you boys do with the women in your life is entirely your business, but you hired her to work for you. If anyone were to break their own rules and become involved with an employee on a personal level, I would have expected it to be Andrew." Thomas lightly laughed.

Luke continued to remain silent. He was turning his glass around, watching the liquor twirl in a whirlpool. Finally, he put his whiskey down on the glass table and began pacing around the room. Luke could bluff on any proposal and business deal but his father wasn't an easy man to lie to. Regardless, Luke didn't even want to deny his feelings for Isabel. He wanted to say what he felt, hoping if he spoke it out loud then it would become real that somehow the boss and employee status lines would disappear between them. But there was something else standing in their way other than their professional relationship. How was Luke to start anything with a woman who continuously kept him in the dark about her past? He wouldn't have cared about her past if it wasn't haunting her present and trying to break into her house through her kitchen window while she was out of town.

"I'm not sure what it is. I can't describe what exactly is going on Dad. I hadn't planned on mixing business with personal affairs, it brings too many complications, but I can't stay away from her, and I can't stop thinking about her. I don't even want to." Luke continued to slowly pace the room while looking down trying to distract his mind with the patterns on the rug. "I care about her," he confessed, "a lot."

Thomas silently watched his eldest son. He was hoping that when his children fell in love, they would be overwhelmed with blissful joy. But life wasn't that simple. It tended to cloud events with its complications. He noticed the struggle in Luke. Though he did not want to pry into Luke's personal life, he still had to ensure the wellbeing of all his children, even those not related to him by blood, like Amanda and Jake. He wished he could help Luke but when it came to love toward a woman, every man had to find his own way. Stillness continued to hover around them until Thomas finally spoke.

"I can't tell you exactly what to do son. Every man decides for himself the importance and delicacy of the woman he cares for. But I've taught you one thing in life and it's when you come across something you want, then you better damn well find a way to have it."

Luke turned around and gave his father a long, thoughtful look. He shook his head and let out a laugh filled with relief. It felt liberating to speak out loud about how he felt toward Isabel, especially to his father who knew Luke would never easily give up on her. His mind was set and there was no changing it now. It was then and there that Luke decided that whatever complications stood in their way, he'd rip through them to lead Isabel toward a life full of joy. He sensed her hesitation, but he would be patient a little while longer. He'd wait for the woman he wanted to finally open up to him and fight her battles along with her until they were both free. He promised himself this as he sat back down across from his father and gave him a knowing nod, finally beginning to enjoy his bourbon.

CHAPTER EIGHT

On New Year's Eve, Isabel stood in front of the full-length mirror in the Brady Estate guest bedroom. She stared wide-eyed at her own reflection, knowing the dress she was wearing was as risqué as the party she had arranged for the night. She smoothed out the red lace patterns of her cocktail dress and admired the detailed beadwork. To say this dress was a little on the sultry side would be an understatement. Luke's attentive interest and appreciative gaze each time he looked at her sure had boosted her confidence and for the first time in her life she felt sexy. She'd always known the depth of her beauty since she was the spitting image of her mother. Therefore, her beauty came by no surprise. But she had never felt sexy before, never felt wanted and desired, yet Luke had managed to awaken the audacious woman who'd been sleeping deep within.

After the Christmas Gala, Luke had become more eager to persuade her. He'd taken her into the city to see her favorite musical, *The Phantom of the Opera,* and indulged her with exclusive candlelit dinners and moonlight walks through Central Park. They worked in the office during the day but by nighttime were transformed into a couple. He never missed a chance to touch her face with his gentle fingers, wrap his arm around her waist as they walked through the crowded streets of New York, or brush his lips against hers when they were out in public. He no longer hid how much he wanted her, and Isabel thrilled for it.

However, he'd yet to visit her bed at night. As eager as Luke had become, he still kept things at a comfortable pace for her. Isabel knew he was waiting for her to be completely ready, and she loved him even more for that but she no longer denied to herself how much she wanted to feel his touch become more intimate. She knew Luke felt the same way, and even though they did not share their nights in bed together, Luke's need for her in the mornings was evident. While walking down the hall to join his family for breakfast every morning, he'd haul her into his room, push her against his bedroom door and kiss her senselessly. Mornings and nights, right before they parted to their own separate bedrooms, had become Isabel's favorite pastimes. Those were the only times Luke kissed her so passionately. She'd follow him into the breakfast room, still flushed, and not miss the knowing glances of his family. His parents went along their casual way as though she was not an employee but their son's girlfriend, Emilia would look at them and giggle, and Andrew would smirk.

Twice, Amanda and Jake had joined them for breakfast as well. Even they were clued in with Isabel and Luke's growing relationship. Their glances made her blush and her shyness oddly caused sweet Amanda to redden in the cheeks and glance cordially away. Andrew and Emilia continued with their obvious interest. Jake would exchange a knowing glance with Luke but just like the way Jake was, he showed no expression on his face. Isabel knew Luke must have told his family of their developing relationship and although a bit nerve wracking, all in all, she enjoyed every minute spent with Luke.

She took a deep breath and headed toward the ballroom where the New Year's bash was taking place. Isabel had taken a chance when planning this party. She decided that since the Christmas Gala was so elegant and formal that the New Year's party would be more like a nightclub and a bit wild. She had researched and found New York's hottest nightclub DJ and hired him and could feel the walls vibrating with loud music as she entered the hall. It was as if Luke was waiting for her. Her eyes instantly locked with his intense green gaze. He took a large intake of breath as his eyes took their greedy assessment of her from head to toe. The lust in his eyes was evident that her appearance affected him. He shot her that smirk she'd grown weak to and motioned for her to join him as he stood with Andrew and Jake by the bar.

"Isabel, you have outdone yourself," Emilia said as she approached with Amanda by her side, swinging her arm around Isabel's shoulder. Isabel liked that Emilia felt comfortable enough with her to greet her as if they were lifelong friends. "This is the wildest New Year's party we've ever had in this house."

"How did you manage to book that DJ?" Amanda asked excitedly as she glanced around.

"I just tossed B. Pentagon's name a few times here and there, and the deal was made. I hope Luke doesn't freak out when he finds out how much money I offered to book him." Isabel laughed nervously. Since Luke hadn't given her a budget she'd gone all out on the event.

"You know, I'm beginning to really like you," Emilia said, nodding and smiling at her. "Don't worry about Luke's money, he's got plenty of it." She brushed it off like it was no big deal. "And anyone who can get my parents to dance like that is good in my book." Emma laughed hysterically. Isabel followed her gaze to the dance floor to see Luke's parents dancing away to the catchy pop music with an elder couple.

"Oh my God. Is that Mr. and Mrs. Harold next to them?" Isabel asked astonished that B. Pentagon's oldest client was dancing like he'd just turned twenty-one, and it was his first time in a club.

Emilia and Amanda laughed so hard, they had to hold their stomachs. "There aren't going to be any surprise male strippers, are there?" Emma rubbed her hands together excitedly and burst into laughter at Isabel's shocked expression.

"Don't take her seriously, she's joking." Amanda giggled and shook her head toward her best friend. "I think."

"I'm telling you. This year's party is going down in the record books. From now on, no one plans these parties but you," Emilia pointed her finger playfully toward Isabel. "But in the meantime, I see three very good-looking gentlemen at the bar watching us. If I keep you here any longer Isabel, my brother is going to kill me. So what do you ladies say we go join them?" Both women smiled and agreed. As Isabel followed them toward the bar, it was the first time she noticed their dresses. Amanda was in a short, green dress very similar to hers, and Emilia was in a black cocktail dress with the back was left completely bare and scooped down dangerously low, exposing more skin than should be legal. She remembered how in her first week at Luke's company, Rachel had informed her that Amanda and Emilia were Yoga and Pilates instructors. *No wonder they have flawless bodies*, she thought. Emilia walked with deadly confidence in her exposed dress acting completely oblivious to how many heads she turned.

As they reached the three gentlemen waiting for them, Drew immediately reached out and pulled Amanda into an embrace. He must have said something provocative into her ear since Amanda blushed tremendously and tried to cover her nervous giggle as Drew grinned at her mischievously. Luke snaked his arm around Isabel's waist and pulled her next to him closely as he leaned in and kissed her cheek.

"Stunning as always. Are you trying to kill me with this dress?" he growled into her ear. Isabel was worried she was blushing more than Amanda now. She watched as Emilia brushed her body suggestively on Jake's and bumped hips with him as she squeezed her way toward the bar. Jake's tattooed arms flexed under his black t-shirt as he tried to maintain a stern exterior.

"Oops! It's really crowded in here." Emma smiled brazenly at Jake and remained pressed against him. Isabel's eyes glanced toward Luke to see if he'd stop his little sister, but he was too enthralled with her, which she didn't mind, of course.

"You want to dance angel face?" Andrew asked Amanda. She nodded enthusiastically, and he pulled her toward the dance floor.

"Some wild party you've got planned here Ms. Stamos." Luke spoke loudly into her ear to be heard over the earsplitting music. "My parents haven't left the dance floor." He laughed happily.

"So I see. Your mom looks great. They look like they're having a great time."

"They are," Luke said. He grinned at her for a while until his eyes became a bit more serious. He pulled her a little closer. "They really like you. My family knows what's going on between us." His green gaze searched her large brown eyes. He saw a sense of hesitation and nervousness. "They approve and want us to make things work. Try putting this whole boss and employee thing behind us." He grinned.

Instant relief washed over her face, and she released the breath she was holding. It bothered Luke to think that she might have suspected rejection instead of acceptance from his family, but then again, Isabel wasn't always the most confident. Lately, she had been, and he was working on making her more assertive. "Would you like to dance?" He grinned slyly. Any excuse to get his hands on her, especially in that dress, he'd take. Isabel's heart fluttered because Luke's eyes, his smile, and his voice all did a number on her. She smiled and nodded, not trusting herself to speak. Luke Brady had become her utter weakness, and it was exhilarating.

Emilia watched Jake over the rim of her delicious Cosmo. "Not working tonight?" she asked as she leaned in closer, still making excuses to press her body against his invitingly. Jake's muscular arm tensed at her closeness. The woman never gave up. She wouldn't rest until she brought him down to his knees, this he was sure of. But if anyone was good at masking their thoughts, it was Jake.

"I'm taking a break," he replied without looking at her. His eyes were always hungry for the sight of her, and he refused to show it. Emilia usually caught his stares, and it motivated her to tempt him more. The woman was a walking hazard zone for him.

"In that case can I interest you in a dance?" she purred seductively.

Jake tossed back his shot and slammed his glass on the bar. Who was she kidding? If he put his hands on her he'd end up dragging her to the nearest, isolated room like a demented caveman and irrepressibly devour her. He looked at her from head to toe with irritation in his eyes as if her being there annoyed him. "No thanks," he smirked. "Better luck next time, babe." He looked away, waiting for her explosion.

That's what usually happened between them. She'd hit on him, he'd reject her, and she'd curse some sort of insult along the lines of him going to hell and stomp away. He hated being so brutal with her, but Jake knew that if he ever got involved with Emilia, he'd end up hurting her even more. As bold and suggestive Emilia kept herself, he knew she was innocent toward a man's touch. She'd challenge him, and when he'd give her a taste of what she was asking for, her innocence and naivety would become evident. He couldn't tamper with her purity. He'd hate himself for it. He was no good for her, and she needed to get over him and keep her distance because God only knew he was on the brink of losing control one of these days. The woman was testing his limits and how far she could push him.

Emma burned inside with rage. She was sick of Jake pretending he didn't want her so instead of giving into his rejection, she did the unexpected. She kept her casual smile in place and shrugged carelessly. "No worries." She gave him the friendliest smile she could manage and watched his face etch with confusion. She turned around to the young man with wavy brown hair standing next to her, enjoying his whiskey and lightly tapping his fingers to the music on the bar. "Hey handsome, you want to dance?" She felt Jake's entire body tense next to her. The young man looked at her up and down and thanked the heavens for his lucky stars.

Jake tried to keep his eyes placed in front of him, refusing to look at Emilia and another man on the dance floor. Something told him he'd have a volatile reaction if he looked at them. After a few minutes of torturing himself, he made the mistake of glancing their way just as the young man's hand slipped all the way down

146

Emma's bare back, dropping just above her curvy rear. Her entire back was exposed and just the thought of another man touching her beautiful skin shook him ferociously. *Jake saw red.* He shoved himself away from the bar and darted toward them. Emma paused mid dance as she saw a very agitated Jake rushing toward her. He caught Emilia's hand and pulled her harshly out of the other man's arms and dragged her to the security room where he kept her the rest of the night.

~*~

Luke and Isabel spent most of the evening pressed to each other on the dance floor. When the clock hit midnight and the entire room exploded into loud cheers and laughter, Luke cupped both hands on Isabel's face and pulled her into a heated kiss. His tongue parted her lips, and he drank in her surprised moan, stroking their loving tongues as they welcomed in the New Year. After their lips broke apart they were pulled away from each other by friends and family hugging and screaming *"Happy New Year"* and cheering with excited joy.

The DJ continued to keep the party going with endless popular songs as Luke found his way back to Isabel and pulled her into his arms again. It was as if it had become impossible to stay away from each other. Her lips still tingled from their shared kiss, and Isabel could no longer deny her desire for him—she was burning inside. This gorgeous man who she had tried to not fall for had been luring her into a whirlpool of emotions, long overdue emotions of wanting, needing and yearning. His eyes were burning into hers. She knew they were in the dead center of the dance floor but was too mesmerized by his smoldering stare to look away. Good thing the room was dark, and the dance floor crowded. Everyone was too drunk on champagne to notice how close he continued to hold her. It didn't matter to Isabel and in this moment, no one came to mind. It was as if she was all alone in that room with Luke's blazing green eyes, Luke's smooth moves as he guided her through another sensual dance, and Luke's strong hands as they held her firmly around her waist and pressed to his hard body. They continued to dance under the seductive, rhythmic beat.

Each movement of her hips sent a shock wave of blistering need through Luke's body. He leaned closer and could smell her fine jasmine scent. It still managed to unravel his senses. Her fragrance had become his undoing.

"If I don't have you tonight, I'm going to lose my mind," he grunted into her ear. He saw it in her eyes, the same raw emotion exploding through her as it did through him. He knew too many lines had already been crossed, that there was no denying how willfully they both wanted each other. He'd tried to stay away, oh how desperately he had tried, but he always ended up right where he was now. *Wanting her.* He made a quick view of the room. It was a good hour past midnight, and his guests still had not budged. He suspected they'd be here for long hours considering the successful turnout of the event, but he could no longer wait. He wanted her now. He took her hand and led her out of the ballroom to the secluded hallways leading to the stairs.

"Come." He let out a harsh breath.

"Where are we going?" she asked willingly following him.

"Upstairs. My bedroom."

Luke stopped at the base of the stairs pulling Isabel roughly toward him. He cupped her face and kissed her fiercely. They somehow managed to make it to the top of the stairs while Isabel struggled with his tie. Both their hands were frantically caressing each other, teasing and attempting to take off clothing. Luke's hands traveled possessively over Isabel's behind where he gripped her firmly. He pulled her closer causing his arousal to push toward her lower stomach. She heard a small struggled moan escape from her own lips. He gripped her bottom and lifted her up as Isabel wrapped her legs around his waist without hesitation. Her heart was beating fast. Adrenaline pumped through her veins at the mere thought of what was about to happen between them. She'd never felt more wanton in her life, never possessed the need to be touched and kissed this way. She needed his strength, needed to feel the power of a man wanting a woman, the way Luke obviously wanted her. She welcomed the effect Luke's lips had on her as they grazed over her jaw and lingered on her neck. She gained an uncontrollable craving to taste his lips and feel his strong body pressed firmly against hers until she realized she wanted more— much, much, more.

Luke kicked the door shut once they were inside his bedroom. He slowly pulled down the zipper of her dress, placed her down and broke contact to look into her eyes. Their shallow heavy breathing was the only sound in the quiet room. The loud music from downstairs still echoed in their ears. They stared at each other both knowing they had reached a point of no return. This was it, either they continued or walked out of this room and pretended it never happened. It was not what Isabel wanted. She was tired of doubting herself and tired of living in fear. She wanted to break the spell of her fragility and to prove to herself and more to Luke that she was not weak. If she desired to make love with a man, then she would have him. No more nightmares. No more panic attacks. No more self-doubt. It was this very moment that she would determine her own strengths and gain her full confidence back.

She didn't give Luke a chance to talk. Before he could break the silence, she launched herself at him. He groaned with pleasure from her boldness as her heated body collided with his. Her hands fisted in his hair pulling him closer, deepening their kiss. He was heavenly, and she felt drunk and driven mad with desire from his taste, from this intensity she felt for him. Luke immediately felt the change of pace and mood. Her mouth was becoming desperate and a deep fear cringed and twisted inside his stomach. He couldn't understand why he felt so much tension inside of her, and it wasn't all due to the thick sensuality floating between them. He felt her trying to lose herself in him and her body was saying it all, that at this very moment, she wanted him, needed him, to help put a deep, dark fear behind her and forget what had happened. And he wanted her just as badly. If this was what she needed, he could give it to her. He could free her mind and ease her pain, but he felt sick to his stomach. She'd been hurt, and he couldn't let her make decisions such as this to wipe out previous fears. She would hate herself for it later which would eventually lead her to resent him. Luke shivered at the thought.

"Isabel wait," he all too quickly released her. "We can't do this," he breathed. "I can't do this."

She was still breathing heavily, with eyes wide open and swollen, red lips. It took every effort in him to not claim her lips again. "Oh," she said. She looked at him confused and instantly backed away when she sensed his hesitation.

He grabbed her hips before she could turn away and pulled her toward him once more. "It's not that I don't want you," he said, reading her mind. "Believe me, every inch of me wants you. All of you. If this was any other situation, you'd be naked and on your back by now."

"Then what's the problem?" She moved forward rubbing her hips against his suggestively and was pleased by her own courage.

He let out a low growl and rested his forehead on hers. She wasn't making this easy and damn it, he was trying to do the right thing. "I can't continue this. Not when I know you've been hurt from something. Someone. It pains me that you don't trust me to tell me, and I can't let you go into this when you have so much built-up tension. Your past is still haunting you. I see it every damn day in your eyes, baby." Luke remembered the video Jake had showed him of a man trying to break into her house while she was here in New York with him. It angered him that Isabel had more issues to deal with than she knew about, that her fears lay deeper than they both realized. "This can't be an escape route. You have to face what problem you're running from Isabel. I can help you," his voice dropped.

"Is that what this is all about? Whatever happened in the past has nothing to do with what is happening between us right now, Luke." *Or is it,* she thought to herself. Did he want her out of pity? Was he too involved with the idea of saving her and being the hero that he would please her in ways he thought she wanted? Or, did he want her out of just lust and nothing more? Isabel shook her head at the unwanted confusion. This isn't how she pictured her first night with Luke.

"Tell me what happened." Luke's demanding voice broke her thoughts. "I need to know. I want to help you get through this. You still don't sleep well, I know you don't. I'm losing my mind trying to figure out what the hell happened to you." He sounded exasperated, but Isabel would not risk revisiting the pain. It hurt enough to tell her mother about the incident and then again to Linda. How was she going to tell Luke? She would not tolerate his pity, and she didn't want a shoulder to cry on. She had embarrassed herself enough already by her weak demeanor, and it pained her to think Luke still viewed her as fragile.

"Why can't you just let it go?" she snapped and pushed away from him. "Did you seduce me up here to get the truth out of me?"

It was as if she'd slapped him hard across the face. His eyes darkened and his jaw twitched. For her to even think it.

"I'm sorry, Luke, that was out of line." Isabel struggled with her words. It was not how she thought of him the least bit. "Whatever happened is in the past. My life changed profoundly once I started working with you. I'm finally starting to feel whole again. Please don't make me relive the past."

"Yet you still don't trust me." Luke shook his head.

"I do trust you, Luke. I trust you with all my heart, but I've placed myself in this bubble that is secure, perfect, and never pops. It's keeping my sanity in check. I'm afraid to speak about the past, afraid it will pop my beautiful bubble, and I'll fall back into reality and everything good that has been happening to me since I met you will disappear. I'll go back to being that lonely girl with a dark, hollow soul. Please don't make me remember. I would much rather have you help me forget."

He stared at her, absorbing what she had just declared. His mind was arguing with him from a million different angles. He finally let out a deep sigh and rubbed his hands over his face. "I just need to know that you're okay. And I want to help you."

"I'm more than okay. You can help me most definitely. Help me forget. Make love to me Luke."

He watched her reach for the straps and slowly peel off her red, vibrant dress. Once it reached her knees, she released it and let it pool to her feet. She was a vision for Luke's sore eyes. He briefly closed his eyes and inhaled deeply. He needed a moment to adjust to the beauty presented before him. Isabel stood there watching him in her black lace bra and matching panties, breathing heavily and waiting for him. He thought he could hear her heartbeat pounding fast inside her chest. *Or is it his own?* He shook his head and closed his eyes once more, hoping for some clarity. Once he looked at her again, Isabel noticed the change in his eyes. Lust and desire darkened his gaze to a darker shade of green. He reached for his tie, yanked it off, and dropped it to the floor. Soon his shirt, pants, and briefs followed. Isabel let her eyes wander over his gloriously naked body, and she realized she was holding her breath. She'd seen his muscular chest before but to view Luke completely bare sent a new wave of excitement through her. He was sculpted and perfect. He reached for her, and he took her hand leading her to the bed. As much as he wanted to savor and cherish every moment, he knew they didn't have much time.

He slowly peeled her bra off revealing her breasts. He leaned forward and kissed her nape then allowed his tongue to slowly run from her shoulder to the top of her breast. He lingered kisses there, waiting for her to hesitate. When her hesitation did not come, he closed his mouth over her aching, swollen peak. Isabel gasped from exhilaration. Her breathing quickened as Luke's tongue expertly swept over one hardened nipple and then moved to the next. She could reach ecstasy just from his homage to her breasts.

"Lie down," he commanded with a husky voice, and her knees weakened. Luke continued to drive her crazy as his lips and tongue caressed most of her body. Not an area was left without his touch branding her. He slowly brought his lips back to hers as his hand began to trace the outlines of her body. She shivered under his gentle touch as he ran his hand between her breasts, down her quivering stomach and then even lower to teasingly brush against her most sensitive area. She moaned from pleasure and arched her back causing Luke's arousal to grow harder.

"Oh God Luke, this feels incredible," she moaned, and it was music to his ears. Isabel screamed slightly, and her body began to shake. Luke knew she was close.

"Don't hold back baby. Just let go."

His words guided her toward release as she cried out loud when sensation washed over her body. Luke watched in fascination as Isabel was consumed by love and heat. It was the most beautiful and invigorating moment he had ever witnessed. No woman had ever stunned him like this before. Her beautiful face as she drifted into pure bliss would forever be etched into his memory. As Isabel was bringing herself back to reality, she gasped as Luke's hips locked into hers, thrusting himself inside. He grunted as Isabel continued to moan helplessly. He placed both hands on each side of her head, waiting until she could adjust to him. He realized that she must not have been involved with a man for a while for it to feel this good.

"When was the last time?" he uttered as he held back the strongest of urges to thrust himself violently in and out of her.

"I was twenty," she managed to say.

Luke grunted. That was six years ago. It lifted his ego to know she hadn't had a man in her life for several years. He felt possessive and vowed that from here on out, no man would ever know the intimacy of having Isabel. She was his and would be his forever. Luke leaned in and took her lips. He groaned into her mouth, still feeling her quiver and tremble. "I can't hold off much longer sweetheart," he grunted.

Isabel kissed him back while moving her hips, inviting him to take her. Her whimpers echoed throughout the bedroom as he slipped a hand under her butt and tilted her up. It drove him wild to watch her body vibrate underneath his. They'd both been anticipating this very moment since they first met. He regretted not feeling this ecstasy sooner but promised himself that this sure as hell wouldn't be the last of it. He'd just had his full taste of Isabel, and he was addicted. He watched her beautiful face brighten as he led her toward the edge again. She fisted her hands into his hair as Luke grunted and continued to finish making love to her for the first time.

Luke buried his face into Isabel's neck as both mind and body found their way back to reality. He grumbled incoherent thoughts when he realized they should soon be going back to the party. He felt Isabel's delicate hands run up and down his back, lovingly tracing every muscle on his bare back.

"We should just stay like this. I don't want to get up."

Isabel laughed. "Me too, but we have to."

He lifted his head and kissed her lips. "Why don't you stay and rest babe, I'll handle the guests downstairs."

Isabel kissed the tip of his nose. "That's sweet, but I'm alright. I'd like to join you."

"I know, I'm just trying to make excuses to make you stay. I finally got you in my bed and want to keep you here." He grinned as Isabel giggled. "Alright, I'll make a deal with you. You can come downstairs with me if you promise when we head back upstairs to bed, you'll come back to my room."

"Hmm," Isabel pretended to contemplate his suggestion. "You drive a hard bargain."

Luke was about to speak when a knock at his door interrupted him. "Shit," he muttered.

"Oh, no. We're busted." Isabel feigned shock but then covered her mouth to conceal her mirth.

Luke laughed as he leaned in and quickly kissed her lips before leaping out the bed. "This isn't over yet, Ms. Stamos." He grinned. "I've got to get back. I'll see you downstairs?"

Isabel nodded. She lay comfortably naked in his bed as she watched him dress. The man sure had a body to go wild for and every inch of that muscular hard body had been pressed against hers just moments ago. Her eyes lingered on the shamrock tattoo on his back shoulder blade. The shading around the Celtic design made it so much more damn sexy. She frowned when Luke pulled his shirt back on, and she could no longer admire it. His body was just too remarkable, and her eyes were hungry for it. Just remembering how it felt being pressed underneath him made her blush and yearn for more. She climbed out of his bed and began dressing as Luke turned around, winked at her, and walked out his door.

When Luke stepped out, Andrew was casually leaning on the hallway wall, his hands shoved into his pockets with the biggest grin on his face. Luke frowned at him. "Having fun?" Drew teased.

"Fuck off Drew," he mumbled.

Drew threw his head back and laughed. "Come on, big brother. Your guests await to bid you farewell." Luke threw his arm around Drew's neck, holding him in a headlock, and dragged him back downstairs.

Shortly after, Luke began escorting his highly pleased guests out of his father's estate as Isabel joined him by the entrance door, watching people enter their limos and wave goodbye. She'd managed to straighten her dress and touch-up her hair and makeup in record time to look decent. Luke kept sending her wicked smirks and knowing glances that made her skin heat and sizzle with need. The guests couldn't leave soon enough, for these two were counting every minute until they could be in each other's arms once more. Finally, they bid good night to Luke's family as every member headed toward their separate bedrooms. Isabel quickly changed into skimpy white lingerie, wrapped her body in a white silk robe, and snuck into Luke's room. She silently congratulated herself for taking Linda's advice and packing sexy lingerie.

Luke was eagerly waiting for her. As soon as she entered his room, his eyes roamed her body greedily. She was a divine vision, and he couldn't get enough of her beauty. He kissed her tenderly and caressed every inch of her silky skin. They did not rush for they had all the time in the world to enjoy each other, and that is just what they did. As Luke lowered her into his warm bed, he made love to her body in slow, leisurely pleasure till dawn.

Morning arrived with a surprisingly cheerful sun for winter, brightening Luke's room. He opened his eyes and watched a very naked and blissfully pleased Isabel peacefully sleeping. She was pressed next to his side as her head lay on his shoulder, and her delicate hand rested on his lower stomach. He smiled contently as last night's events recapped his memory. She must be well exhausted for he kept her up all night. He couldn't help himself; they were both insatiable last night. He began kissing her warm lips until she woke up. Isabel quietly hummed as pleasure slowly worked its way through her body. When Luke deepened his kiss she moaned.

"I can't get enough of that sound," he whispered against her lips. "It makes me want to never stop pleasing you."

"Who said you have to?" Isabel challenged him.

Luke chuckled. "Don't worry, love, I'm not done with you yet. Not by a long shot."

Isabel straightened up quickly and looked over to his dresser where the clock announced it was almost noon. "Luke, you have a meeting at twelve-thirty. You're late."

Luke laughed. "Don't worry sweetheart, it's close by. But I'll get up now." He kissed her again and rose from his bed. Isabel immediately missed the warmth of his body. "I'm going to take a quick shower. Please do me a favor and don't join me. I won't be able to stop myself and then I really will be late. Isabel giggled and Luke grinned. There was that giggle that melted his heart.

Minutes later, Luke stepped out of his bathroom with just a towel wrapped low around his hips and was pleased to see that Isabel was still lying naked on his sheets. "You're taunting me with that body of yours. At least throw a cover over you or I'm going to take you again," he warned and earned a seductive glance from her. She arched her back and stretched lazily which caused her plump breasts to push up higher. *Oh she knows very well what she is doing to him. The woman is after his heart.* He grumbled and muttered to himself as he headed toward his closet. Isabel laughed, but when Luke's towel hit the floor, she gasped at the sight. Luke's body was much hotter with tiny, wet specks of water spread all over him. She was half tempted to seduce him back to bed and lick every speck of splash she could find. But for now, she enjoyed the view of watching him get ready. She loved every minute of watching Luke dry himself then suit up for his meeting. The man made every piece of clothing so damn sexy, especially suits.

Once he was ready he leaned over and kissed her lips. "Meeting might take long. Stay here and catch up on some rest since we fly back tomorrow afternoon." She nodded and accepted his lips again. Closing her eyes, she lay back into bed, getting ready to fall back asleep. Luke smirked and after kissing her lips once more, he told himself he needed to leave or else he would spend another hour just devouring her lips.

A few minutes after Luke had left, Isabel realized she couldn't sleep without him next to her. She instantly missed the feel of his body next to hers in his warm bed. She sighed happily, rolled out of bed, and headed for Luke's massive bathroom. There was a hot tub with massage jets in there, and it had her name written all over it.

CHAPTER NINE

It was close to eight in the evening when Luke got back to his father's estate. He yanked off his tie and handed his briefcase to the doorman that greeted him. It had been one hell of a long meeting. Dawson Inc. was an international architectural firm Luke had been trying to obtain as a client for the past year. The owner of the company was a bit paranoid about trusting outside businesses. The last company that handled Dawson Inc.'s prints and advertisements had cost Brent Dawson a few clients along with a lawsuit. Therefore, he was skeptical with everyone who tried to do business with him. But Luke, being the determined man that he was, remained relentless and kept trying to persuade Dawson, because he didn't take no for an answer. He made one proposition after another until his deal was so appealing that Dawson called for a meeting. Luke didn't mind the added attention and work that was needed to book this client. Once he had Dawson's signed contract in his hands, immense opportunities awaited B. Pentagon as Dawson Inc. would become one of their largest clients. Luke already had in mind to open two new branches to solely handle this account. If all went well, he would continue adding B. Pentagon locations across the nation. Hell, since Dawson had extended his business internationally, Luke might even broaden his horizons and follow suit.

It sure as hell was difficult to keep focused, though. When Luke dealt with his clients, especially large accounts, he gave them his undivided attention and dedication. But today, his thoughts kept slipping back to Isabel and how one night with her had changed so much. Her beautiful smile and dark eyes kept taunting him throughout his meeting and by the time it was six in the evening, Luke was anxious to see her again, to touch her soft delicate skin once more, to taste her sweet lips, and hear her silky voice. Maybe even tempt her back to his room and make her moan again. The sounds of her sensual whimpers still echoed in his head. God, he couldn't get enough of her.

His thoughts trailed to the danger waiting for her back home. He'd tapped his foot nervously throughout the entire meeting, thinking of what he was to do with her situation. He needed to keep her close and safe and though she was far away from whatever had provoked her nightmares, tomorrow he would be taking her back toward the very danger that awaited her. He swore he would not allow her to even get close to anything remotely threatening but was losing his mind with all the uneasy emotions swirling through his head. He was desperate for her. He wanted her and needed her just as much as he felt she did for him. Luke couldn't deny that he was falling in love with her—that explicit, overwhelming, mind consuming, body and soul type of love. And the thought of her shutting down and pushing him away if he tried to help her again instilled incredible fear.

Just as he walked toward the staircase that led to the upstairs bedrooms, Andrew was walking down. "Hey. How did it go?"

"Pretty good." Luke nodded. "Dawson's a pain in the ass, but he'll come around soon enough. Do me a favor though."

"Sure bro, what do you need?"

"Knowing Dawson, he might call for another meeting soon, and I'll already be back in San Diego. He'll want to go over what I already told him twice. Contract details are in my briefcase so I'll leave them here just in case he calls for another meeting. We fly back tomorrow," Luke informed Drew.

Andrew nodded solemnly. "Not a problem. I'll go over it with him again. I'll take care of it. I got a call from Donald Layton an hour ago." Drew grinned. "I close the deal for the Langmon Hotel tomorrow."

"Sweet." Luke laughed. If anyone understood the satisfaction of booking a new client, it was his brother Drew. They talked business and upcoming events a little longer. It was looking like another promising year for B. Pentagon and both Brady brothers were content, yet relentless.

"So where is everyone?" Luke asked.

"Mom and Dad went to the Country Club with the Henderson's this morning and haven't been back since. Emilia's at Amanda's, and I'm heading there myself."

"What about Isabel? Where is she?" *She can't possibly still be in bed,* Luke thought.

"Uhh. She's here," Andrew said, scratching his chin. "Luke, I need to ask you something." He lowered his voice and looked down the hall.

"What?" Luke drew his brows together.

"I know it's probably none of my business but something happened, and I'm just fucking confused." Andrew scratched his head this time and looked down the hall again.

"Will you just fucking spill it out Drew?" Luke snapped, losing his patience. Andrew was obviously stalling, and Luke was trying to keep calm. Something told him he wasn't about to like what he heard.

"She completely freaked out." Andrew shook his head still stunned.

"What do you mean?"

"I didn't do anything to her, and she freaked out. Maybe I caught her off guard, I don't know, but I didn't expect her to react like that. I felt terrible," Drew continued to ramble, half lost in his own thoughts.

"Andrew, what the fuck are you talking about? Can you explain this shit a bit more clearly because you're confusing the shit out of me. What the fuck happened?" Luke snapped again. His reactions involving anything that had to do with Isabel being hurt were pretty violent.

"Will you calm the fuck down?" Andrew hissed. "I'm trying to tell you."

"Hurry," Luke breathed and waited for his brother to speak again.

"It was just us two here at the house. Like I said, Mom and Dad have been gone all day. Emilia called to invite me to join her at Amanda's. I didn't bother calling your cell since I know how shit is when you're dealing with Dawson. I went looking for Isabel to see if she wanted to come with me to Amanda's. I didn't want to leave her alone since I had no idea when you'd come back. I found her at the far end of the library staring at some books. The room was pretty dim, and she had none of the lights on. I called out to her, but I guess she didn't hear me. It was weird as shit bro, she wasn't even moving, just standing in one spot looking at the same book. I went closer to her, and the second I touched her shoulder, she lost it and completely freaked out. She started gasping and couldn't breathe like she was having some sort of panic attack, Luke. Totally scared the shit out of me. I didn't know what to do."

Luke's breathing had become rigid. "Did you touch her again?"

Drew pulled his head back in shock. His brother's words struck him as odd. *What the fuck?* "For fuck's sake Luke, I'm not about to make a woman who's having a panic attack even more uncomfortable. You think I would be crazy enough to try to touch her when she is already shaking with fear?" Drew spit out.

"I know man, I'm sorry. I don't know what I was thinking." Luke brushed his hand roughly through his hair. This woman was going to make him lose his mind.

"Before I could help her she bolted out the fucking door and locked herself in her room. I didn't know if I should go after her. I tried talking to her through the closed door, but she said she was sorry, and she was fine and wanted to be left alone." Drew sighed heavily and ran a hand nervously through his hair, subconsciously mimicking his brother's move. "I mean I get the whole getting scared or startled part. It's odd as hell but I can somewhat in a weird way understand it. But what I didn't understand is the way she looked at me."

"What do you mean?" Luke was almost afraid to ask.

"She looked at me like I was some kind of rapist or something Luke, like I was going to hurt her." The alarmed look in Drew's eyes was evident. Women didn't look at him in that way so this was a true shock to him.

"Fuck." Luke let out a line of curses.

Andrew silently watched him shake his head and curse, hoping it would help Luke cope. "So what's her deal? Why did she react like that?" Drew asked when he thought it would be safe.

"I don't know. She won't fucking tell me." Luke was getting tired of repeating that line. He felt as though long sharp nails were clawing at his skin. His patience was wearing thin, and there were too many unanswered questions to Isabel's past that just kept piling higher. Just when he thought she was doing better, some odd shit like this happened.

"So when did this happen?"

"About two hours after you left," Drew informed.

Luke looked at his watch and it was nearly eight-thirty now. His meetings had lasted longer than he had anticipated. Every minute that passed by was counted with eager anticipation of his return to Isabel. He was starting to sound obsessed, and he knew part of him was. He didn't like leaving her alone, for obvious reasons like this. Why couldn't she see how some of her reactions were unhealthy and unstable? He had to get to the bottom of this once and for all.

"Where is she now?"

"I saw her go into the office where you two have been working."

Luke gave a curt nod. "I'll go see how she's doing."

"Luke, if there is anything I can do…" Andrew trailed off seriously. "I didn't mean to scare her like that. I'd never hurt her."

Luke nodded again and squeezed his brother's shoulder. "I know. You don't have to explain it to me. I know," he repeated.

Luke watched his brother shake his head and leave. He headed toward the office where he knew he would find Isabel and began mentally preparing himself. He was uncertain how to approach the situation. He had tried to ask her directly what she was hiding more times than he could count, and she had not given him the answers he wished for. *You need to tread lightly Brady*, he thought. He found Isabel wandering around the large office, examining the family portraits scattered on various walls.

"Isabel," he called out to her, half expecting to receive the same reaction Drew had. When she turned around and smiled warmly for him, instant relief relaxed his nerves. He walked toward her and wrapped his arms around her waist, pulling her close to him. How much he had missed her during those few hours. He nuzzled her neck and then kissed her lips.

"I've missed you," he confessed.

Isabel's heart melted. If only he knew what he meant to her, what his love and attention did to her heart, and how lonely she had felt without him there. "I've missed you too." She kissed him lightly. "Meeting went well?"

"Better than expected." He grinned a boyish grin, making Isabel laugh. Luke always got excited when talking about new clients. "What are you doing in here? Not working I hope. I wanted you to relax on our last day."

Isabel smiled. Luke was always caring about her. She turned in his arms and grabbed a picture off his father's desk. "I've been wandering around your house admiring its beauty and family portraits, this one in particular." She nodded her head toward the picture she held. Luke looked over her shoulder to view the picture and saw the frame that had been resting on his father's desk for the past few years. The picture was of him, Andrew, Emilia, Amanda, and Jake when they were younger, many years ago. His mother had taken it during one of the many summers they spent together. A few months after Andrew had rescued a very vulnerable Amanda who was being terrorized by her grade school bullies. They had welcomed her into their family and into their lives with open arms. Isabel admired the picture. They were all pressed tightly together. Amanda was pulled into Andrew's lap as she shyly looked into the camera. Luke had one arm wrapped around Andrew's shoulder and another holding Emilia to his side. Emilia had one of her arms linked into Jake's as Jake stood, hands shoved into his pockets with a grim hooded gaze, watching the camera. They were all smiling except for Jake. His seriousness was evident even from a young age. Isabel admired the beautiful faces looking at her through the picture.

"Jake seems so serious," she said.

Luke sighed, "He didn't have much to smile about back then. He had a rough couple of years growing up."

"That makes me sad to hear," Isabel said genuinely.

"He's okay. He's Jake. He fights and survives."

"You all seem like you've been close forever." Isabel continued to look at the picture. It was as if it was telling her a story of Luke's childhood.

Luke smiled as he rested his chin on her shoulder and watched the picture as well. "Yeah, we have. I love Jake and Amanda as much as I love Andrew and Emilia. They're all a part of me."

"It must have been nice growing up closely with such great people. I didn't have too many childhood friends since we traveled a lot, and it became difficult to keep in touch. Both my parents have no extended family, no brothers or sisters. I imagine I must have some long distant cousin somewhere but who knows." Isabel laughed weakly.

It pained Luke to hear her speak like this. The extent of her loneliness was so evident. Even growing up she didn't have much companionship. Her father died at a young age, and he all but imagined how difficult it must have been once it was just her and her mother. Her mother had her art to escape to but what did Isabel have? Luke tightened his arms around her, embracing her into his body by pressing her back into his hard chest. She had him now, and she'd never be alone again or feel unsafe or scared, even if he had to make it his life's mission to prove to her that there was more out there for her. He loved this woman, and her pain had quickly become his.

"Drew was really worried about you," Luke whispered into her ear before he could stop himself from saying it. He felt Isabel tense inside his arms and slightly regretted bringing it up but he had to. It could no longer be ignored. They had to address the issues at hand. "He's worried he hurt you. Or he screwed up in some way."

After a few agonizing moments of silence, Isabel slowly placed the picture frame back on the desk and released a heavy sigh. "He didn't do anything wrong," she whispered. "I'm the one who should be apologizing to Andrew. He's been nothing but kind and welcoming toward me and didn't deserve the way I reacted toward him." Isabel turned back around in Luke's arms to face him. She smiled warmly at him when his eyes watched her full of concern. "I'm fine, Luke. Embarrassed that I reacted like that, but fine."

Luke searched her brown eyes for answers he was yet to find. There was too much he wanted to know and it was time Isabel began sharing. "Why did you quit law school?" he asked randomly.

"What?" Isabel was confused where the conversation had led.

"Law school," Luke repeated. "Scotts said you dropped out before moving out of town. Why?"

Silence hung heavy in the air. Isabel quickly pushed her way out of Luke's arms, and he reluctantly let her. "Scotts?" Isabel's voice cracked from alarm. She ran a shaking hand over her forehead realizing she was quivering from anxiety and fear. The name brought back too many unwanted memories. "When did you talk to Preston Scotts?" Her voice rose an octave while she tried to maintain a grip on her growing panic.

"A few months ago when he called me. He was wondering why you had ran off."

"He called you? Why? Why would he call you? Does he know where I am now? Oh God, they know where I am. They know where I am." Her entire body began to shake from fear. If Scotts knew where she was, then surely so did others. The vile feeling of vomit was threateningly rising in her throat. She was going to hurl if she continued this way. She wrapped her arms around her waist and rocked back and forth, hoping to control herself.

Luke was instantly in front of her, firmly gripping her arms. He couldn't watch her suffer like this, it was too painful to witness, and it was ripping him apart. "Isabel look at me. Look at me, damn it," he harshly whispered, demanding until she looked baffled into his eyes. "You believe me when I say I will never let anything happen to you, right? That I will never let anyone hurt you?" She slowly nodded her head. "Say it," Luke demanded with more sternness in his voice. "I need to hear you say that you believe me."

"I believe you," she confirmed with a soft weak whisper.

"Good." He shook his head. "It's killing me to see you like this, do you understand? It's ripping my heart. You can't go through this alone anymore Isabel. It's time you trusted me. Tell me what happened," he murmured.

"Okay," she whispered, surprising him that she had finally agreed. She slowly sank into a seat when Luke nudged her to sit. He then kneeled in front of her and tightly held her hands in his.

"I was researching on a case Scotts was working on. As I was working from home, I realized one of my files had been left at work. No one was at the office, considering it was close to midnight, but it didn't matter to me. I was always there during random hours. When I got there, I figured I was already in the office so I might as well complete my research." She paused to take a deep breath. Luke didn't speak and silently held her hands.

"I realized the case I was working on was very similar to a popular litigation suit Scotts had won a decade ago. Everyone at the firm still talked about it so I was familiar with it. I went to our file room in the basement where we kept hard copies. Scotts is old fashioned, and for some odd reason, he didn't like certain files scanned into our computer systems. Anytime we needed to refer back to an old case, we dealt with the paper files in the filing room downstairs. No one really ever went to the basement; it was dark, dusty, and the old building pipes always made cracking sounds. I never cared. Fear was never an obstacle in my life. I guess since I was so independent from such a young age, I'd grown numb to certain things that should have scared me." Isabel took another breath waiting for Luke to speak. When he remained silent she continued.

"When I got there, I realized I wasn't alone. I heard voices and naturally became more curios than frightened. But the moment I realized the sounds I was hearing was of a woman crying and struggling, instant fear paralyzed my body. My mind screamed at me to get the hell out of there but my feet walked me toward the noise." Tears began slowly filling Isabel's eyes. It was causing Luke unbearable pain to watch her suffer while telling the story. He knew she must be reliving every moment as each word left her lips but he didn't dare interrupt her.

"We had a college student named Marcy Brooks who was completing her internship at our firm. A petite, cute, little blonde with a very bubbly personality. She had to be probably twenty years old. I found her naked, bleeding on the floor with her hands tied behind her back. A man was hovering over her from behind. I recognized him as Scotts' son Dean. He was raping her." She choked out the last sentence.

Luke took a harsh intake of breath and began to physically shake. He jumped to his feet and walked to the desk, planted both hands firmly on the desk and leaned heavily for support. His breathing had become rigid, and he stood there silently ordering himself to stay calm.

"Then what happened?" he asked through clenched teeth without looking at her.

"Luke, I don't think—"

"What, happened?" he roared, making her flinch.

Isabel swallowed the lump in her throat. "I started screaming," she whispered, "Something along the lines of 'leave her alone' but when I saw the gun, I ran." She twisted her hands in her lap. Isabel couldn't explain the amount of relief she felt for finally opening up to Luke about her past. But the look on his face placed more fear in her now. He looked possessed, breathing in and out like a wild animal.

"You ran?" he finally asked.

"Yes."

"Did he run after you?"

Silence. "Yes," she whimpered.

"Did he catch you?" he said without looking at her.

More dreadful silence, then finally she spoke. "Yes"

Luke's blood was boiling. He didn't trust himself to move, and his judgment was clouded and fuming with rage. He attempted to compose himself but the severe anger shook him to his core.

"Did he hurt you?" His jaw tightened.

Isabel took a deep breath. Tears stung her eyes and pooled down her cheeks. "Not as much as he hurt Marcy," she whispered.

Luke slammed his fists on the table, causing Isabel to jump. He picked up the first available object and launched it across the room. It crashed with a loud noise against the wall. He walked to the window overlooking the gardens trying to concentrate on a single spot until he could gain control of his breathing. He scrubbed his hands over his face as a low, cynical laugh escaped from his mouth.

"I'll kill him. With my bare hands," he decided. "I'll kill that fucking bastard." Violent thoughts clouded his mind for the next few minutes as images of Isabel walking into a rape scene troubled his mind.

He finally turned to Isabel. "I want to know the rest." He went back to her, surprisingly calmer, and kneeled in front of her, taking both of her shaking hands in his. He carefully kissed her knuckles, looking into her swollen tearful eyes. He gently wiped the tears from her cheeks and cupped her chin forcing her to look at him. "I want to know everything Isabel. Don't ask me to explain why, but I need to know everything that happened with you," he explained softly and was surprised by his own gentleness. A minute ago he wanted to tear the entire room apart.

"Please," he pleaded with her.

She nodded. "He slammed me against the wall and placed his hands firmly around my neck, choking me. He said if I told anyone what I'd just seen, he'd do worse to me than he did to Marcy. He was so wild and demented, and his grip around my throat kept tightening. He reeked of alcohol, and his eyes were bloodshot. He would have done it then and there. As I felt my head spinning with no oxygen reaching my brain and my chest cramping, I knew he was trying to choke me to death. He'd lost complete control. He jolted off of me once we heard the evening security down the hall. He quickly untied Marcy and helped place her clothes back on, finally leaving through the back staircase. I watched her trembling and choking with sobs while she pulled her clothes over her bruised, bloody body. It was evident he had beaten her before brutalizing her sexually." Isabel choked out a sob as she remembered vividly.

"Before he left, he placed the gun to my head and said he meant every word, and I believed him. I rushed out of there before the security guard saw me. I don't even remember how I made it home that night but I did and wallowed in my own pity for a week. I didn't eat, I didn't sleep, and the fear had knocked any sense I had left in my brain. The thought of calling the cops wasn't even an option. I was weak and a damn coward. Just imagining him doing that to me sent me into wild panic attacks until I would hyperventilate and pass out. I felt partially dead." Isabel watched Luke's face flare with pain and anger. She knew she was pushing him toward rage, but she was finally opening up and didn't want to stop talking.

"I finally dragged myself to call my mom. She found me sprawled on the floor in my cold apartment, drenched in my own sweat. I can still remember the sounds of her screams when she walked in and found me. She took me to some hospital out of town. I was too disoriented to understand what was happening but apparently I'd had a seizure and it was a miracle I was even alive. I stayed in the hospital for about a month to recover."

"Did you receive any therapy after you were out?" Luke rubbed his hands over his face.

Isabel nodded. "My mom introduced me to Dr. Finch, my therapist. She made sure my whereabouts were covered, and I had security tracing my every move. My mother had enough money to hire all the right people and ensure my safety around the clock. My panic attacks and hallucinations had become uncontrollable. I constantly woke up screaming in the middle of the night, thinking I was being choked. That's why when you witnessed me having a nightmare, I really thought I couldn't breathe."

"How often does that happen, you not being able to breathe?"

"Almost every time I have the nightmare. Sometimes I struggle and other times I wake up instantly and realize it was just a dream. I had sessions with Dr. Finch every day until I got better. My mother hired some lawyers who located Marcy. She denied everything of course and said Dean was her lover not her rapist and I had misunderstood what I saw. They couldn't find Dean. He had disappeared off the face of this planet, but I always felt as though he was somewhere watching me."

Luke's jaw twitched. "Does Scotts know what his son did?" Luke asked.

Isabel let out a long difficult breath. Telling the story had given her a massive chest ache. She rubbed her hand between her breasts hoping to ease the growing pain. "I don't know, he was out of town at the time. If he found out after I was gone, I really don't know, but I've been fine putting this all behind me, Luke. You can't understand how much my life has changed thanks to meeting you. You can't begin to understand how much you mean to me. You filled the empty hole in my heart," she whimpered.

Luke's breath hitched. He stared into her swollen brown eyes with his intense green stare, burning into her. His heart ached to see her quivering lips and tear stained face, her eyes no longer holding the secrets he terribly wanted to discover. And now that he knew, he didn't know how to handle it. He wished he had been there in her past to hold, protect, and save her from any demons she was fighting to survive. He stood and pulled Isabel into a tight hold. She buried her face in his hard chest and began sobbing with heavy relief.

"You're going to be okay, sweetheart." He stroked her hair and pulled her further back, forcing her to meet his gaze. "If anyone wants to get near you, they'll need to go through me first." She nodded. He brushed away a tear on her bottom lip with his thumb, lowered his head, and took her lips in the most gentle of ways, sending her head over heels in love with him.

That night, Luke couldn't sleep. Isabel's revealing of the truth had the wheels in his head turning. He had to find a way to keep the woman he loved safe. Just thinking of what she had witnessed and the extent of her struggles was enraging. She should have never suffered to this degree. As he made slow, thorough love to her, his every thrust into her was his way of showing his desperation to keeping her close. He then watched Isabel drift to sleep while his wide, awake eyes lingered on her sleeping form till dawn.

~*~

Light broke through his windows, and it was Luke's indication that morning had arrived. He hadn't had a minute of sleep as his mind had been too preoccupied to worry about the time. He softly kissed Isabel until she stirred awake, whispering against her lips how much he'd missed her while she was asleep. Isabel smiled and stretched leisurely. The man sure knew how to give a damn good wake-up call.

"We leave at noon darling. It's almost eight," he announced after briefly looking at his watch. "You okay on time or should I delay our flight?" he asked kissing her again.

"No, I should be fine. I'll go pack now." She rose from his bed, picked up her robe off the floor and slipped it over her slim body. She slowly opened the door, looking down the hall for any sign of someone seeing her leaving Luke's bedroom. She turned around and gave him a giggle that made him laugh. It felt like they were teenagers sneaking in and out of each other's rooms.

Luke didn't have much to pack, so after he showered, shaved, and prepared his luggage, he went to the office to gather their files. He made a few important calls regarding Isabel's situation then walked down the hall toward the front entrance to make sure the limo had arrived to take them to the airport. He spotted Jake walking out of the security room.

"What's up man? Why are you still in New York? I thought you left last night," Luke asked surprised.

Jake shrugged. "I had a few things to take care of and just crashed here for the night. You got a minute?"

Luke glanced up the stairs seeing if there was any sign of Isabel. "Isabel's packing. We're heading back to L.A. in less than an hour. I've got some time."

"Good because I think you're going to want to hear this first before you head back," he said as he walked toward the security room, knowing Luke would follow.

"What's up?"

Jake waited a moment before talking. He wasn't hesitant, he was just trying to mentally prepare himself to how Luke was going to react. "I found a match to the fingerprints on Isabel's kitchen window."

Luke went still and in an instant his eyes were raging. "And? Who the fuck is it?" He raised his voice.

Jake scratched his chin. "Dean Scotts." He waited a moment in case it hadn't clicked. "Preston Scotts' only son."

Luke stood still, aware that his breathing had become irregular. It was as if all the blood had drained from his body leaving him numb. Something crawled inside of him, scratching away at already marked bruises—Dean Scotts, the bastard that Isabel witnessed raping another woman. The fucker was after her now.

"Luke, did you hear me? I take it by your abnormal silence that you were somewhat expecting that answer."

Luke nodded. He placed his palms flat on the desk and heavily leaned in. "This isn't fucking happening. She won't survive this if she finds out. I'll kill that son of a bitch if he ever comes near her again."

Jake knew better than to ask questions, and he rarely needed to. With the way Luke was reacting, he sensed Isabel was in danger from this Dean character. He'd be damned if any harm came to her. Any woman who had managed to get his best friend in this state of mind had his respect and protection.

"That's not going to happen," he told Luke. "Neither you nor I will let it. We need to resolve this shit, and we will get to the bottom of it."

"What else did you find on that piece of shit?"

Jake shook his head. "Well not much at first. A few speeding tickets, a DUI, some public fighting at random bars, a shitload of properties—no doubt that Daddy paid for, since he doesn't have a single check signed to his name—and a healthy trust fund." Luke just nodded.

"But I dug a little deeper," Jake said, pausing until Luke looked at him, "and found something dear ol' daddy did his best to cover up and hide. I just knew there was more to this asshole than meets the eye, and if he's sniffing around Isabel's house, there has to be more to it. I was able to come across some assault charges that aren't in his police records."

"Do I need to ask how you came across those files?" Luke asked, shaking his head. Jake's immense amount of connections sometimes astonished him.

Jake smirked. "No."

"What did you find?" Luke was almost afraid to ask.

"Ex-girlfriend Andrea Barnes filed a lawsuit against him for sexual assault and battery," Jake said.

Luke's body shook with anticipation while his mind worked overtime at the possibilities of there being another witness against Dean other than a not-so-cooperative Marcy.

"He messed her up really badly," Jake continued. "She needed stiches on her forehead, surgery for a broken arm, and a hell of a lot of physical therapy. I saw the pictures, and it sure as shit wasn't pretty. I didn't bring copies since it's classified and when I say I had to do some deep digging, I mean it. Scotts buried this shit so deep it took me a few days to get my hands on it."

Luke continued to stay silent. Jake knew Dean's involvement with Isabel ran deeper than any information he could find but there were no reports on paper.

"So you going to tell me what happened and save me the trouble of finding out myself?" Jake asked.

Luke released a heavy sigh. There was no point withholding information from Jake because they both knew that in a few days, he'd have all the answers. He'd go through a meticulous background check, investigate every person who's ever stepped foot inside Scotts' firm and it would lead him to Marcy, eventually. Plus, Jake was on their side and would use his connections to help Luke in whatever he had in mind.

The frantic need for retaliation and justice kept boiling his blood so he told Jake everything, not leaving out a single detail. After the torturous moment of explaining to Jake what Isabel had been through, he was livid with a whole new amount of anger.

Jake stood still as a statue. Tattooed arms crossed across his chest, he listened to what he had already suspected based off of his research. He wouldn't mind ending Dean's life with his own hands, but this was Luke's battle to fight, and they would handle it how Luke saw fit. After contemplating his raging thoughts, Jake scratched the back of his neck.

"We've got two options, Luke. Option one, I introduce you to the most aggressive and hostile attorney that ever existed who will ruthlessly rip Dean, his daddy Scotts, and his whole firm apart, giving Isabel and rest of these women the legal justice they deserve or option two, you leave this to me, and I handle it my way. You just say the word and this fuck disappears by midnight tonight with no trace or trail of him ever even existing."

Luke stared at his best friend of many years. Though he knew the extent of Jake's need to serve and protect, at times it baffled him the amount of power Jake had. His offer of option two was wickedly tempting, so tempting Luke almost agreed to it. But he needed to think this through. Scotts wouldn't be an easy battle to fight, but Luke's desperation for righteousness was greater.

"I'm going to need to meet this attorney of yours, as soon as you can make it happen. We'll talk in L.A. In the meantime, I'm taking Isabel to my place. There is no way in hell she's going back to that house."

Jake nodded. "Alright."

CHAPTER TEN

As they settled into Luke's private company plane, Isabel sighed with relief and leaned against Luke's arm.

"I love New York, but I'm excited to go back home. I miss it, all of it." She looked up into Luke's green gaze, and he smiled warmly down at her as he pulled her closer. "I miss my beautiful view of the beach right from my living room windows. I miss the salty sea breeze and burying my toes into the soft sand. I miss answering the phone and saying, 'Mr. Brady's in a meeting right now, can I take a message?'"

Luke tilted his head back and laughed.

"I'm serious," Isabel said, poking his ribs with a tease, "I miss Linda, Ginger, Brian, and all of our crazy staff, even the mail room girl who constantly calls out sick making me run the mail down myself. Yup, I even miss her." Isabel nodded and smiled.

"Babe, we've only been gone two weeks," Luke chuckled, "how could you possible miss it to that extent?"

Isabel sighed as she rested her head on his broad shoulder. "I just do. They feel like family. They like me. We're a team, and we work well together."

Luke stayed silent. He lowered his head and pressed his lips to her hair, inhaling her sweet jasmine scent. At times, he tended to forget the lonely life Isabel had lived before moving to San Diego. Sometimes he took things like always being surrounded by people who admired him for granted. But not Isabel. This beautiful, delicate woman who should always be cherished, appreciated life's most simple moments, and he was a better man for knowing and loving her. Never in his life had he possessed this immense need to show someone how much love and affection pumped through his veins for them, but he did for Isabel. He wanted to hand her the world on a shiny silver platter, to always love and protect her, to show her how someone as sweet and gentle as her needed to be treated. He didn't think life had dealt Isabel the fairest of cards, and he decided he was going to change the deck—manipulate all the cards—until she was constantly served with a royal flush. He vowed to himself that Isabel would not live in despair and fear any longer.

But how was he to deal with the issue at hand without frightening her away? It clearly was a sensitive subject for Isabel, a subject that took a while for her to trust him with. They couldn't ignore it anymore, and he needed to figure out some way of dealing with this without sending her into a full-on panic attack. She'd had a seizure for heaven's sake, and he had to avoid saying too much and ending up harming her. He'd rather cut off his left arm than cause Isabel any further pain.

"Sweetheart, we need to talk about what you told me," Luke whispered softly into her ear. Isabel immediately tensed and began to pull away. Luke tightened his grip to hold her in place. "No, don't do that. Don't pull away from me. I want to make things better."

Isabel squeezed her eyes shut tight. She wanted to control her breathing but the dreadful threat of panic was making her weak and she hated it. "We already discussed everything. There's nothing left to say."

"You are still having the bad dreams. I know all of this isn't behind you, maybe if we could just…"

"No, Luke." This time when she pushed away from him he reluctantly let her go. "No," she said with a louder, shaky voice. "You need to let this go. I'm not talking about this anymore. Please leave it alone, it is hurting me, don't you understand? Just stop pushing it."

She hated how tears began stinging her eyes. She wanted Luke to let her move on, not keep bringing up her weakness like it was a simple topic of discussion. An involuntary sob escaped her lips at the thought of looking so weak and pathetic to the man she was desperately in love with.

Luke watched Isabel struggle with her emotions and cursed himself silently. He hadn't meant to upset her. He couldn't afford for her to pull away from him, he'd worked too hard to get her this close, to get her to open up to him and trust him, and he'd lose his damn mind if Isabel distanced herself.

"Okay, okay baby, it's okay." He pulled her back into his arms and breathed in relief when she went back to him. "I'm sorry I brought it up. We won't talk about it."

How was he going to get around this without her hurting this badly? His only choice was to collect his thoughts, figure out a well-developed and thorough game plan, and then deal with it. He hadn't yet figured out how exactly to handle this without sending Isabel running out of his life. She feared her past, buried it deep, and hid from it while he kept trying to dig it back to surface.

~*~

When they arrived back to San Diego, Luke's limo and driver were waiting to greet them. Luke helped his driver place their luggage in the trunk and held the door open for Isabel. He slipped in after her and drew her close. Isabel smiled in contentment. Luke always found some way to touch her or hold her, and the amount of love she felt for this affection was exhilarating.

Luke played with the tips of Isabel's hair and leaned in to gently kiss her lips. "I've told my driver to take us to my house. If you don't mind, I'd like you to see my place."

Isabel grinned up at him. "That would be great. I'd love to see it."

"I'd also like you to spend the night. In fact I'm hoping to convince you to spend a few nights with me at my home."

Isabel's eyes widened as she inhaled a deep breath. "Really?"

"Yes, really." Luke's eyes became serious. "I've woken up next to you twice, and I can't imagine not having that every morning. I want your beautiful face to be the first thing I see when I open my eyes. I didn't want you just last night Isabel, I want you every night."

His words baffled her. She stared at him with enlarged eyes. Luke's fondness toward her left her speechless at times. She never imagined being wanted to this extent, never imagined a drop-dead gorgeous man with such a caring heart like Luke to walk into her life and changing everything.

"I'd really like that," she managed to murmur back.

Luke leaned his head until his lips touched hers, and he whispered against her lips, "I wasn't going to take no for an answer."

He parted her lips further and stroked his tongue against hers. Isabel's moan heightened and intensified the overpowering need he had for her. He couldn't get enough of her delicate moans and cries, and the powerful male in him roared with loud satisfaction that he was the one to make her this weak. He tightened his hold on her.

"I can't wait to get you home and have you again. I'm aching for you."

Isabel tilted her head back and hummed in pleasure when Luke's mouth roamed to her neck, and he licked her beating pulse. He glided his hands down her body until his strong hands landed on her thighs. Isabel gasped when Luke picked her up and moved her onto his lap with one swift movement. Without even realizing his intention, she was straddling his lap, her skirt hiked up past her rear and her aching center pressed to his growing erection. The intimate position awoke the brazen woman in her. She didn't hesitate to rock her hips back and forth rubbing her area of need against his. Luke growled and gripped her rear helping her move back and forth against him. The heated friction was driving them both into a wild frenzy.

Isabel slid her hand between them and palmed his bulge through his pants making Luke groan. "Why do we have to wait to get home when you can have me now?" She ran her tongue against his bottom lip and then gave it a playful bite.

Luke breathed against her lips, "You drive me crazy you know that? I want you so damn bad. You're killing me here."

"Then take me," she challenged him.

Since the moment they had met, it was Luke pursuing her, but her bold eagerness had left him ecstatically bewildered. Luke fumbled with the buttons on the side of the limo until he had his driver on intercom.

"Yes Mr. Brady?"

"Keep driving until I tell you to take us home," he demanded and watched Isabel's eyes widen in surprise.

"You asked for it." Luke grinned wickedly, and his palms gripped her butt tighter pulling her closer into him. He slid his hand lower and smoothly ran a finger over her dampened panties. He groaned in satisfaction when Isabel moaned in appreciation. "Two can play that game," he growled. "Let's get rid of these." He hooked a finger into the string of her panties and tugged it down. Isabel moved and wiggled around in his lap until Luke successfully pulled her panties off, slightly ripping them. All the while their lips hadn't left each other. They continued to suck and lick and taste so fiercely as though their lives depended on it. Their soft murmuring sounds had turned into heavy rapid panting while they devoured each other's lips. The tempo increase neared insanity as they groped and felt each other.

Luke thumbed her bare center and hummed with satisfaction when he found her ready. She threw her head back and cried out at the feel of his touch, "Oh God. That feels so good. Luke, I want you, I need you." She cried out again when he slipped a finger into her entrance and began caressing her from the inside. The moaning sounds she was making were foreign to her own ears. She did not recognize the sex-crazed woman she became when Luke had his hands on her but oh how she craved and longed for his touch. The way Luke touched her was worship all on its own. He not only got enjoyment from her, but he also took care of her. Luke was an intense lover and everything he did to her intensified her pleasure more. His desire and raw need for her grew with each touch and kiss. He could feel her tense against his moving hand and knew she was close.

"Oh God," Isabel moaned. "Please, I need you."

"Not yet." He kissed her lips. "Your body needs to be nice and relaxed first before I can take you."

"Please, Luke," she begged again through uneven breaths.

"Stop fighting it. Relax and enjoy what you're feeling."

His words guided her toward her release. Isabel threw her head back again and shuddered violently against his hand. Her body had a mind of its own as she rubbed her release against his palm gaining every ounce of pleasure she could obtain. Too lost in her own wild euphoria, she didn't realize that Luke had unzipped his pants. When she felt the tip of his bare skin begin to press against her throbbing center, she jolted with a newfound desire. Luke nudged himself against her entrance.

"Take it in easy, your body isn't ready…"

Isabel didn't hesitate the very least to proceed.

"FUCK!" Luke howled.

She moved her hips and went up and down in rhythm, not pausing for any rest. Isabel felt the fire building inside of her so fiercely it frightened her. She was almost afraid to finish in fear of what it would do to her body, not to mention her heart. What she felt for Luke was two cents short from crazy, and she was lost in him. His touch. His feel. He first owned her heart and now he owned her body. She whimpered and chanted his name over and over again begging him for some mercy.

"That's it. Just like that," Luke growled. "Oh damn, that's so good."

"Oh yes," she cried, "oh Luke …"

Isabel finally went limp in his arms while Luke tightened his grip around her waist, holding her to him. Stimulating bliss buzzed through both their bodies as they breathed deeply trying to gain an ounce of clarity.

"That was the most erotic experience of my life." Luke buried his face into Isabel's neck and breathed in her sweet scent. The heavenly scents of their lovemaking filled the limo. "You are going to be the end of me," he whispered against her soft skin.

Any fear, doubt, or uncertainty Isabel ever witnessed when it came to her feelings toward Luke washed away instantly. His words warmed her heart, and it danced with joy at the understanding that what she felt for him was mutual. Luke gently helped Isabel fix her clothes and settle back into her seat while he adjusted his pants. He informed his driver to take them to his home. He tucked Isabel into his side and kissed her cheek.

"That was incredible," he said.

"It was." She smiled softly and jolted in her seat, pushing away from Luke when realization hit her hard. "Oh my God."

"What?"

"Your driver. He must have heard us. Oh God." She covered her mouth with one hand.

Luke chuckled. "Well it's a little too late to worry about that sweetheart." Isabel slapped his arm for laughing and Luke just laughed louder. "Relax tiger, the window panel separating us is soundproof. I had it made that way in order to keep privacy. I use this limo for business Isabel. When I invite top clients for business arrangements, at times we discuss deals in the car until we reach our destination." He pulled her back into his arms and ran a hand inside her thigh. He pressed his lips against her ear and whispered, "This is the first time this car has experienced some mind-blowing sex."

Isabel relaxed and giggled. "That was pretty epic wasn't it?"

"If we weren't two minutes away from my house, I'd take you again. Once we get home I expect a sequel."

Isabel looked up at him with shocked amusement. "You can do that again?"

"Sweetheart you have no idea," he growled.

A few minutes later when they arrived home, Luke dragged Isabel to his bedroom without giving her a chance to see the rest of his house first. He demonstrated to her over and over again just what she did to him. He was losing his mind with the overwhelming need to continuously own her body and make her whimper and beg for him. Every sound she made during their lovemaking was sublime music to his ears. The crazed love he felt for her was both exhilarating and welcoming. This was a new experience for him, to love a woman so passionately, so profoundly, to want to make her his in every way. The thought of ever losing her, of her ever being faced with danger again awoke an unknown fear deep inside. He had to figure out a way to keep her safe, to keep her by him.

Luke woke with Isabel still in his arms. They had spent most of the day in his bed, only taking bathroom breaks. He'd ordered dinner from Isabel's favorite Italian deli near his office building, and they ate together in soothing, peaceful bliss. The wide, floor to ceiling windows of his bedroom allowed soft sunlight to illuminate the room.

Luke watched Isabel, lying on her stomach, as she slept silently in his bed. He'd never felt more content in his life. He pushed her long, brown hair away to be able to skim his palm up and down her bare back. Her skin was as smooth as silk underneath his touch. Every moment spent with her made him feel more connected to her, and now that he had her in his bed, he couldn't imagine a single night without her there.

His phone, resting on the night stand next to him, chirped, informing him he had a new text message. He slid the touch screen open with his thumb and saw Jake's text.

'Dean Scotts just checked into Hotel Moneta. It's barely a mile away from Isabel's house. I just know he's up to something. I'm watching this fucker.'

Luke was pressed with a newfound anger. That scum was settling himself closer to the woman he loved with no doubt of scheming an evil plot. He had to warn Isabel. But how, without sending her into full-blown panic? She refused to hear him out and if Isabel sensed danger was close, it frightened Luke that she might flee again.

'Watch him. Keep me informed. I'm going to need to speak to that attorney of yours,' Luke texted Jake back.

'I already spoke to him. He's on top of this shit. He'll be in town soon.'

'Okay good. Thanks man I appreciate it.'

'I told you neither of you are in this alone. We'll bring this fucker down if it's the last thing I need to do.'

Luke shook his head at Jake's reply and smirked. His dear friend sure had a determined streak when it came to protecting those he cared about. At times, he wondered if he asked Jake for the full truth about what he did, if Jake would give him an honest answer. Once, Jake had informed him that it was better if he and the rest of the family were kept in the dark about certain aspects of his life. Luke figured there would always be a part of Jake no one would know or understand. His life had been different from the rest of theirs, and if his friend needed to keep a part of his life hidden in order to survive, then so be it. He never thought that the lost, lonely boy he met years ago would grow to be such an unconquerable man. At times, Jake was detached from the rest of the world. He'd physically be there, but mentally he'd be somewhere else. They were all used to it by now, and they were all curious as to why Jake disappeared for months without a word, but no one questioned it other than Emilia. His little sister's curiosity and lack of censoring her verbal thoughts was going to land her in trouble one day.

Luke felt Isabel stirring from sleep so he put his phone away. After they showered together, Luke pulled one of his shirts over Isabel's naked body and led her into his kitchen where he made her breakfast. She didn't have a chance to see his house when they arrived so she looked around as they passed through the living room. Much like his office, Luke kept his house modern in design. There were black leather couches with crisp white pillows and she noticed that most of his furniture was dark in shade while the walls and curtains were pure white. Surprisingly, the contrast made the place amazingly masculine. The white drapes were pushed back behind handles revealing a massive balcony overlooking the Pacific Ocean. She saw the waves rising up high and splashing toward the shore. The view was breathtaking.

Isabel watched Luke in nothing but baggy gray sweatpants that sat dangerously low on his hips as he worked his way around the kitchen. She watched his bare back muscles flex as he expertly

188

flipped pancakes off the pan. She was enthralled by his Celtic shamrock tattoo engraved on the back of his left shoulder blade. It was sexy as hell and so damn captivating. She blinked in surprised shock at the moon-shaped nail bites carved near his tattoo and on the rest of his back. Her cheeks reddened as the memories returned of how shamelessly she had asked Luke to take her over and over again. Luke turned around and shot her a knowing glance. The intensity of his green gaze and his cocky smirk let her know he'd caught her fantasizing about their lovemaking.

"Keep thinking those thoughts and we'll be late to work," he warned.

Isabel squirmed in her seat but couldn't help the uncontrollable need she constantly had when he was around.

"That's a risk I'm willing to take," she breathlessly spoke.

Before she could blink, Luke had rounded the counter and hauled her up into his arms. He crashed his mouth into hers and devoured her lips with a kiss that made her toes curl. He cupped her butt and slid his hand to the back of her bare knees, lifting her up and setting her bottom on his kitchen counter. Their tongues swirled together as Isabel let out a small whimper. She felt Luke's hands slide up underneath her shirt and palm both of her breasts as he began to fondle and squeeze them, loving what his hands were doing to her. Isabel arched her back, pushing her breasts further into his touch. Luke lifted her shirt over her head and stared at her eagerly, running his eyes up and down her naked body.

"You're so beautiful," he whispered in appreciation. He took a taut nipple into his mouth and sucked relentlessly, causing Isabel to moan louder. He ran his hand to her needy center where he found her wet and ready, as usual.

Isabel roamed her delicate hands up and down his ripped abs and hard chest, loving the way his muscles tensed at her touch. She could touch his rugged body for days and not get tired of it. *What woman in her right mind would?* Every inch of him fascinated her. She felt him place a flat hand on her quivering stomach and push her down, pressing her back on the hard counter.

"Lie down," he commanded in that demanding voice he got right before they started making love. "This is going to be quick."

Isabel whimpered at his words. Before she could comprehend a coherent thought, Luke slammed into her. She arched her back and screamed from unbearable pleasure. Luke groaned as he pushed into her again. He lifted her knees until her bare feet were flat on the counter. He pushed her quivering thighs further open and grabbed her hips to get a better grip as he continuously pushed forward, loving the way his fast rhythm was shaking her entire body. He could feel the pressure building up in both of them. Just as he had predicted, it was going to be fast. She felt too damn good on him and the fast friction was doing explicit things to both of their bodies.

"Yes!" she screamed in pleasure. "Oh God!" She cried out as release shook her body so roughly that tears streamed out of her eyes. "Oh yes, Luke." Finally, his release joined hers as the loud screams of their lovemaking echoed throughout the entire house.

~*~

Luke shot knowing glances toward Isabel with a satisfied smirk on his face and a gleam in his eyes as he drove them toward his B. Pentagon building. Isabel fiddled with her hair as she exchanged shy glances with him. Her cheeks were still bashfully pink from their lovemaking, and she was radiating with a glow. Once they made it to the building, Luke handed his keys to his valet service and grabbed Isabel's hand, watching her eyes widen in surprise. She gave him a pleasant smile as he lifted up their joined hands and kissed her knuckles as they walked toward the elevator. Isabel wasn't oblivious to all the wandering eyes that just witnessed Luke's intimate gesture. Everyone in the building recognized Luke and since she was his assistant, they recognized her as well. She just hoped she wouldn't soon become the topic of discussion. The same stares continued as they made their way toward the top floor, and Luke still didn't release her hand. A few, such as Matt, Ginger, and Brian were already working behind their desks. Matt gave Luke a nod and appreciative smile as they walked past everyone toward the back of the building, closer to Isabel's desk. When they finally reached her desk, Isabel released the breath she was holding.

"Babe, you're all flushed and red." Luke chuckled.

"I'm sorry, I'm just not used to this much attention. I feel like everyone is watching us," Isabel said, sitting at her desk.

"Get used to it, it's going to be like this for the next couple of weeks I assume." Luke leaned on her desk and stroked her flushed cheek. Linda chose that moment precisely to make her entrance. Isabel, seeing Linda's silly smile, looked away from Luke's intense gaze. Any fool would recognize that look a man gives to a woman he's intimate with.

"You two have a good weekend?" Linda asked with amusement in her voice.

"Um, yes, it was wonderful," Isabel answered but avoided eye contact with either of them. "How were your holidays Linda? We missed you."

"Don't mind her Linda, she's still recovering from the eventful morning we had in my kitchen an hour ago." Luke laughed when both Linda and Isabel gasped in surprise at his bluntness. "What? You expected to sneak around and hide?" He lifted Isabel's chin and gently brushed his lips against hers. "It's not my style, sweetheart. The whole damn city can know that you're mine now." After watching her face burn with fresh embarrassment, Luke casually strolled back to his office with the widest grin on his face.

"Oh. My. Lord." Linda clapped her hands together. "I have a conference call in two minutes, but I want every detail during lunch," she called out as she hurried toward the boardroom, pointing a stern finger at Isabel. "Every detail."

The rest of the week went by with Luke constantly insisting that Isabel spend the night at his house. It took two days until she was finally able to convince him to take her home to get a new set of clothing. She had been living out of her luggage from New York, and it was sprawled open in Luke's walk-in closet. She didn't understand why Luke seemed so tense once they arrived at her mother's beach house. He kept looking around and checking all the rooms as if he was searching for something. After they left, Isabel realized he hadn't left her alone in one room for even one second. She even offered to cook for him and have a cozy dinner by her fireplace, but Luke came up with an excuse that he had work to do and needed the paperwork in his office and would feel better knowing she was nearby.

On their way to his place, Isabel realized Luke's uncertainty must have been due to her telling him about a possible break-in the night they went to Marcio's. Maybe this was the reason why he was so persistent to have her near him at all times. An unwanted feeling of insecurity and disappointment caused a bitter anxiety inside of her. She had assumed Luke wanted her close because he was in love with her, couldn't get enough of her, and he enjoyed his time with her, but she couldn't help but wonder if Luke's particular possessive demeanor was because he was a good man, wanting to protect her, especially since he had seen her at her most vulnerable. Did he think he had finally molded her into a confident woman, and that if he were to step aside, she'd go back to the helpless, lonely soul she was before him? This thought both scared and angered Isabel, mainly because she worried he was right. It saddened her to think Luke was concerned about her and wanted to comfort her instead of her being a strong independent woman that lured him in. Her defenselessness was what drew Luke to her, and she hated feeling insecure again, as if the last few days hadn't happened.

Luke sensed Isabel's change of mood as he drove toward his home. "You okay baby?"

Isabel looked at him and saw the concern in Luke's green eyes. "I'm fine." She managed to smile. She could see that he didn't believe her, but he just nodded and didn't continue. Once they were back at his place and she was back in his bed and into his arms, Isabel gained her confidence back as Luke demonstrated what a thorough and caring lover he could be once more.

~*~

Friday finally arrived and Isabel sat at her desk working on an editorial draft Linda needed. It sure had been a long week. There had been some pressing issues waiting for Luke when they had returned, and it had kept them very busy most of the week. She had never looked forward to the weekend as much as she did now. She used to anticipate Mondays where she could finally come back to the office after a long, lonely weekend and be surrounded by people again, but Isabel was now excited since Luke had informed her that his brother Andrew would be in town and wanted her to spend the weekend with them.

She tapped her pen on the printed files on her desk while reviewing the draft copy before her. When she lifted her head she noticed a young gentlemen, dressed in an expensive suit and briefcase in hand, walking toward her desk. He looked familiar. When his icy blue eyes met hers, she remembered him.

About two years ago, when she was still working for Scotts, on a legal trip with the law firm to Chicago, Scotts had teamed up with this man, Travis Reed, to defend a corrupted tycoon CEO against charges of major corporate fraud. Travis Reed was the main attorney, but Scotts was hired to tag along since the CEO was a close, personal friend. Scotts had invited Isabel to witness the trials as a learning experience. Isabel remembered how the young, ruthless attorney had ripped the prosecution team apart. The jury had been easily swayed by his charm and charisma and who could forget that thick, wavy, blond hair of his. The women on the jury were all but drooling each time he approached the bench. Isabel remembered how fascinated she had been as she had witnessed how Travis Reed managed to make the scumbag CEO turn out to be the victim instead of the criminal they were accusing him of being. The prosecution team sat there, wide-eyed and stunned, and even the judge had sided with Reed. Scotts offered him a partnership in his L.A. firm, but Reed had refused to leave his practice in Chicago.

"Hello," he said. He sent Isabel a curt nod before he entered Luke's office unannounced and shut the door.

What the hell is that about? Isabel wondered. She checked Luke's schedule and didn't notice any scheduled meetings. *Must be an old friend on personal business*, she mused. No one just walked into Luke's office unannounced, they always waited to be invited.

As she worked for hours with the rest of the staff, Luke's double doors remained closed. She caught herself occasionally glancing toward his doors, wondering what could be so important for Luke to be locked up with a corporate attorney for this long. She hoped the company wasn't in legal trouble, but Luke hadn't said anything to her. *Then again, why would he? He sleeps with you, he didn't make a declaration of love or commitment*, she told herself. He had only contacted her once, asking her to hold all his calls.

When lunchtime arrived, Luke emailed asking her to order them, including her, lunch from one of the delis he had a tab with. When the deliveryman arrived with their lunch, Isabel took the bags to Luke's door and knocked. He opened the doors wide but somewhat stood in her way.

"Hey babe, thanks for ordering lunch." He leaned in and swiftly kissed her lips as he grabbed the bags from her hand.

Isabel couldn't help but glance inside his office where she saw Reed sitting on Luke's wide, black leather couches. The wide, glass coffee table was covered with scattered paperwork.

"Is everything alright?" Isabel met Luke's gaze and murmured.

"It's great sweetie. Just a business lunch. Did you order something for yourself?"

Isabel frowned. "No, I'll just go to lunch with Linda."

Luke hoped that panic wasn't written all over his face. Just the thought of Isabel walking around outside in public without him to protect her terrorized him. He had achieved keeping her close every minute of the day since they got back and much to his advantage, the office had been hectic and busy so he managed to keep Isabel indoors even during lunch hours.

"Oh uh, actually sweetheart, I'm waiting for an important call from Rick. You mind if you girls order lunch and eat here? I really can't miss it."

"Sure." Isabel solemnly nodded and was further confused when she saw the immense amount of relief on Luke's face.

He cupped her face and whispered against her lips, "Thanks baby." After a brief, yet intense, kiss he released her and gently closed his doors.

The time ticked away as minutes turned into hours. Rick never called, and Luke's doors didn't open again.

CHAPTER ELEVEN

Isabel watched the clock as another hour passed by. The floor was empty. Everyone, including those who were usually forced by Luke to leave, had already gone home to start their weekend. Isabel had assumed her and Luke would be leaving together, but he had yet to contact her and open his doors. She really hated to disturb him, but she didn't want to leave without letting him know. Just as she was gathering her items, Luke's door flew open. His eyes immediately went to the purse in her hands.

"What are you doing?" he asked, alarmed. "Were you planning on leaving?" Worry was etched across his face.

"Oh, hi. I was just about to knock on your door, but I didn't want to interrupt. You seem really busy so I'll just see you tomorrow. I'm sure you have your hands full and my house isn't that far, I'll just walk home," she hurried with her words.

Luke was instantly by her side. He took her purse from her hands and placed it back on her desk. "Isabel, if you left without me that would really have pissed me off." He cupped her face and tilted her face so her eyes met his. "You arrive with me and you leave with me. Is that clear?"

Isabel nodded in misunderstanding. She was going to argue back at his demanding voice, but the fear and worry written across his face stopped her from doing so. Luke sure was acting strange. *What is up with him today?* she wondered.

"Well, uh, are you almost done?" she asked hesitantly.

"Not quite," Luke paused. "I was actually coming out here to ask you to join us inside my office. Mr. Travis Reed would like to talk to you."

"Me?" Isabel's eyes widened in surprise.

Luke pulled her into an embrace and kissed her temple. "Just hear what he has to say sweetheart."

Isabel stiffened but was too stunned to speak. Even when Luke pulled her toward his office, she entered wordlessly. Her body switched to complete numb mode. Her back straightened and her fists clenched by her side. *Panic was mere seconds away.* Her mind started to assume what this was about but she was refusing to believe it. This man couldn't possibly be here for that reason. Luke wouldn't do this to her. He wouldn't put her through this when she had continuously begged him to drop the subject and let her move on, let her live her life.

"Travis Reed. It's a pleasure to meet you Ms. Stamos." Reed extended his hand, and Isabel hesitantly accepted his greeting.

"I know who you are," Isabel spoke with a shaky voice, "and I can already assume what this is about." She shot Luke an accusing glance, and he immediately winced when he saw the pain of betrayal in her eyes. *She must hate me already,* he thought.

Reed cleared his throat. "Alright. Well then, we will skip the formalities and get straight to business. If you will please have a seat Ms. Stamos so we can discuss this more comfortably."

"Call me Isabel," she said and against her better judgment she joined them, "And forgive me for correcting you Mr. Reed, but this subject has no means of being discussed comfortably." She hoped her voice was as cold as she intended it to be. A nervous shift of stance from Luke let her know she'd made a clear message of how much she disliked this.

"No forgiveness needed since I agree with you," Travis Reed continued. "There's no other way of saying this Isabel other than we have decided to reopen the case against a Mr. Dean Scotts. We've already contacted Marcy Brooks. She's agreed to cooperate and testify."

Isabel let out a cynical laugh. "She's not going to do it. She said the same thing last time to my mother's attorney, but the minute the cops became involved she became very elusive."

"I have reason to believe I've gained her full cooperation this time. Quite some time has passed, a great deal has changed and—"

"With all due respect Mr. Reed, what are you going to do that already wasn't attempted a year ago?"

"Isabel, we have new evidence that will—"

"Did you think I did not try to fight then?" This time she aimed the question at Luke.

Reed controlled his frustration when she interrupted him again.

Her eyes become cold and aloof, radiating the dark bitterness that was forming inside. "You picture me as this helpless girl who was harassed and did not attempt to fight it? That I wallowed in self-pity until the pain disappeared? Well, news flash, it didn't disappear; it didn't vanish into thin air. It's still there, very real, and very deep." She didn't mean to tremble but sheer panic weakened her. Her body shook as unwanted memories began flooding her mind once more. This was exactly what she didn't want. To relive every moment and pain and Luke was forcing her to do so.

Luke remained silent with clenched fists. Of course he knew the pain was still there. He'd witnessed her in pain one too many times but for her to admit it did something to his heart he was unable to explain. He didn't want her to hurt any more.

"Ms. Stamos," Reed tried again. "I know what you are going through. Believe me, you're not my first client to live through this. I assure you I'll do everything in my power to put this to an end."

"What are you even doing here Mr. Reed? You're a defense attorney for major corporations. Your job is to defend corrupt tycoons from ending up in jail. Your business does not involve sexually harassed victims. Why would you want to represent us?"

Travis shot a brief look toward Luke then turned his gaze back to Isabel. "You want the truth?" He waited until Isabel firmly nodded. "Just calling in an honest favor for a close friend, one who cares a great deal about you. Mr. Callaghan and I have immense connections, especially in the court of law, along with law enforcement departments. This can easily work in our favor."

"Jake?" Isabel's brows furrowed from misunderstanding. "What does Jake have to do with this?"

Luke cleared his throat. "He knows all about this."

"What?" her voice rose with alarm. "Why? Why would you tell him?"

"I didn't. He figured most of it out on his own," Luke admitted with clenched teeth.

"That doesn't make any sense." Isabel shook her head refusing to make eye contact with either man in the room.

"Isabel, please…" Luke begged.

She squeezed her eyes shut as tight as possible, willing the tears to not come. "I'm sorry Mr. Reed, but you have no idea what this is like. I've put this all behind me. You can't rely on Ms. Brooks because she is not a dependable witness and I refuse to live through this again. I apologize that Mr. Brady and Mr. Callaghan have both wasted your time. Though I appreciate your commitment to an old friend, I can assure you there is no case here. I've seen what Scotts can do."

"Ms. Stamos, with all due respect—"

"Please, Mr. Reed. I can't do this. Please understand." Her voice had minimized to a whisper.

Travis looked helplessly at Luke. Luke briefly closed his eyes, shutting them tightly then nodded to him to let it be.

Travis frowned. "Well if you change your mind, just let Luke know." He released an exhausted sigh and got up to leave. "Brady," Travis said and nodded farewell to Luke.

"We'll keep in touch." Luke nodded back.

Isabel remained rigidly seated on Luke's black leather couch with her back defiantly straight until she heard the elevator doors close behind Travis.

"You had no right to do this Luke, I told you to let it be." She jumped to her feet and lashed out on him the second they were alone. "Why are you trying to drag me back into this?"

Luke shoved his hands through his hair. "This needs to be done and we need Reed's help. It's more serious than you're willing to admit."

"No, it isn't. You're trying to dig up my past and bring it back to the surface when I asked you not to. What is it? Do you like seeing me helpless and vulnerable? Does it feed your ego to constantly save me and play hero?" she yelled at him, letting the words slap him hard across his face.

Luke's lips thinned into a straight line. "That's enough Isabel. Now I understand you're upset—"

"Upset?" she shouted. "Of course I'm upset Luke, this is none of your business."

"And I suppose falling in love with you is?" he yelled back. "I suppose watching the woman I've fallen crazy in love with suffer through this is none of my business?" His loud voice echoed across the large room. Her stunned, baffled face was all the satisfaction he needed. His words had really shut her up. "That's right. I'm in love with you. And it's killing me to see you this way. Do you understand that? I can't see you this way Isabel." He reached for her, but she took a step back. The rejection felt like a knife through the heart.

Isabel took a few steps back, maintaining a safe distance. "You're not in love with me. You see me as helpless and want to save me," she cried out. "You pity me."

"For fuck's sake Isabel, you can't be that insecure." Luke scrubbed his face with both hands.

"Well what the hell are you doing with an insecure woman Luke? What is a big-time, corporate hotshot like you doing with a woman who can't keep her emotions and panic in check?" She had turned her weakness into anger out of defense. She would not allow his confession of love to give her false hope. Luke didn't understand what he was saying. He saw her as weak and wanted to protect her because that was the type of man Luke was. He didn't love her.

His face heated with fury. "You know that's not what I meant."

"I don't care what you meant. I'm sick of reliving this memory with you. It's like a never ending nightmare." She shook her head.

"It's a never ending nightmare, because you still have the fucking bad dreams every damn night," Luke barked with rage.

"Well it will no longer be your problem."

Luke raised his brows. "What the hell is that supposed to mean?"

"It means you don't have to witness what I'm going through so you no longer feel responsible to help me." She grabbed her purse and jolted toward the elevators.

Her words sent a scorching, hot terror to cut through his senses. "Isabel."

That one word and the saddened tone in his voice was enough to stop her dead in her tracks. Her back toward him, she clutched her purse as tears began spilling down her cheeks. She could feel the anger, mixed with panic, radiating from Luke's body a few steps behind her.

"You're running away again sweetheart," he said in a struggling gruff voice.

Isabel shut her eyes tight, urging the pain to go away. "It's the only thing I know how to do," she whispered. "Please let me go. Please don't come after me." She hurried through the elevator doors.

Luke watched the doors close and take away the woman he loved. He shook himself to wake up and ran after her.

"Luke."

Linda's call had him spinning toward her. He thought they had been alone all this time. Linda must have come into the office and heard them. He watched her pale worried face as she held folders in a tight grip.

"Shit," he cursed. "I can't right now. I need to go after her."

"Luke, let her go."

"I CAN'T," he roared, making Linda flinch.

"Give her some time. She's just scared. You and I will never fully understand what she is going through. It frightens her."

Luke gave Linda a long, hard look. He shook his head in disbelief. "She told you." It wasn't a question.

Linda nodded. "Give her some time," she repeated. "I'll see to it she gets home safely."

Luke hesitated but eventually caved. He blew out a struggled breath and nodded. "Please text me when you're both securely home."

Linda didn't question Luke's odd need to be informed of Isabel's safety so she agreed and hurried after her. Once she was gone, Luke picked up the nearest phone and placed a necessary call. Some arrangements needed to be made.

~*~

Jake sat across from Luke. He took a long swig from his beer and watched Luke's brooding face. His best friend had called him and told him the meeting with Reed and Isabel hadn't gone well. Jake had greeted Andrew at the airport and informed him of his older brother's current situation, leaving some details out. Now all three sat in Luke's living room with cards passed out on the table, open beers, and a bottle of tequila with shot glasses in the middle, as they engaged in a silent, moody poker game.

"I told her I love her." Luke broke the murky silence with his eyes casted low, focusing on his cards.

Jake and Drew exchanged a quick glance but remained quiet.

"I told her I'm in love with her, and she thinks it's out of pity," Luke continued. He took a quick, frustrated drink from his beer then placed it roughly back on the table. "She all but threw

Reed out of my office. Then, she said it gave my ego some kind of sick fucking boost to find her helpless and in need, that I somehow must get a rise out of all this shit. I've never seen her that cold." Luke shook his head still in utter shock.

Jake's lips twitched, realizing Brady had met his match. So it seemed shy Isabel had a temperamental side, and this somewhat pleased him. They remained silent for a while, allowing Luke to gather his thoughts. Jake had informed Andrew about the situation Isabel was presently in.

"She's just afraid, Luke." Drew hoped he could somehow help his brother. He'd never seen him so torn, especially over a woman. It was a foreign situation for all three of them to be in. None of them were experts on relationship. Have a question about casual, no-strings-attached sex? Sure, Andrew Brady was your guy. But damn, not when it came to relationships.

"She witnessed a brutal rape scene. Dean raped some college intern that used to work at their firm. Isabel walked in on the whole thing while it was happening. The shit she saw was disgustingly vicious. Dean caught her and threatened her. The young girl that was raped became too freaked out to confess. Isabel's mom, Vivian, and her attorneys did everything they could but nothing helped. Dean disappeared, but now he's back and Isabel has no fucking clue," Luke told Andrew and watched his face transform into awareness. He assumed Jake hadn't given Drew full details, and his guess had been right. Luke swallowed the lump in his throat. He couldn't inform them about Isabel's health condition, about how she suffered a seizure all alone curled up on her apartment floor. If Luke repeated that scene, if he allowed his brain for one minute to picture her in that situation, he'd be sick, throw up, and pass out. The woman he loved had been through so much, and she still continued to suffer.

Jake pushed out of his chair and walked over to the window. He scrubbed his hands over his face and then crossed his arms over his chest. He was trying to stay composed, and he could feel Luke's and Andrew's eyes burning holes in his back. They both knew how violent and irrational he became when an innocent person was harmed. His natural, yet very bizarre, instinct to want to protect constantly consumed him. Jake had felt helpless his entire youth and when he became a man, he vowed to never become the victim and to serve and protect others as far as his capabilities allowed him to. He felt a cold sweat threatening his body and knew something needed to be done. He'd go crazy thinking of an innocent, beautiful woman like Isabel being at the mercy of some sick bastard like Dean.

"Jake, I can hear the wheels in your head turning buddy," Luke called out to him.

Jake just shook his head. "We've got to do something Luke, you have to tell her about us seeing Dean in the surveillance cameras. She needs to be aware that her safety is in jeopardy."

"Yeah, you need to tell her," Andrew agreed finally, realizing how deep the significance of the situation was.

Luke sighed heavily. "I'm afraid if I tell her, she'll start running again and this time, it won't be two hours away to the next city. I'm scared she'll run so far I won't find her. Something tells me that's exactly what Isabel would do. I don't want to cause her any more anxiety. She already doesn't sleep well. I was hoping that once she knew we'd found the college intern Dean raped, and that she was willing to partake in the trial, Isabel would be more willing, but she's not. And the distance between my house to hers is the most I'm willing to suffer. I'm afraid to picture what I would do if she completely disappeared."

Andrew watched his brother confess the depth of his feelings for this woman. He understood Luke's need to protect Isabel because he'd been obsessed with protecting Amanda since the minute she'd walked into his life. *But to be that madly in love with a woman where all rationality leaves you bare?* It frightened the hell out of Drew.

"So I guess that's it?" Jake shouted, gaining the attention of both brothers. "You're just going to let some sick fuck like Dean Scotts get away with this shit? When he's out there sniffing outside your woman's kitchen window?"

Luke's eyes turned cold. "I'll go to hell a thousand times and come back before I let that scum anywhere near her. I've already got security posted outside of her house watching out for her," Luke confessed.

Jake relaxed a little and sat back down. "Yeah, I know about them," he said.

Luke watched him knowingly, and a small grin spread on his face. "Who do you have out there Jake?"

Andrew laughed. "Let me guess. Just a few of L.A.'s finest right?"

"You have P.D. watching her?" Luke asked.

Jake tossed back a tequila shot not bothering to chase it with beer. "No," he said firmly. "A few agents." He met Luke's gaze dead-on.

"Secret service?" Andrew called out. "As in CIA? Fuck Jake, when are you going to explain the reason behind all these connections?"

Jake tried a casual shrug. It was ineffective, because there was nothing casual about him. "Trust me Drew, you don't want to know. You'll sleep better at night."

Luke studied him through a narrowed glance but did no further questioning. After high school, Jake had joined the Army. He had been gone a few years and returned a different man. Something about him had become lethal. His entire family had their suspicions that Jake was involved with more than just the army and lately, he was proving these suspicions to be on target.

Luke didn't question it though. He nodded to his friend in an unspoken bond of trust and gratitude. He felt better knowing more eyes were watching Isabel. She could be as stubborn as she wanted to be, but she still had a very active threat too damn close to her. Especially since Dean was staying at a nearby hotel and was closer to her than Luke was. The thought made Luke uneasy.

"So what about the witness? The college girl. What happens to her?" Drew asks.

Luke picked up his beer and looked away, contemplating his thoughts.

Jake shook his head as he laughed. "I knew it."

Andrew raised his brows, catching on. "You're still going through with the trial aren't you? Against Isabel's wishes. But how are you going to use Isabel's surveillance cameras as evidence in court without her consent?"

"I still have another witness, don't I? Reed is a smart man. We'll figure something out." Luke nodded, attempting to reassure himself more than his brother. He wasn't going to give up that easily.

Jake nodded in agreement. "This is going to be an open and shut case, real quick. Alright Andrew, let's play some fucking poker. Your brother's lovesick face is going to make me hurl soon," Jake said, chuckling.

Andrew threw his head back and howled in laughter. "Hope that shit isn't contagious."

"Both of you can go fuck yourselves," Luke barked, but his lips twitched with amusement as he dealt the cards.

~*~

Isabel was nervous about going back to work the following Monday. She hadn't spoken to Luke since their disagreement Friday night. He tried to contact her both a few times Friday night and all day Saturday, but she wouldn't budge. Finally on Sunday, he hadn't bothered reaching out to her. She thought about calling in sick but couldn't convince herself to do so. That would be another form of running, and she would not run any more, just like she refused to let her past further haunt her. Luke didn't understand what he was doing. He was digging up buried bones without seeing the effect it had on her. She refused to live through that again, and Luke would just have to let this go.

The office was beginning to fill. She saw Linda walk in and give her a sympathetic smile. God, she hated it when people pitied her, and it was all Luke's fault. Soon, the entire office would know she had an affair with the boss that didn't end well. Isabel wanted to tell herself she was wrong for putting her guards down with Luke, but she just couldn't. She still believed Luke was the best thing that had happened to her, and she was still desperately in love with him. She'd never felt more loved and cherished the way Luke had treated her. But now, that fine line of love and empathy were beginning to blur.

Her heart broke to think Luke was only into her because he had a good heart and wanted to help her. She recalled the past few months with him and realized the only times Luke had been there for her was to help her, console her, and protect her. Had she been an average woman walking past his way with a casual smile on her face, he would not have been drawn to her but Luke had placed himself in this obligatory stance to save her. *And damn him*, she thought, *she doesn't need him for that*. She could deal with her demons on her own. She wanted a man to love her and want to spend time with her, not a man who thought he was in love with her because he somehow felt responsible for protecting her.

Isabel's eyes began to sting with tears. She quickly wiped them away and got her powder compact out to fix her makeup. There were dark circles underneath her eyes that even makeup couldn't cover. That's what happens when you lose sleep and don't eat well for a couple of days.

When she heard the elevator ding on the top floor she took a deep breath. Instinct told her she'd see Luke walk through those doors and just as she had assumed, he walked in with his usual confident, domineering stride. Part of her half-expected and half-hoped to see him as torn as her, but Luke looked the exact opposite. He looked determined, and she couldn't help but notice the angry sulk on his face. This Luke was much more intimidating and scary. He walked straight toward his office without acknowledging his staff, something he rarely did. He stopped at Isabel's desk and placed a file on her desk. He gave her a curt nod.

"This needs to be completed by the end of the day," he said, pointing at the file, no greeting, and no warm smile. He looked like a typical, tyrant boss. Isabel noticed a new gleam in his eyes that she had never recognized before. Luke had never been this angry with her. She was about to speak when he interrupted her.

"Hold all my calls. Cancel any meetings I have today. Anyone that needs to see me, reschedule for tomorrow. I don't want to be disturbed for the rest of the day." With no more words, he walked through his double doors and closed them shut.

This flared Isabel's anger. Who the hell did he think he was? He could just sleep with her and pretend like nothing happened? Well she had words of her own, and he would hear her out. Without rethinking her actions, she pushed away from her desk, opened his office door, and closed it shut once she was inside.

Luke was already behind his desk with his coat hanging by the door leaving him in his nicely fitted white dress shirt. He looked up with raised eyebrows. "Is there a problem Isabel? Were my instructions not clear enough for you?"

"Is that how you speak to a woman you claim to love?" The words were out of Isabel's mouth before she could stop them. She saw a mixed emotion of hurt and anger flicker across Luke's face. His green gaze turned wild as he took in a deep breath no doubt trying to obtain control.

"According to you, I am not in love with that woman, I just pity her." Luke folded his hands on his desk and continued to watch her with a haunting gaze.

She bluntly stared back, unable to speak. Isabel knew there was no point in arguing. The office was completely full by now and if things ended like Friday night, she and Luke would be yelling at each other, and it would further tangle her in the gossip vine. So she took a deep breath and changed her tactic.

"I want you to remove the men you've placed as guards in front of my house," she said sternly.

"That's not going to happen." Luke turned his face away from her and began looking through his files as if that was the end of discussion.

His curt response further aggravated her. "Luke, it is my life, and I won't be watched like I'm some sort of child. They even followed me to the drug store. I want them off my property."

Luke blinked in surprise. The thought of Isabel leaving the house had stupidly not crossed his mind. He sat back in relief, thankful that the men placed to protect her had taken it upon themselves to follow her.

"I checked the property lines babe. No one is trespassing." He gave her a fake no teeth showing smile.

"You are unbelievable. You can't force that service on me. I'll call the cops and have them removed for making me feel uncomfortable. There has to be some law against it and plus, they are loitering."

Luke laughed and shook his head. "Cops are on Jake's payroll sweetheart. But you can sure as hell try." He leaned back in his chair and gave her a challenging smile.

He was enjoying this, she realized. She was out of any further conversation she could have with him, as he seemed to have an answer for everything.

"Fine. Have it your way." Without allowing him to speak again she walked out. She had to go figure something out.

Luke stared at his closed doors. Right when Isabel walked out he let out the breath he was holding. It wasn't easy staying strong when he was breaking down inside. She looked tired and restless, like she had been suffering. She also looked thinner than she was a few days ago. Luke cursed and violently tugged at his hair. Just imagining what she must be going through at nights, curled up afraid and all alone in her bed, was fueling his rage. This wasn't right. *How can she not see the obvious love he has for her?* he thought. *How can she insult him and call his love pity instead?* It drove him disgustingly mad. He should be there for her, holding her through the night in case she woke from a nightmare, to comfort her. But the woman was being too damn stubborn. He tried reaching out to her over the weekend, but she would not budge. She wanted to play hardball, so that was what he would do.

Luke worked silently inside his office, occasionally receiving calls from Reed's staff to keep him updated. He had told Reed that he wanted to be informed of every little bit of progress and just as promised, he was getting his updates. He had to hand it to him, the man worked fast, and he was immensely impressed by Reed's capabilities. Luke continued to work effortlessly until his eyes glanced toward the time, and he noticed it was almost noon. His email dinged informing him he had a new message. It was Isabel.

Hello Mr. Brady,

Just checking in with you to see if there is anything you need before I leave for lunch. Please let me know if I can order lunch for you.

Thank you,
Isabel Stamos, Executive Assistant
B. Pentagon Print and Advertising

Luke suddenly found himself very alarmed. Isabel had an hour lunch that she usually took with Linda. They mainly leave the office and walk to any of the cafés down the street. Just the thought of Isabel being away from his watchful eyes sent a jolt of panic through him. No way in hell was he having her leave the office. His hired men had been watching her every move, but if he could avoid any risks then he damn well would. He quickly began to type…

Isabel,

The office is busy due to our two weeks of absence during the holidays. I will require you to please take a working, paid lunch and remain in the office for assistance.

You may order lunch for both of us from anywhere you would like. Please have them deliver directly.

Thank you,
Luke Brady, Vice President
B. Pentagon Print and Advertising

Isabel stared at her email. *Seriously? Working lunch?* Luke had never required a working lunch from anyone before. She was the one handling some of the distribution of work and didn't realize the office was busy to that extent. She'd barely even had any calls.

Linda approached her desk and gave her usual cheerful smile. "Ready to head out?"

"We can't, Luke sent out an email asking us to have a working lunch. We have to stay here."

"What email?" Linda looked confused.

"This email," Isabel said, pulling it up and watching Linda read it. She began to laugh, and Isabel raised her brows. "What?"

"Oh honey," Linda continued to laugh, "You're the only one that got that email."

"What? What do you mean? How do you know?"

"Well I sure as hell didn't get it. And look..." Linda pointed toward a few people who had grabbed their purses and coat jackets and were headed toward the elevator.

"What the fuck?"

Linda burst out laughing. This was the first time she'd heard Isabel curse and look so angry. *It sure was entertaining.*

"You two are too damn much. Guess your man wants to keep you close. He's getting all possessive on your ass. That's kind of hot." Linda winked and began walking away.

"Yeah, real hot," Isabel said through gritted teeth as she made her way back toward Luke's office.

"Why am I the only one required to take a working lunch?" Isabel slammed Luke's door shut. Luke looked at her, unimpressed, as if he'd expected to see her.

"Rick, let me call you right back, I've got a bit of a situation in my hands." He gently placed his phone down and looked at her. "This is the second time you have interrupted me when I have asked to not be bothered today."

"You are being unreasonable."

"And you are being stubborn, not to mention unprofessional."

Isabel raised her brows defiantly, "Oh, I'm being unprofessional?" She hadn't realized her voice had raised a notch. "You're the one being a tyrant."

Luke released a heavy sigh. "Are you done ranting, Ms. Stamos? I got off a very important call for this."

Isabel wondered if she looked as hurt as she felt. "So this is how it's going to be? We're going to be rude and uncivilized toward each other?" Now she wanted to cry because her confident voice had weakened, and she hated that.

"We are civilized. I'm your boss, and you are my assistant. Therefore, I am telling you that the office is busy and you are required to take a working lunch to accommodate the situation."

"But I'm the only—"

"There are no buts, Isabel," Luke interrupted her abruptly. "There is nothing to discuss."

Isabel grinded her teeth together, "Fine. You win again, Luke." And just like that, she walked out.

Luke stared after her once again. It didn't feel like he was winning when she resented him so much, but guaranteeing her protection would have to come before gaining her love. The least he could do was love her from a distance.

~*~

Luke and Isabel continue to work under these mind-numbing, nerve-wrecking circumstances for the rest of the week. Luke ensured that Isabel stayed indoors at all times, but she was beginning to become defiant. She'd find different excuses to leave the office and disappear to another floor, and Luke had to send Linda to find her. Luke began including Isabel in meetings she normally would not be part of. When on telephone conferences with executive staff from different offices, Luke would ask Isabel to join and take notes. She'd roll her eyes but silently comply. But the most difficult of all was a conference call Luke had with his father when he'd asked about her. He'd asked Luke how Isabel was doing and that Kathryn and him were sending their hellos. Luke's eyes never left Isabel's as he lied to his father that Isabel was doing great. Isabel continuously shifted restlessly in her seat, refusing to meet Luke's intense gaze. When Friday finally arrived, she couldn't rush out of the office fast enough. It was the first time since her first day working at B. Pentagon that she'd left the office without asking if Luke needed anything first.

CHAPTER TWELVE

Isabel peeked through her curtains, looking at the sleek, black town cars that were still parked outside her front door. She counted about five of them surrounding her house. She shook her head in disgust at the lengths Luke had gone to keep tabs on her. She wasn't sure if she felt flattered or disturbed by his boundless need to protect her. As she was about to draw away from the window, she noticed a familiar motorcycle pull in front of her house and the rider hop off the bike. She recognized Jake's hard, muscular body immediately. No one but Jake had that much ruggedness yet could handle a bike with such finesse, so it wasn't difficult to identify him before he took off his helmet. He casually strolled toward her front door and Isabel slightly opened it to greet him.

"Luke sent you?" she questioned suspiciously.

"Nope, he doesn't know I'm here." Jake smiled casually even though Isabel gave him a skeptical look. She didn't look like she was ready to let him inside anytime soon. "What, you don't trust anyone who's an acquaintance with Luke now?"

"No," she immediately replied and then regretted it once Jake raised a brow. Isabel sighed and held the door open for him. "I'm sorry, that was rude of me. Come in Jake, please. It's not your fault your best friend's an ass."

Jake chuckled. "Damn you're really pissed off huh?" Jake leaned in and placed a sweet kiss on Isabel's cheek. "You look like shit babe." He grimaced. Luke had said Isabel was losing weight, but he hadn't expected to see her this thin.

"Thanks." Isabel rolled her eyes. She self-consciously looked down at her oversized, unattractive sweater and ran her hands over it attempting to smooth out the wrinkles.

"Sorry, I didn't mean to make you feel bad. You're still very beautiful Isabel, don't get me wrong, it's just that you've lost weight since I last saw you. Your face has paled and your pupils have dilated. You're not sleeping much." Jake shook his head.

Isabel narrowed her glance. "You're too damn observant," she accused.

Jake sighed. "Trust me, it's not a desired talent." If he could make himself oblivious to all the wrongs in the world, he'd sleep better at night, but his restless energy came from his overly observant skills. Not much happened that didn't catch the eye of Jake Callaghan.

"Come, let's go to the living room." She walked away from Jake's probing eyes even though she knew they'd follow her. "Can I get you some coffee? I just made a fresh pot."

"Coffee would be nice," Jake said as he plopped down on her white couch and waited for Isabel to return with a tray of mugs and a pot of fresh coffee. He smiled to himself, remembering the first time he'd met her at this house and how she had offered him coffee. Back then he had been under a different impression of who Isabel Stamos was and what she meant to his best friend. His entire perspective of her had changed in a matter of months, and Isabel had gained Luke's love, now holding an importance not just for Luke but Luke's entire family. She'd left quite an impression on everyone during the holidays. And Jake wasn't immune to her either. Jake never opened up or was close to anyone other than Luke. On occasion, he'd let Andrew and their father Thomas in as well. Emilia tried her hardest to get to him, but the walls he had built against her were too high. Isabel, on the other hand, had somehow someway managed to chip a block off his icy heart.

Isabel placed the tray down and joined Jake on the couch. "So if Luke didn't send you, why are you really here if you don't mind me asking?" Isabel asked with suspicion lacing her voice.

"Trust me, if Brady knew I was visiting his woman late at night he'd try to kick my ass." Jake chuckled. "Lucky for you, I'm not scared of him, and I'd kick *his* ass."

Isabel giggled, despite wanting to. She really liked Jake. He rarely spoke but when he did it was with brutal honesty. He was the type of man she should fear being around, but she was oddly at ease with him, maybe since Luke and his family trusted him immensely. She studied his tattoos again, the ones etched on his arms. This time she was close enough to see the writing she had seen before that was in a foreign language she wasn't familiar with. She frowned while studying them. Jake's tattoos were as much of a mystery as he was, but she didn't dare ask him the meaning behind them. Something told her that it was a boundary not many would attempt to cross.

"Luke's worried about you," Jake's deep voice cut through the silence. "You've really pushed him away."

Isabel exhaled deeply and pulled a pillow into her lap, hugging it close. She missed Luke so much. His sweet kisses, his gentle touches, the way he made her body come alive with the slightest touch of his hands. In a short amount of time, he had become her world, her lifeline, her reason to get up in the mornings. Now she spent sleepless nights alone with dark thoughts haunting her.

"He became too overbearing. I didn't know how to cope with that," she confessed.

"They can't help it, it's in their nature to save people. That's just how the Brady's are," Jake told her.

Isabel pondered that thought, pleased she'd been able to meet a man who came from a family of good morals, distressed that she was right as to why Luke was so determined to help her. "So I was right, he's doing this out of pity. I'm helpless, and he wants to save me. It's in his nature, just like you said." Isabel saddened with pain too unbearable to overcome.

"No, you're wrong," Jake answered sternly. "He's in love with you. Trust me, I was shocked as well to find out that Luke's in love, but he is, and it's killing him that you won't believe him. He's just trying to do the right thing and be able to keep you at the same time. You're a smart woman Isabel. I thought you'd figure that one out on your own."

Isabel was taken aback by Jake's sudden determination to prove her wrong. She clearly heard an insult somewhere in that statement, but she agreed with him reluctantly. "When did you become such a wise ass?" she muttered.

Jake grinned. "I've been called worse."

Isabel lightly laughed and then the room went back to being silent. She knew Jake was just being considerate and remaining quiet so she could gather her thoughts. She restlessly tossed the pillow aside as she got up to pace her living room. The tiring stress of the past few days was weighing on her. Her mind and heart were having an internal battle, confused about whether it was her or Luke who was at fault for the sudden strain on their relationship.

"What are you thinking about?" Jake finally broke through her thoughts.

"I'm just confused and a bit lost, not to mention petrified. I didn't want to do this. I didn't want to live through it again," she said, looking at him.

Jake nodded reassuringly. She didn't need to explain she was referring to taking Dean Scotts to trial. "I'm going to help you. Luke won't be the only one there to support you, I promise."

"Why? Why are you so determined to help?" Isabel asked. She was glad her question didn't come off as offensive but curious instead.

"Because I know what it's like to be the victim."

Isabel's eyebrows rose. Jake's response had just shocked her. One look at the man and it was nearly impossible to picture him as any type of victim.

"I was fourteen years old, had no parents, and lived with a drug addicted, alcohol-infused uncle. He gained custody of me when my parents died." Jake spoke with cold bitterness in his voice.

Isabel watched Jake's chest rise and fall from his heavy breathing. He was no longer looking at her, as if those two sentences had taken him back to a time he'd much rather forget. She didn't speak as she slowly walked back and took a seat next to him on the couch. She gave him a comfortable distance, because Jake's entire body had gone rigid with intensity.

"He'd come home high and beat the living shit out of me." Jake let out a humorless laugh and scratched his chin roughly. It was still difficult to talk about, he realized, but he needed to let Isabel in so she could understand that it was okay to be scared and learn how to overcome your fears.

"I had just met Luke and sometimes we'd walk home from school together," Jake continued. "They always had a driver pick them up, but Luke knew I walked home alone and refused to go with their driver, so he'd walk with me. Sometimes he'd convince me to allow their driver to drop me off. Their parents worked long hours at the time and wanted to make sure Luke, Andrew, and Emilia all got home safely."

Jake paused. He had to order his body to relax. These memories brought a whole new level of anger and hatred for the man who single-handedly scarred his life, in more ways than anyone knew. He sighed heavily and continued.

"One day, Luke and I decided to go play ball at a nearby park. We stopped at my house first so I could grab some gym clothes. I assumed Joe, my uncle, wouldn't be home. But when we got there and I saw his old truck parked out in the driveway, I told Luke that Joe didn't like guests and to wait for me outside. I can't explain to you the fear I felt walking into that house." He looked at Isabel when he confessed this, and she nodded her head silently willing him to continue.

"He was never home during that time so I felt that something bad was about to happen. Luckily, the piece of shit was too high to do much damage. He yelled at me and slapped me around a few times, but I managed to grab my shit and get out. He came after me as I ran outside, cursing and saying 'Wait till you get home.' Luke saw him and tried to ask me what was going on, but I told him I didn't want to talk about it. We played ball for hours until the sun went down. Not much conversation took place, we just played."

"Finally, Luke said he had to go home before his parents got worried so we walked back to my house. He asked me if I was sure I wanted to go in, and I assured him I was fine. I was embarrassed as shit, thinking Luke could see my fear. I always hit Joe back even though I wasn't as strong as him. I always managed to fight back, but the more I did, the angrier he got. I went inside, regardless of how scared as fuck I was. I was fucking relieved when there was no sign of him. Just as I walked into the kitchen, he came at me from behind, knocked me to the floor, and pounded his fists into my face. I managed to get up and fight back, hitting him with every available object I could find, but he still managed to get a hold of me. His heavy fists repeatedly landed on my face, and I was on the verge of blacking out when I heard someone yelling. It was Luke. He came back." He looked into Isabel's eyes and smiled.

Isabel slowly smiled back. Jake had really cold, green eyes, but his eyes warmed at the memory of Luke coming to help him. She knew this held great value and fondness to Jake and something told her that he was surprised Luke came after him, as if the idea of someone coming to his aid was so foreign and impossible.

"He shoved my uncle off of me. Joe was a coward to hit anyone else so he didn't stop us when we ran out of there, and we didn't stop running until we reached Luke's house. My heart was pounding the entire time, thinking he could have followed us. Or worse, Luke could have gotten hurt as well. I ran in after Luke when he broke through their front door. All hell broke loose. His entire family heard us. I think I lost it. I must have collapsed to the floor, because everything passed by in such a damn blur."

Silence fell heavily between them. Isabel saw Jake's jaw twitch. This was just the tip of the iceberg of his past and problems. This wasn't all that haunted Jake, but she figured this was the easiest to confess. Any fool could see Jake's problems were deeper than that. How much deeper could there be? Child abuse was bad enough.

"What happened then?" Isabel spoke softly.

Jake exhaled harshly and leaned deeper into the couch. "Luke's father did everything in his power to send Joe to jail. A warrant for his arrest was issued that same night, and they found drugs and an unregistered gun in the house. That added to the charges, for not only beating a child, but exposing a minor to such indecency. Thomas fought for custody, and he did everything in his power to make sure I didn't end up in foster care. God knows how much money he spent on lawyers to gain custody of me." Jake shook his head in disbelief. He pushed away from his seat and paced just like Isabel had earlier. "He was relentless. He made a promise to me, and he kept it. I always thought Luke was my hero until I met his dad." Jake laughed warmheartedly. Luke's family had been his savior in every possible way. They saved him. Not all of him but whatever lay on the surface had been saved. Everything else buried deep inside could never be salvaged.

"This isn't about just you anymore Isabel," Jake said, turning to her. "This is also about the intern Dean raped. Just imagine how scared she's been all this time."

"I tried to help her Jake, I swear I did," Isabel cried immediately, jumping to her feet, needing him to understand. "I know I was weak and waited too long, but I tried to do the right thing. She didn't want our help." Isabel's voice broke into a whimpering sob, and she clamped her mouth shut with both hands. Time had not erased the guilt she still felt for Marcy, a young, beautiful, vibrant girl who had been at the mercy of a disturbed, sickened monster.

Jake hurried toward her. He pulled her into his chest and stroked her trembling back. "I know you did, sweetheart. I know you did. But maybe we can try again?" he murmured.

Isabel pulled away from him and looked into his light green eyes. She always pictured Jake as emotionless. One could never read his expressions because his eyes were always aloof. He was a distant man who barely let the outside world in but she now knew of the man inside, the one who had suffered as a child. He had willingly shared a small part of his past.

"Thanks for sharing your story," Isabel said and wiped away her tears.

Jake nodded. "You're welcome. So what do you say? You'll join us during the trials against Dean and confess against him?"

Isabel took a step back when realization hit her. "Wait, what? The trial against Dean?" She shook her head in misunderstanding. Then her face became still as a stone. "Luke and Travis Reed have still been going through with this haven't they?"

"This is Brady we're taking about," Jake smirked. "He put his mind to it, and you can throw all the tantrums you want babe, he's still going to go through with it."

Isabel wanted to be angry and feel further betrayed but she couldn't, not when the realization of how much Luke loved her radiated within her. He wouldn't give up, even if she had. He was still fighting to get her the justice she had only dreamed of, and he did it all out of love. She saw this now and felt like an idiot for being so immune to it, for being insecure and pushing him away.

"Every night I go to bed with Marcy's shattered imagine still lurking in my thoughts," she said and surprised Jake with the sudden change of subject. "She comes into my dreams, angry at me for not helping her. I see her lying there, naked and bleeding, and she screams at me to help, but I just stand there. I blame myself every day for not going to the police that same night." More tears stream down her face.

Jake cursed and shook his head. "That's some fucked-up shit to carry around all this time." He gently wiped a tear from her face with his thumb, amazed at himself for being able to show any affection toward another human being. His responsiveness was usually nowhere near gentle. When Emilia did something to put herself in danger and piss him off, he'd usually yank her away into another room to yell and scold her, but Isabel seemed so fragile, he was afraid she'd break.

"I'll confess during the trials."

Jake's brows rose, shocked and relieved all at the same time. "You will?"

Isabel nodded her head confidently. "Yes, I will. It's time this was finally behind me. Thank you Jake."

Jake grinned from ear to ear. "Anytime. And thank Luke instead."

Isabel frowned and looked at him nervously. "Can this stay between us for now? Trials haven't started yet, and I need to wrap my brain around a few things. I need to mentally prepare myself before I can walk into any courtroom. If you could please not tell Luke yet about my change of heart?"

Jake smiled. "Sure thing. Alright, I'm going to get going." He leaned in and kissed Isabel's cheek. "Thanks for the coffee."

"Thanks for the talk." Isabel smiled and walked him toward the door.

"Turn the alarm on," Jake demanded as he pointed to the console on his way out.

Isabel rolled her eyes but laughed lightly. "There are like fifty men outside my door."

"Don't make me come back and install another camera," Jake called over his shoulder as he walked toward his bike. He watched Isabel laugh but promise to turn it on. He winked at her and settled onto his bike. He didn't leave until Isabel shut her door, and he heard her alarm beep.

~*~

Luke stood outside the courtroom with Travis Reed. Any minute now the trial against Dean Scotts would begin and piercing nerves coiled his insides. Reed had worked day and night to gather an impeccable amount of evidence to convince the judge to issue an arrest warrant within days. Luke couldn't explain the amount of relief he felt when he got that life changing call and had been informed that Scotts had been arrested. For the first time since Isabel and he had arrived from New York, he was able to slightly breathe normally. His situation with Isabel at the office had become insufferable. Walking past her every morning knowing he no longer had a claim on the woman he loved was slowly killing him. Watching her lose weight and work like a lifeless zombie sitting behind her desk was the worst type of torture he could experience. But something had changed about her. She'd stopped arguing back. Her actions were sad and defeated, instead of the defiance she had shown him ever since the day he introduced her to Reed. Every time she looked at him now, it was with new pain. She didn't argue with him when he told her to stay in the office during lunch hours. Something had shifted for Isabel, and Luke was scared to the core that she was getting antsy enough and would run away again. It terrified him that she had finally given up any fight that was left inside her. Even her bold behavior toward him the past few weeks was gone and replaced by a meek, silent shadow.

Now he stood outside the courtroom, wondering when this torment would end. He watched the scum arrive with his father along with his team of partners. It looked like Daddy had brought his whole firm with him. Luke's hands itched to wipe the smirk off of Dean's face when they came face-to-face. Luke wanted the bastard to know he was the reason his ass was going to jail, and though they had exchanged a few words, Luke kept his composure intact.

Reed, their lawyer (more like Marcy's lawyer), had gathered compelling evidence and gained her complete participation and trust. Reed was very confident and knew they had the case in the bag. It seemed like a simple win. A few of Jake's trustworthy men had managed to get into Dean's room at the hotel he was staying at to see what the bastard was up to during his stay. After finding what they had suspected all along, they worked quickly toward his arrest warrant. The hotel's owner had allowed police to search his room, which provided Reed with further evidence to use against Scotts and his polished clan of attorneys.

Dean was not prepared to hide his illegal activities before the police broke in and confiscated his cell phone, laptop, and unregistered handgun. What they found gave Luke even more momentum to continue this case against Isabel's wishes. He might end up losing her completely in the process, but at least he would ensure her safety.

Luke wondered what the cocky piece of shit was so confident about. There was no way in hell his daddy was going to be able to get him out of this mess, but it just goes to show what a ludicrous, self-centered idiot Dean really was and how careless of a criminal he had become. No doubt his brain failed to function coherently when under the influence. He could have been smart about it, but his overly arrogant personality didn't think he needed to take precautions.

"The fucker thinks he's untouchable." Luke grinded his teeth together. Reed patted him on his shoulder and told him to have patience, promising him it was going to go well.

Luke's mind trailed back to Isabel and how for so long, she refused to acknowledge him. She arrived to work and only speak to him regarding work related issues. Any time he'd call her into his office, she'd be distant and cold and not even look into his eyes. It pained him to watch this woman, who was once so expressive with her large brown eyes, acting completely remote. No emotion flickered across her face, and Luke was beginning to wonder if she even was mentally present when they communicated. But this was a risk he was willing to take in order to protect her. He'd just love her from a distance and cherish the fact that after this trial, she would be safe. Her security and peace of mind were much more important to him than his own needs.

"We start in about five minutes," Reed informed him and Luke nodded.

He decided walking further away from the courthouse for those remaining minutes would be good for him. He needed to clear his head and gain all the patience he could gather. Once the trial started and the jury was informed of Dean's actions, Luke was going to need to keep his composure. God knew how desperately he wanted to beat the man to death for inflicting pain upon innocent women. Now every time Isabel flinched from fear, Luke had a face to place with the blame, and he desperately wanted to inflict that pain back onto the person who was causing it.

Over and over, Luke contemplated handling this Jake's way. Jake had an immense network of people that would wipe Dean Scotts and his very existence off the face of this planet. Luke was still unsure what his best friend did when not working for B. Pentagon. He had his theories and assumptions, but each time he got closer to gaining some truth, Jake informed him he'd be better off not knowing. Jake had once explained that if Luke had been a man with no family ties, Jake would have involved him in what he did, but neither of them would want to place Luke's family in danger. Luke's ties with his family were strong and any threat coming toward him would drag his family in danger as well.

But Jake considered himself a nomad, a man detached from the rest of the world, living by his own law. As much as Jake considered Luke's family his own, when push came to shove, he would disappear out of town for months at a time and return randomly. No one questioned him. They were used to how Jake operated.

But Luke decided he wanted to do this the legal way. Jake's way would have led them to do everything behind closed doors and not a damn soul would know about it. *No*, he thought. Luke wanted to make every aspect of this public. He wanted to smash Preston Scotts and his disgusting, filth of a son to the floor, burn them down to ashes, and have the entire nation know what kind of scum they really were. He knew there was no way Scotts was bullshitting his way out of this one. Reed's evidence was just too damn strong.

Luke took a few steps outside and came to an abrupt halt. His green gaze locked with the large brown eyes he'd fallen hopelessly in love with. Isabel gave a shy smile to the shocked look on Luke's face. She turned around and said something to Jake who was standing next to her, and he nodded in reassurance. Isabel nodded as well, and they both headed toward Luke. Luke thought his feet were glued to the floor. He couldn't bring himself to move toward her. They stood in front of him, and Jake slapped him on his back.

"Brady." He nodded. "I'll give you two a minute." He looked at Isabel and nodded again as if his nodding continued to give her positive confidence.

"You came," Luke said. He tried to clear the hoarse sound in his voice but failed.

"I should have been here sooner." She paused and waited for a while, silently thanking Luke for giving her a minute to gather her thoughts and order her lungs to breathe. "This is difficult for me Luke, but you are right. I need to put it to rest. I'm willing to testify."

Luke took a deep breath. It felt as though he hadn't been breathing for days, like he'd been suffocating without her. He didn't say another word. He stepped forward, cupped her face, and placed his lips on hers. He kissed her hungrily and a little frantically. He'd missed her so much; her taste, her smell, her beautifully expressive eyes. Everything about her. He allowed his lips and tongue to linger over hers and gain back the familiarity of her touch, along with the uncontrollable need to show how much he wanted her. Isabel matched his craved embrace with her own eagerness. She realized Luke really did love her. He had done everything to shelter and protect her, and she had pushed him away out of fear. Her insecurities had taken a toll on her but no more. No longer would she ignore that she needed to face this and put it behind her, to move on with life with no more fear, doubt or regrets. Luke would help her get there, and she would not refuse him this time.

Luke pulled away from her lips and buried his face into her neck. He wrapped his arms tightly around her thin waist and inhaled her sweet jasmine scent. "God, I missed you so much." He'd missed holding her. He felt her small hands run up and down his back. Those small momentous minutes felt like a lifetime for Luke. He didn't want to let her go, dreading the concern that she could easily slip out of his hands and out of his life again. He didn't want to release her, but he had no choice once he heard Jake calling them to go inside. He reluctantly pulled away but still kept his arms wrapped around her fragile waist. He gazed into her eyes, allowing her to see the amount of love, lust, and longing he had for her.

"Are you ready for this baby?" he murmured.

She placed a gentle hand on his cheek and smiled. "As ready as I'll ever be."

Luke took both her hands and kissed each of her fingers. "Come on, let's go. I've got you." With his arm wrapped tightly around her waist he pulled her into the courtroom where faith and justice waited to make their earth-shattering decision.

~*~

As far as Isabel knew, the easiest part was agreeing to testify. The worst part was seeing Dean Scotts for the first time since that dreadful night. As she stepped inside the room, her panic hit her with such a fierce impact, even Luke's strong arms struggled to hold her up. He immediately rushed her away from the courtroom to the nearest women's restroom. Isabel had asked for a moment of privacy and slowly closed the door on Luke's frightened face. She leaned against the sink willing her breathing to stabilize. Small sweat beads broke across her entire body, and she shook severely. She could vaguely hear Jake and Luke talking outside the closed door as Jake's stern voice argued with Luke, stopping him from going inside, to grant her a moment to gather herself.

Isabel thought that any minute, Luke would burst through the doors to come to her aid. What she least expected was for Marcy Brooks to walk into that crowded narrow restroom and look upon her with sad, knowing eyes. To Isabel's shock, she stood right in front of her. And much more to her surprise, she looked well. Isabel didn't know what she had expected. Maybe a thin, fragile girl who'd changed her vibrant blond hair to a dull brown, hiding behind overly large clothing. But before her stood a young woman whose beauty radiated much like it did when they had first met.

"Marcy," Isabel blurted out in a rasping voice. "How are you?" *Stupid question,* she thought. "You uh, look so well." She was nervous, she realized, since she'd expected Marcy to look at her with accusing eyes. Here before her was the same young woman who'd been haunting her dreams and instead of hate radiating from her, Isabel felt calmness from Marcy.

"Don't let the appearance fool you, the inside is all torn apart," she whispered but managed to smile.

Isabel took a long, hard look at the young intern who had once seemed so carefree and full of life. But now it was Marcy's eyes that gave it away. She might be hiding well behind her fancy clothes and nicely styled hair but had failed to cover the hollow glance in her gaze.

"You don't hate me?" she finally asked the burning question.

"Hate you? Why would I hate you?" Marcy shook her head. "You and your mother tried to help me, but I refused. I'm so sorry Isabel, I'm sorry I turned away from you. I was just scared."

"I know, I've been there too. I still am." Isabel let out a mocking laugh. "It took me a while to agree to this." She paused. "So how are you really doing? Other than looking evidently great."

Marcy grinned. "I'm healing. Dr. Finch works wonders. He's been so patient with me, and his methods of coping have really helped me accept what was done. I didn't want to acknowledge it but now I finally have."

"Dr. Finch?" Isabel asked. *What is the irony of them both seeing the same doctor?* she wondered.

"Your mother has been paying for all my therapy sessions," Marcy confessed. "After I refused to press charges, a few days later she came back to my apartment and said she couldn't stand the thought of me living through this alone. I guess she realized I was in denial and that was worse than admitting what really happened. She left Dr. Finch's card at my door and said if I ever sought any help, she'd help pay for it. She begged me to go see him, and at first I refused, but eventually caved and made an appointment."

Isabel was shocked at what Marcy had just said. Her mother had never mentioned Marcy again or the fact that all this time not only was she keeping track of her therapy sessions but also paying for them. Isabel's heart swelled with pride and love from her mother's kindness, making it difficult to speak.

Marcy's eyes began watering with unshed tears. "I don't have a mother so I hope you don't mind that I've been borrowing yours from time to time. She checks on me weekly." Marcy took a deep breath as the uncontrollable tears escaped from her eyes and poured down her cheeks. "She's my guardian angel," she sobbed.

"Oh sweetie," Isabel cried and pulled her into her arms. She held onto Marcy as if her dear life depended on it. "She's my guardian angel as well," she whispered as they both clung to each other, silently crying and soothing the pain away. To think that all this time they could have helped one another but both were scared to face a menacingly, disturbing man. After what felt like hours had passed, as each woman gained her composure, they heard the soft knock on the restroom door, and Luke's gentle voice saying they had to proceed. Marcy and Isabel gave each other confident, reassuring smiles and walked their way toward a room that held the very man who'd scarred them deeply.

The tranquil April sun shone and brightened the private beach, making the little specs of sand glitter like tiny diamonds. A soft wind carried a sense of sedative calmness through Luke's open bedroom balcony doors, making the white curtains gently dance. Daylight had arrived with the promise of reassuring yet another pleasant, spring day. Isabel moved in her sleep, forcing Luke wide awake. He woke with a jolt only to find her still snuggly pressed to his naked chest. He released a sigh of relief and rested his head back on his pillow. He turned to watch Isabel's beautiful face and smiled to himself when he realized her naked, sedated body was still a willing prisoner of sleep. Time had most definitely been on their side. With time, he had struggled yet helped the woman he loved not only face, but also overcome, her biggest fears and finally find peace and harmony. A once panic-ridden woman, Isabel was now the opposite. It was difficult for Luke to watch her adjust to her raging emotions. He'd awake at night to find Isabel, curled up into the fetal position, crying from her haunted dreams. But the nightmares had evaded her as so had the very man who'd planted that seed of panic inside her brain.

The trial against Dean Scotts had irrevocably ended. Isabel had witnessed their attorney, Travis Reed, reveal one immaculate piece of evidence after another, shocking the jury along with the judge. He kept the trial going, hoping to continuously add to Dean's sentence, and had succeeded tremendously. Trial after trial, Isabel sat between Luke and Jake, clutching Luke's hand, as both masculine men protectively sandwiched her. Neither let Isabel out of their sight for months in worry that Preston Scotts might become desperate and try something stupid and harm her.

The astonishing evidence found in the hotel room Dean was staying in was presented to the jury, revealing the menacing steps he had taken to plan an explicit attack on Isabel. Hundreds of pictures of Isabel were found as he had clearly followed her and psychotically noted her every move. Luke had forced himself to not dwell on the facts presented before him in worry he might jump out of his seat and kill Dean, regardless of where they were. Isabel had started losing weight as she relived that frightful night from the bench testifying. After her testimony, Luke had asked her to no longer join them during the trials, but Isabel had refused. While Marcy Brooks had quickly fled the courtroom after her duties were fulfilled, Isabel realized staying and witnessing every bit of information became a coping method for her. She'd faced the last wrath of her demons until they had finally surrendered and left her in peace.

But what sent a wild tremor quaking throughout the entire courtroom was the surprise witness Reed had presented. It was an unknown witness to even Luke and Jake, and they exchanged an amazed look of wonder. A man they did not recognize approached the bench, placed his hand on the bible, and swore his oath. Isabel recognized him though. Her breath choked in her throat as she heard the security from the night of Marcy's attack confess he had helped Dean destroy any footage the cameras had captured in exchange for a large sum of money. This being Reed's final witness and after delivering his closing statement, Dean was justifiably sentenced to rot in a prison cell for decades to come.

Finally, Luke and Isabel were gifted with peaceful nights. The threat that had heavily hung over their heads was eliminated from their lives. Luke brushed his hand on Isabel's bare back and lightly kissed her naked shoulder. It hadn't taken much convincing to persuade Isabel to move in with him once the trials had started. Now he made sensual, sweet love to the woman who'd captured his heart, every night and every morning.

Isabel fluttered her eyes open to see Luke's mesmerizing green gaze watching her. One of the greatest benefits of living with Luke was seeing the intensity of his green eyes amplify once he'd awake from sleep, not to mention the explicit things he did to her body before and after they went to bed. She gleefully smiled at him, and Luke leaned in to kiss her plump lips. He brushed his thumb softly over her rosy cheeks as he deepened his kiss and released a low chuckle when Isabel hummed from satisfaction.

"Good morning love," he murmured.

"It's always a good morning waking up next to you Brady," Isabel smiled.

"Is that right?" he teased and leaned into her, sinking them deeper into the mattress.

Isabel clung to his biceps. "Yup. You make my mornings very memorable," she purred as she traveled her hands up and down his back, feeling his muscles tense. Her eyes hungrily admired his hard chest and abs as if she was preparing to devour him.

Luke raised a brow and feigned disappointment. "Why do I suddenly feel like I'm being used for my body?"

"Oh, that's because you are," Isabel sighed casually as she allowed her hands to dip lower, causing Luke to growl.

"Well in that case, I better live up to your expectations Ms. Stamos," he grunted and kissed her lips with a bit more force, causing Isabel to gasp. Just as his hands began to roam and pleasure her naked body, Isabel's stomach picked that very instant to loudly growl. Luke pulled away and laughed.

"Talk about a cock-block."

"I'm sorry." Isabel giggled.

"Don't be." Luke kissed her forehead. "As punishment, you get to make breakfast."

"Hey," Isabel said and frowned, making Luke laugh again.

He kissed her pouty lips before rising to sit up, pulling Isabel with him. The covers fell, pooling around her waist, but she didn't bother to cover her revealed breasts. Her confidence with nudity carried no boundaries when with Luke, and he thrived on that fact.

"So why am I stuck making breakfast?" she continued.

"Because you're so cute when you cook." Luke tapped the tip of her nose while enjoying her reaction.

Isabel yelped in disbelief. "Cute? You think I'm cute? Jesus Luke, you'd call your sister or cousin cute, not the woman you're sharing a bed with." She crossed her arms under her chest.

Luke threw his head back and laughed. "The fact that you're so bothered by the word is cute itself." Though he was enjoying teasing her, Luke grabbed Isabel and hauled her against his chest when she attempted to leave their bed. He cupped her face and kissed her before she could escape. He wasn't satisfied until he heard her whimper when he parted her lips and greedily swept his tongue over hers. He pulled her far enough to stare into her widened eyes. "You're the sexiest and most beautiful woman I know and your sensuality makes me so incredibly crazy that sometimes I question my own sanity."

His words had stumped her. "Wow," she whispered, "you deserve a breakfast buffet for that one."

Luke chuckled and kissed her cheek. "Okay but before you go, I've got something for you." He reached over and opened the side drawer where he took out a white envelope. "This is for you," he said, handing it to her.

Isabel furrowed her brows when Luke gave her a sly smile. "What's this?" She hesitantly took the paper.

"Only one way to find out sweetheart," he said and gestured for her to open it.

Isabel nervously smiled and pulled out the neatly folded paper that was tucked inside. She became further confused as her eyes scanned the writing, "This is your private plane's flight schedule for the next few months."

"Keep looking."

"Well at least tell me what I'm looking for." Isabel shook her head. "Is there a problem with the…" She stopped breathing as her entire body became as still as stone. Her eyes froze at the center of the paper on two specific words. She blinked a few times, thinking that if she adjusted her vision, the words would disappear. But they didn't. Right there, listed under the upcoming June month on Luke's official flight plan was a scheduled round trip flight to Naxos, Greece; the very Greek island Isabel had told Luke about on their flight to New York; the island that held her most cherished childhood memories. It was where her father was born and where her beloved grandparents were buried. She hadn't stepped foot on that land since her father had passed away. Neither her nor her mother had the heart to return, but now Luke was asking her to go with him, to visit the very place that defined who she was and to rekindle her roots. Her heart swelled with vast emotion as she attempted to blink away the tears but failed.

"Why?" she managed to ask.

Luke gently ran his hand up and down her arm. "Because I'd like to go there with you. I'd like to visit the one place you've spoken so fondly of and add our own memories."

Isabel covered her sob with her hand as tears flooded down her face. The overwhelming joy and liberation she felt was indescribable. Luke pulled her closer and her feeble body went willingly as she instantaneously wrapped her arms around his neck.

"This is the most incredible gift I have ever received," she cried. "Thank you."

Luke gently swept his hand down her hair while his other arm wrapped around her waist, bringing her closer. "Oh sweetheart, you don't have to thank me," he murmured. "Just be with me. That's all I want."

"I'll always be with you," she vowed as Luke's embrace tightened.

Isabel held onto Luke as memories of her past and present sprinted through her thoughts. If it hadn't been for Luke Brady, the man she had spontaneously met on a destiny filled July afternoon, she'd still be the lost soul she was before. But now, she was cradled inside the arms of the very man who'd saved her in every possible way; a man who had restlessly persuaded and challenged her to become stronger. He fought her battles and clashed with her demons, and now he presented her a life full of happiness. It was safe to say that Isabel had found her other half, and Luke Brady had filled the emptiness in her heart.

ACKNOWLEDGEMENTS

And where would an Indie Author be without her support group? My biggest supporter of all is my husband Argo. Your optimistic attitude manages to pull me out of the darkness I have crawled into, and give me hope. Thank you for believing in me. You are my silver lining.

To my dad Harout and my mom Hasmik for being the best parents a girl could ask for. The love you both have given me has been my shield during challenging times. You encouraged me to keep writing, and for that, I thank you.

To my sister Ani, you've always been an inspiration to keep my head strong and confidence high. If I said I know a person who has overcome more obstacles in life than you have, I would be lying. Your support gives me courage to face challenges. Thank you for being the sister of my heart.

A big thanks goes to Adelina for accepting my plea to proof read my manuscript. I'm lucky to have a good friend like you who also has a hard time ignoring the voices in her head. Who better to understand my moments of joy and moments of frustration than a fellow writer herself.

I cannot begin to explain how grateful I am for my editor, Jenny Sims from editing4indies.com. You stepped in, dissected my book, and pointed out all the errors I was completely oblivious to. Thank you for your patience and constant help. I truly cannot wait to work with you again.

I also want to thank other friends and family along with any reader who has reached out to me just to say how much they enjoyed Luke's and Isabel's story. I want to personally thank any reader who supports Indie Authors. You guys rock! Thank you so much for your support and kindhearted words. There would be no 'self published' world for Indie Authors without you.

ABOUT THE AUTHOR

To learn more about this author, visit her on
www.goodreads.com/aneta_krpekyan

Instagram @anetakrpekyan

www.facebook.com/AnetaKrpekyan

Stay tuned for Andrew's and Amanda's love story as Part II in the Brady Trilogy